Slamming into the balcony rail below my suite, I hurdled over the banister.

After gripping a locked patio door, I yanked up an iron chair and caved through the glass.

Crriiissshhh!!

With shards hailing over me, I ditched the chair, and rolled to the floor. As the drive flew from my pocket, I snatched it up and glanced over to a man.

He sat on the sofa, eating popcorn, and watching television with subtitles.

While swallowing the drive, I bolted for the door.

Popcorn flew everywhere as the man jumped to his feet. "Hey!" He shouted.

As I put on his house shoes, I dashed out of the room and into a gory hallway…

EVOLVING | CRANE

VSN | 2

Book Two | Archipus

Dave Temperance Welch

A river of mangled agents decorated the hall.

Thinking the elevator was busted, I sprinted through the bloodshed and straight for the stairs.

Ding!

The feeling of my enemy raced behind me as the hairs stood on my head.

"Aagghh!" I shouted as the male assassin reached for me.

Shoving the staircase door open, I gripped the handrail. Before I leapt over, the assassin kicked the door off the hinges.

Floom!

The door whammed into my back, tumbling me over the rail.

Plummeting to my death, I reached for everything, banging against the sides of the stairwell.

The ground came quick.

Swack!

Dedication

To all my fans. And my haters.

"...."

-Zacuther

Ka-Thunk!!

The door crashed on top of me, breaking my nose.

Bleeding profusely, I stood slowly as the door slid to the ground. But I tumbled back to the floor. After a fall like that, I *should* be dead. That was twenty stories… the fuck is up with me?

Sirens blared as I rolled over to my stomach, I stood again, peering up the stairwell and to the exit sign.

Barging out of the door and into the sun, I searched for the parking deck.

"Fuck!" I hollered, turning frantically in circles, wiping my nose as the cartilage shuffled about my skin casing.

"There!"

While jogging over to the parking deck, I noticed Agent Woods parked behind the toll booth.

"Hey!" I screamed, running up to the car, banging on the window.

After peering into the vehicle, my hope collapsed.

Blood seeped from my counterparts' throats, as I stumbled back from the car…

Table of Contents

Prologue

After Space Void, the Feuler became the most wanted slug in all of Layian history.

Knowledge of such a massacre, expedited the Symbassy's plans while drafting some of the deadliest beings into the fray.

In spite of this aftermath, the Xaris opposition, 7-Dial, developed his own responsive tally, activating Project M.O.S. But millions of galaxies were already victims of the Symbassy's intangible reach.

Now, in the wake of consuming Earth, the malicious Xaris swamped the land with their deadly venom. And sadly, Canieya Lawson bared witness to their spread of vile diversions.

But out of all their diversions, came one in particular.

This diversion was a horse.

And that horse's name...

... was Archipus.

CHAPTER 1:

Wraith

Part 2

Shoving through the door and into the parking deck, I untied the keys from my gory nightgown. While progressing forward, I spun around, anxiously pressing the auto start.

Bom! Bom!

The horn sounded, jolting my adrenaline.

Vvrrrrooomm!!!

The car cranked and the lights flashed, as I sped over.

"Shit!" I shouted, reaching out for a door handle. I pressed my thumb against a small panel and the door opened fast.

"Welcome, Canieya Lawson." The car spoke as I hopped in.

Fom! -Slamming the door.

"Nooo… You're one of those smart cars." I mumbled.

Glimpsing over the Massenburg with an ignorant feeling of undue, I buckled myself in.

"Would you like for me to drive?"

"Nawl! I got it!"

"I'm sorry, can you repeat that?"

"Shit! I don't have time for this. Emergency!!"

"Would you like to contact the authorities?"

"Bitch! Yes!" I shouted, firmly gripping the steering wheel. A gear popped up from a compartment by the console.

"Applying manual override."

Snatching the gear into drive, I stomped the gas and took off like a rocket.

Ripping out of the parking deck, I saw him again.

The male assassin stood in front of the hotel, watching with eyes of detest. He rubbed a piece of cloth in his hand, savoring every facet of its making.

Flying through the stop sign, I whipped into traffic, flipped on my hazards and peered into my rearview. Police filled my view but-

That bitch! She was running right behind me.

"Not you!" I hollered, flooring the gas.

Blowing my horn, bobbing and weaving in and out of traffic, I peered into my rearview again. She was gaining on me.

Running a red light with a sharp turn, I caused about two wrecks, hoping to lose her. But I only made her more defiant.

She dashed onto the sidewalk, crashing through the patrons' setting like a raging bull.

She bolted back into the street, dodging between the cars. Losing her was not going to be easy. She violated the laws of physics.

Traffic came to a standstill. But I couldn't stop, that bitch was right behind me. In my attempts to avoid the gridlock, I swerved into oncoming traffic.

"Get out the way! Move! MOVE!!" I hollered as the cars flew by. "MMooooovvveee!!!!" I screamed, dodging a high-speed collision.

Diiizzzsshh!

Bashing over the median, I whipped back in the flow of traffic.

"This intersection is active. We recommend that you stop and wait for a clearing."

"No, ma'am! Code ten-one! Ten-one!"

"Code approved."

The windshield lit up with holograms projecting from the glass as I flew through the red light.

Bom-Bommm!

"Agghhh!!!" I howled, lifting my head to a semi.

The truck missed by a thread as I peered into my rearview mirror. That deadly female sprinted clean under the truck.

Then, a bright gleam flicked in my eyes.

And there she was, speeding beside me like a machine.

"Hell NO!" I screamed, glancing over to my speedometer. I was doing a 130 when I tried to run her skank ass over. She yanked out her nunchucks. Knives unsheathed from the ends. She flipped into the air, slicing through my tires as she rolled to the ground.

Ssskkiiissttshhh!!!!

"Shit!" I cried, as the Massenburg spun in circles.

"You have two flat tires. Would you like to auto inflate?"

"YYYYeeeesssssssss!!!!" I screamed, fighting to keep the car steady.

"Inflating."

The tires inflated as I sped on. But my driving remained reckless.

Another intersection approached swiftly. The light was green, but the intersection was clogged with officers. The diagram suggested to make a left, into this crowded intersection. But I couldn't stop.

Vmf!

The male assassin appeared in front of the blockade. Then, the bitch queen appeared in my rearview mirror.

Boy, I got mad, stomping the gas to the floor.

The male assassin charged straight for me.

"Motherfucker!"

He hopped on top of the car, sinking his sword into the roof.

Shinnck!!

The demon blade staked into the armrest, slicing my shoulder open.

"Agh!" I shouted, as my blood painted over the seats.

His hard body tumbled atop the car, as I yanked from left to right.

In a flash, the sword entered again, slicing through my forehead and nose, staking between my thighs.

Shucckk!

"Aaaggghhh!" I hissed with blood skeeting over the steering wheel.

The heat from the katana forced my legs open.

He yanked his sword from the roof, just as I pulled the E-brake.

Flinging from the roof, he stabbed his sword into the car's side panel, and gripped the hood with so much strength that he mutilated the metal.

Bllissshhh!!

The bitch queen shattered the rear window with her bladed nunchuck.

Instantly, I dropped the E-brake and backed over her.

Bum-Bf!

She hurled under the car as I drove over her again, speeding on to the sidewalk.

"Move!" I yelled, smashing into tables and chairs. My adversary balanced atop the hood, gripping his sword with both hands.

Darting back into the street, I slammed on the brakes, flinging him off the car.

Ka-Foom!

He crushed into the road and hopped to his feet in one motion.

A mass of wreckage waved through the street and into the police barrier, causing a ripple of devastation.

My assailant tore out of the ruble, without a single scratch on him. Before I knew it, he was sprinting towards me again.

Hoping to run his bitch ass over, I floored the gas.

Within a flash, he jumped in the air and filtered through the glitchy windshield.

While mounting the sidewalk, I passed through the barricade. The demonic merc landed in the passenger seat, ramming his katana into my jaw.

Pikkc!

The blade punctured the driver's window.

"Aagghh!" I wailed as he yanked his sword free, fracturing my jawbone.

The blood came fast as he stabbed me over and over.

Fainting and waking, I struggled to keep the car from crashing. But he covered so much space, I could barely move.

He punched me in the head, cracking my skull like a shell.

Stabbing into my chest, he pierced through the seat. As he yanked his sword out, he gripped the handle with both hands and my adrenaline surged, wiping my pains away.

I weaved the seatbelt around his wrists, and fastened it.

Click!

He came to a dead stop, as I pulled the E-brake, drifting the car to a spin.

"Passenger eject!" I hollered. The door flew open as I took the razor clamp from my hair, and sliced through the seat belt.

Snip! Snap!

He bolted out of the car and crashed into the street.

Crrroooommmmm!!!!

The passenger door shut as I dropped the E-brake and spun off.

Tearing the string from my nightgown, I tied it over my head and around my chin to keep my jaw from drooping. *"You are in desperate need of medical assistance. We're notifying the nearest emergency unit."* The Massenburg spoke.

As my adrenaline pumped, my blood ran like a faucet.

"Agent Lawson, you are showing a loss in consciousness. To ensure hospital arrival, please engage the autopilot feature."

"Agent Lawson, please pull over."

At 200 miles per hour, the Massenburg flipped out of control, twisting into another shape. Dozens of airbags deployed as I bounced like the globe in a pinball machine.

The Massenburg screeched to a static halt. As the sirens roared from afar, I bled in silence…

CHAPTER 2:

Gastropoda: Gray Garden
Part 2

Compos Mentis, I awoke.

Through my flawless perception, I could see every molecule, the deepest of atoms- fundamental units.

The equations of life and its creations spawned before me. It wasn't derived by technology but more of a natural distinction, an essential composition of ceaseless bloom.

The wall in front of me was simple. I could pick it apart, molecule by molecule. But the image designed within the wall came as a riddle of unidentified iotas, modicums of mind-expanding eventualities. The more I stared into the logo, the more the lacuna world around me deciphered. My branch of endowment came clustered with speedy advancements.

The expeditious gift stopped when I felt a tiny itch burrowing out from the top of my head. My senses, my ability to detect quadrupled and at several different intervals.

A voice spoke…

Xon.

To my feet I stood, glaring into the image infused into the wall.

Then, his presence manifested, this unrestricted, omnipotent, and divine being.

A heavy door opened and closed as he entered, speaking in Layian, in which I fully understood.

"REB," he said.

Turning to the direction of his voice, I witnessed a man floating with no arms or legs. He simply hovered along, and I understood how.

To my immediate right, REB stood.

He was a tad taller than me, bulky and defined. His head was bald, and his chin was bold. His face had narrow lips and thin white glowing eyes. And at the top of his head sat a skinny pair of antennae with a small yellow bulb resting on each end.

He wore a light blue speckled short sleeved condenser shirt. The shirt was of some type of armor as it came integrated with a black anchor, covering his chest and his upper back. The anchor looked just like the logo infused into the wall in front of me.

REB wore a thick brown utility belt and a pair of dark khaki cargo pants with several pockets on them. He had on a pair of light blue and white handguards with black trimming. He wore a pair of brown reinforced toe combat boots, with buckles and straps to ensure firm fitting.

His skin was light gray and green, along with white and dark gray blotches. On the sides of his head sat a colorful button that must've been utilized for some sort of technological purposes.

REB stood with his palms facing up.

The floating man stopped and looked into REB's hands. His palms and fingertips were filled with unknown colors.

The man nodded his head in affirmation and REB dropped his hands to his sides.

Then, the floating man scowled over to me with a hint of befuddlement in his eyes.

"Xon."

But I was already standing...

He glided over and looked me in the eyes. He floated even closer, so close that I could see his chemical makeup.

His skin was ashy, brown and full of ancient engravings. He was nearly naked all but for the loin cloth that covered his pelvic region.

He peered deep into my eyes, and I stared right back. For a while, there was nothing. Nothing but an empty silence...
Bupkis.

The floating man said nothing more. He glared down to the ground then he glided away slowly. He glanced back to me and his eyes of inquietude hurried off.

"Infiltrate and Retrieve. Azix. Rayefill," he announced as he floated on.

In the opposite direction, there stood two immaculate beings beside me. A male and a female slug.

The male stood next to me. His face was clean with thin lips. His skin was gray and green with small black spots. And his eyes were squinty and glowing white with a hint of neon.

His body was covered in a marble blue bodysuit- revealing only his bald head, hands, and feet. The suit was extremely compact and crafted with vents that glowed with neon lights. The lights flickered and flashed and then faded into a purplish hue.

On the left pectoral of this suit, glowed a neon green medallion. The ornament was a tad smaller than the inside of my palm. The emblem had been fitted into the suit and in the center of this token sat the same image. The same anchor, designed into the wall ahead.

The floating man stopped right in front of this being. He stared into him. Then, he looked him up and down. "Flawless…" he whispered.

The floating man drifted slowly over to the final being withstanding this line up. He stopped just in front of her.

She had a smooth, curvy, and seductive face. Her lips were more defined. Yet her eyes glowed with that same squinted streak of brilliant white. She was bald just like the rest of us, and with a pair of fully extended, ultra-thin antennas resting in the top of her head.

She wore another bodysuit, covering everything but her head, hands, and feet. This outfit was extremely form fitting with tiny holes embedded in the suit. The skintight uniform was smoke gray with tiny burnt orange lines defining the contour of her quadriceps, her midsection, shoulders, forearms, and biceps. Then, from her breast area and on to her back, the glowing lines captured the same anchor. The same design on the wall before me.

The floating man had been staring at her for a while and so had I. "Perfect," he gulped with a shimmering voice.

I... Something else was drawing me, something that I couldn't explain. There was so much power inside of me and with no way to express it or harness the capacity of...

Why is this...?

"I am Guitussamii. You can call me Colonel G," he announced as he backed up to the wall in front of us.

"You and I are family. Family of this genealogy housed in this training facility. We are committed to each other. One does not- without the other. You are empty but filled with galactic aptitude. I am your coach. Your instructor and your lifeline, trained to dig into your mother's second sight. She will nurture you and the septillions of Gastropods that are constantly replicating themselves, deep within your super concentrated skin. Your body will adapt into a complete understanding of cosmic anomalies in which you will potentially use- to do the impossible.

I will fill you with Layian ESP, the uttermost spectral force of thought transference and redirection. The feature has already been embedded and I aim to fully expose your brain to these vast abilities." He lectured.

"You will own the innate coding for every macro galaxy, solar system, planet arrangement, species foundation, and means of access to the internal and external alien psyche. Past and future technologies will bow to you. The illusion of time will yield to your mercy. We are the best and we will become the purest combination of elegance and strategic violence, with an integrated knowledge of control over every galactic domain." He declared.

"This!" He yelled. "Behind me, is your definition. It is an ultra-current, real term, and constantly updating index of cosmic particles, chemicals, and enzymatic elements- fabricating into ontology as new galaxies materialize, proliferating into the forever inchoate universe. Studying and understanding these cellular arraignments will equip you for interdimensional travel.

You are the anchors designed to establish equilibrium for all walks of life, to all realities and to every corner of the expanding multiverse." He noted.

"You, the anchor, will foster aid and ensure the continuation of preexisting and newly forming galaxies by the Layian understanding of atomic elements.

Under no circumstances should you defer from your root cause, your ground zero for being. When we crumble, you will be our bottom, the last and final seat for our cause. Further advancement resides in teamwork- your unyielding catalyst for Layian communication.

I have been awarded sanction over the anchor's development. You, Men of Slugs, are and forever will be, the ending sentence -the eyes that we look into when every reality fails." He avowed.

"And class begins now." He mumbled with an assertive tone.

From there, we left the cell and ventured down a massive corridor. With Colonel G leading: Reb, myself, Rayefill and Azix followed behind, like a supreme functioning unit.

As the setting opened a few things caught my eye. In passing, I witnessed bronze- and yellow-colored hues about this mechanical hall. The objects and machines were clean and well manufactured. The walls and the grounds around us were fitted with dense Layian composites. But it felt like I was treading on clouds.

We marched by several holding cells. Most doors were shut, but one. One door was in the process of shutting...

Peeping into this chamber, I saw an athletic human, being hoisted into the air by several Inatechs. The man was cursing and screaming in German. He was so angry, that he nearly fought off the Inatechs, that struggled to subdue him.

"*Lass mich los. Verliere mich!*" He hollered as the door shut swiftly.

I could still hear him screaming at the top of his lungs, "*Ich bin die uberlegene Rasse. Ich bin Hitler! Ich bin Hitler!*"

Moments later we came to a bisecting hall and Colonel G spun around to face us.

"Approach the line," he ordered.

Side by side we stood, stepping on to this gooey black chemical that ran all the way through the hall.

We stood still for a moment. Suddenly, my feet plunged into the black stripe. Then, I heard something… something, deep.

"… Ccccrrrraaaannneeee…" a voice rumbled so that it shook my body.

Fixed on the line traveling through the bisecting hall, I followed the black border. My sight ventured into a room at the end of the hall. And there, in this room, sat a massive creature.

He rested like a dog in a profile position. Facing the wall in front of him, the creature stared into an engraved image. It was the same anchor as before.

The monstrosity (while sitting) was a little shorter than me. It had a huge head with squinty white glowing eyes that were as wide as both of my hands. The creature was built as a man. But his arms and legs were massive. His face was strange as his ears sat on top of his head. It had a pink and brown fleshy snout for a nose with the jaws of a wild dog. His hair was long. They stopped midway down his back. They were sharp and pointy, like hundreds of large aloe leaves.

His hands were unseen. They were tucked in between his legs which were as large as engines. His feet were massive but still in proportion with the rest of his immense body.

His skin was dark green and gray, with small lime green, orange, blue, and teal green speckles covering his back and shoulders. The color combination was profound and well balanced with the creature's image.

For so long did I ogle at this, failing to realize what I was seeing.

Suddenly, the monster turned his head over to me slowly, and in an ominous- perilous manner. But what made the creature so peculiar, was the smile that he wore.

The creature had a grin, a leer from ear to ear that exposed nearly all of his sharp white teeth- a metallic luster of adorable death.

The smile looked to be eventually painful as it had yet to weaken from muscular fatigue. In fact, the smile seemed to intensify…

It was then, that we made eye contact.

Immediately, an eerie feeling overcame me…

31

There was a presence, or a phantom. Some... spirit of the night. A small being, skipped and frolicked about, singing some sort of lullaby of dismal condition.

This murky, barefooted being wore a thin, bloody nightgown, with long filthy hairs covering its face. The sighting may have petrified me, but I had no impression or knowledge of sentimental feelings.

The monster peered into me with that undying smile as the being sung and skipped. Suddenly, the phantom vanished into the air. But the monster continued to ogle. We both stared with vacant expressions, omitting that troubling smile of his.

The elongated hall began to shorten... Then, the monstrosity turned away from me, staring back to the anchor encrusted into the wall. The beast was obviously still grinning, demonically...

Guitussami cleared his throat, shouting, "Your path!" Quickly I turned away from the monster.

"--Has been provided," he added while standing in front of us, rolling his eyes away from me.

"The anchor will guide you through the pilot study, testing and training, finally completing your true understanding of Layain ESP. Now!!!" He hollered. "As you can see, this line of God particles has already soaked into your body's systematic mass. This is the first step to unlocking your fluidity. You are rigid. The

Blackline will provide you with ultimate mobility, keeping your mass dense and virtually indestructible." He explained.

Guitussami spoke in a tongue that I could not comprehend.

Suddenly, we zapped into the goop and at an undefined speed.

The darks of God came...

CHAPTER 3:

Archipus
Part 1

Dartmoor, England
Devon County SW

Twenty miles south of Dartmoor National Park rests a large medieval farmhouse. Early in the misty dew morning, amongst a forestry setting, Perry arrived in a rickety stagecoach.

"Hooo!" The driver mumbled as he pulled the reins, bringing the horses to a stop.

The stagecoach driver was very old, skinny, and ungroomed. He had about two or three teeth and one of his eyes was glass. He wore a brown flannel shirt, some thick gray corduroys, a black brim hat, a dark gray overcoat and some black tractor boots.

"Not too many people come out here. Word is, they got some fine horses," the driver stated as Perry opened the door.

"You look like a man on a mission. And I'd hate to slow you…" the driver inserted as Perry stepped out of the stagecoach.

He turned around and lifted two leather duffle bags from the coach. He sat them on the ground and shut the door.

Perry was a dashing man who worked solely off timing. He wore an all-black snakeskin over coat; some black leather gloves, a black scarf (covering his face), a pair of black slacks, black dress shoes, a black top hat and a pair of black goggles.

"Mighty fine bags you got there. Any chance you sell 'em?" Asked the old driver.

Perry picked up the bags and walked to the front of the carriage. He stopped momentarily, glaring across the distance at the oversized farmhouse.

"You've got a bit of a ways to walk, young sir. Did I tell you that I have a daughter? She looks a bit like me, but girlier. She has been single now for about six years. I've got a picture in my back pocket. Wait a second here let me get it," the driver addressed as he dropped the stagecoach reins.

Perry was still gazing at the farmhouse while the driver reached for his wallet.

"You ready? She's a looker."

"No need." Perry interjected, turning to face the driver.

The old man froze.

"Report to this spot in precisely one hour."

"One hour? That's fine, sir. But I have no ways of telling time." The old man admitted.

Perry sat one of the bags down. He reached into his coat pocket and pulled out a platinum pocket watch. He opened the watch and looked at it.

"It is 9:00. By the time I depart, another minute will have transpired. Do you understand?" Perry asked.

"Yes, sir," nodded the old toothless man.

Perry closed the watch and handed it to the driver. "Keep it as payment. If you are even a second late, I will detonate you." Perry exclaimed as he snatched up the duffle bag. He took off, walking briskly over to the farmhouse.

The stagecoach driver glanced down to the watch as it ticked precisely to one minute. He closed the watch and tucked it into his shirt pocket. Then, he grabbed the stagecoach reins and slapped the straps on the horses' back.

"Kcik! Kcik!" He sounded.

The horses sped up into a light gallop. The driver turned the stagecoach around, only to stop in the same exact spot.

Facing the opposing direction, the old man locked the stagecoach wheels. He sat back into his seat and kicked his legs up over the stagecoach ledge. He lowered the hat over his eyes and put his hands behind his head. And there he waited.

Fifteen minutes later, Perry approached the large double doors of the farmhouse. He grabbed the oversized gold knocker, shaped like a horseshoe. And-

Bok! Bok! Bok!

The knock echoed through the manor. Then, the sound of several locks released, as if someone forgot which way to turn them.

Suddenly, the door opened…

Perry's eyes started high, but his head lowered to capture a small child.

The kid was barely four. He stood there looking straight ahead, wearing only a diaper.

"Where's Yuely?" Perry asked.

The kid just kept looking straight ahead, breathing subtly, scratching his side.

"Let him in Capris!" Shouted a voice from the rear.

The kid held the door open, stepping slowly to the side.

Perry barged in, knocking the poor kid to the floor.

He sat his bags down and glanced over the medieval farmhouse.

"Welcome!" An old, degraded voice shouted.

Perry looked to the top of the stairs and there stood a man.

He was about seven feet tall. His skin was thin and pale. He was bald and boney even to the point of frailty. His eyes were green, and his face was clean. He wore a long wool trench coat, some rugged brown string up boots and some dark brown jeans.

"Yuely. I presume."

"Yes, sir. Been waiting for you." He replied as he looked to Capris.

The kid was still lying on the floor, staring in the ceiling.

"Capris! Go get your brothers. Tell em' to prep Archipus."

The little boy jumped up and took off to the rear of the manor.

Perry shut the door behind him and picked up his bags.

Yuely hurried down the stairs, "This way. We got at least ten minutes before we reach the stables."

"How's Horace?" Yuely asked as they rushed down the hall.

"He's fine."

"Man, I'm happy to see you. Your friends act fast."

"Yes. We are pressed for time even now."

"I see your concern. We can use the golf cart out back."

The two entered another long hallway, filled with vases, paintings, and pictures of horses with their owners. At the end of the corridor, stood a wooden door. Yuely opened the door and stepped outside into another breezeway.

Just to the right sat a small golf cart.

"Sit your bags on the back there and hop in. We can speed this up."

Perry sat his bags down carefully while Yuely powered up the golf cart.

They sat eagerly, speeding down a graveled path.

Moments later, they reached the far ends of the farmland. Perry studied over the doors to the stable as he unloaded his bags.

Yuely walked casually over to the door, pulling out a hefty keychain. He shuffled through the keys as Perry approached with haste. Yuely opened the door as soon as Perry neared. He stepped aside, ushering Perry in.

But Perry slowed in his observance of the massive stables.

A dimmed lighting complemented the ease of yellowish breezes, brushing lightly over the herbage covering the floor. The entire structure was built of live oak and black locust wood which blended well with the medieval construction. There were twenty stables total, ten on each side of the corridor.

"Ohhhh, this is impressive."

"Yeap. He's about five stables down."

"Wonderful! Yuely, I have to use the restroom. I've been holding it since my initial departure," Perry declared as he glanced up to Yuely.

"Well then, you take this here hall here to my left. It's the first door on your right," gestured Yuely with direction.

"Splendid," nodded Perry as he hurried down the hall with his duffle bags in hand.

Perry shoved into the bathroom quickly.

Directly in front of him sat a counter with two sinks.

He sat one bag on the counter and the other bag on the floor. He took off his leather gloves and tucked them into his back pocket. Then, he took off his coat and placed it next to the duffle bag on the counter.

While gazing into the mirror, his watch ticked to a silent alarm and his goggles switched to a computer tone.

He opened the bag on the counter and took out a pair of odd medium gloves. He put the gloves on, while squatting to open the bag on the floor.

Carefully, he lifted a strange machine. It was about nineteen inches wide, eight inches deep and about a foot in height.

He sat the device on the counter, beside the duffle bag. Then, he turned on both sinks.

The waters entered an expedited cycle of molecular reactions. The liquid evaporated into a gas, which then powered the machine.

Perry waved his hand across the front of the machine and a drawer ejected from the base. Inside the drawer where two cylindrical slots.

Perry reached into the bag on the counter and pulled out a black canister. He sat it in the far back of the counter. He placed his thumb on the top of the canister. A mist lifted as the can collapsed into a mound of blocks. They flipped and flattened away, leaving two hovering flasks behind.

One vile held a bright glittering red fluid while the other held a bright green substance.

Perry grabbed the red liquid and filled the cylinder slot in the drawer at the base of the machine. He grabbed the green flask and poured it into the other slot at the base of the machine. He waved his hand across the front of the contraption and the drawer closed into the machine. With the two fluids inside, the machine ran with a hum. Perry sat the empty flasks in the duffle bag on the counter.

Another drawer opened from the side of the machine.

The slot was full of a thick black substance. Perry grabbed a clean flask from the duffle bag on the floor and sat it into the black spongy liquid. The flask submerged slowly into the dark mixture. Seconds later, the flask lifted out of the substance with a strange burgundy solution inside of it.

Perry placed a cap over the flask. Kneeling to the bag on the floor, he pulled out a syringe. He loaded the flask into the automatic syringe and placed it on the counter next to the odd machine. Then, he waved his hand over the machine.

The slot closed back into the contraption as the device powered down. Then, the waters ran from the sinks as normal.

Meanwhile, Yuely stood against the opened stable with his head down and his eyes closed. While gnawing on the end of a wheat steam, he waited patiently for Perry.

"I hate to see you leave Archipus… You were my best friend," said Yuely as the great Clydesdale softly neighed.

"I know. I love you too."

Just then, Perry entered the stable.

He stood next to Yuely as his eyes followed up to the ceiling.

"Getting your goodbyes in?" Perry asked while glancing over to Yuely.

"Yeah..." He responded with sorrow as he took the wheat straw from his mouth. He sat up from the wall and walked over to the great Clydesdale.

"He's a huge amount of beauty."

"He?" Quizzed Perry as he gripped his duffle bags, walking about the horse.

"Yeap. He is a rarity. Strong as a keg of moonshine." Chuckled Yuely.

Perry sat his duffle bags to the grainy turf, asking "How tall is he?"

"He's ten feet easy... Maybe twenty-two hands."

"Incredible." Perry sighed, gently caressing the Clydesdale. "Did Horace make you an offer?"

"Yes, he did. Actually I need the money."

"How much did he offer?" Perry quizzed as he advanced over to Yuely.

"Well, he told me one million. He put half in my account already just to keep him here." Yuely explained while Perry looked at his watch.

"Uh-huh," said Perry as he tapped the face of his watch.

He stopped just in front of Yuely, patting the old man on the shoulder. "Freeze delay." Perry whispered. "Good man. Time will solve all your problems." Perry spoke as he turned away, walking slowly over to his duffle bags.

Yuely froze...

"By the way... my name isn't Perry. It's Attica. Attica James. I'm not from here. Honestly, I'm from nowhere near here. But on behalf of an illustrious group of beings, I... *be*." Attica lectured as he turned to face Yuely.

"I guess you're wondering what happened to you... Are you, Yuely?" He asked while adjusting his goggles.

Yuely stood unresponsive.

"That's rude," Attica noted as he reached into his coat pocket to retrieve the automatic syringe.

"I have a gift Yuely, as well as some high-tech weaponry." Attica explained. "I can stop, abrupt and even undo the timing of events. Control Z on the keyboard. This includes elements, objects, and in some cases, beings. In your case... I have only altered the functionality of your internal clock. You have about two minutes before your entire body malfunctions. I've traveled over a quadrillion galaxies, just to administer this Life Osmolality to Archipus."

He stabbed the Clydesdale in the rear with the automatic syringe, injecting the vial substance into the horse's blood stream.

Archipus didn't make a sound as Attica continued to empty the flask.

Attica removed the syringe and put it back into his coat. Then, he hoisted up the duffle bags.

"You see, Yuely, because of the Feuler and the events of Space Void, your reality (this world) has been placed on an expedited path… This solar system is overdue for an upgrade. And, well… I should say, in the immortal words of every Xaris, with every upgrade comes the removal of the older version. The outdated, prehistoric central processors." He explained while stepping over to Yuely, who had yet to move.

"That feeling, Yuely, that's your puny lungs failing and your blood thickening to clay. Your heart has slowed and all the moisture in your body has evaporated. It'll take a laser to cut you open." Attica noted with a muffled voice.

He stood in front of Yuely just as the large Clydesdale began to fall.

"This is but a small portion of things to come. The only reason I'm still talking, is because I know you can still hear me.

45

And, I had another minute to spare," Attica voiced as Archipus hit the ground.

Whom!

The sudden clunk sent tremors through the stable, vexing the other horses.

Attica sighed with passion. "Time's up," he whispered into Yuely's ear.

He skuttled out of the stable as Yuely dropped like a bag of cement.

Bomfff!!

Miles from the grand farmhouse, a small dot emerged across the herbage.

The old stagecoach driver snored on in comfort as the distant dot neared.

"Arise!"

The old man jumped up in a hurried fashion.

"Oh! That was fast."

"No, it wasn't. It's 10:01. That's precisely one hour of Earth time that I have mastered." Attica proclaimed.

The man sat with a loss of words.

"You can't tell time. Can you?"

"No, sir. I can't. But my daughter is teaching me a little. I've got a picture here in my pocket." He responded while leaning over to retrieve the photo. "She's looking for some di-"

"-Show me that photo, and I will detonate you." Attica interrupted.

The old man froze as Attica sat his duffle bags on the ground. He opened the door to the stagecoach and carefully sat the bags into the seat. "We are leaving," he disclosed as he climbed into the coach, shutting the door behind him.

"Yes, sir," the old man mumbled as he gathered the reins in his hands. "Ya!" He shouted, slapping the whips against the horses' back.

At all...

Communication of the Clydesdale diversion, journeyed beyond the telescope's lens.

By the time this report reached the Layo Galaxy, the Xaris had already progressed to other existences.

The automatons prevailed, and with diligence, did they convey their execution, through subliminal- digital means. But, the source of their real problem lay beyond simple schemes.

Killing the one responsible for the Space Void massacre became more than just a task.

The death of the Feuler became a must...

CHAPTER 4:

Gray Nativity

Twenty cycles north of Riaxon lies the Center Market.

This land of trade provides sources for business needs, routes to the Unitran, thousands of entertainment and shopping venues, and living spaces for beings over the galaxy.

At this moment, the multiverse land of commerce, and the most congested strip in the galaxy, Garlken Tymus (or The Straitzs), opened to the public.

One individual came, incognito in fashion.

A chef.

Or a butcher, to say the least.

Some came to love him as one of the best cooks to ever work for The Zygote (a high-end restaurant located in lower Riaxon). Some saw him as a hero, the one psychotic enough to stand against the Symbassy's tyrannical reign. Others hated him for being the first to single handedly spawn off an undying feud. And yes, the tragic events of Space Void followed him internally, branding him as the one and only Feuler.

He stepped on sluggishly down the congested Straitzs wearing a heavy smoke gray cloak, shrouding him in mystery. His eyes held the same burning glow with that faint yellow tint, inviting your visual into the rift of visage.

Others passed him as if he was invisible, while a few beings were more than aware. From the darks of a gloomy alley, a pair of eyes studied the butcher's every move.

The Feuler had been wandering about The Straitzs for a while before he stopped to gather groceries.

Kavav's Market sat within a crater, miles deep into the Layain turf. It was a massive, circled depression that was full of different levels. Every rift (along the sides of the crater) had been converted into shelves to hold the millions of spices, minerals, potions, and more. The crater was also packed with Transportal systems for easy travel. Kavav's Market remained well-lit as it was surrounded by several suns that never set at the same time.

The Feuler entered the market slowly just as Kavav stood in the center of the crater.

"Come! Come! My Friend!" he shouted as the other beings poured into the large crater. "Take your time, my friend. Let me know if you need anything."

The Feuler held silent as he searched through the fresh food section. He walked slowly down a long rift that led towards the butcher's area.

He stopped at the meat display.

"What'd you say? Oh… yes!" The Feuler speculated as he leaned over to observe a piece of flesh.

51

"Can I help you find something, sir?" A butcher asked from behind the meat display.

"Who cuts?"

"I'm sorry... who whats?"

"Who cuts the parillion, you, or the machine?" The Feuler explained as he reached out to touch the bloody ration.

"Well, the machine, sir." The young butcher spoke as he approached the partition, whipping his hands free of meaty debris.

"Why you ask?"

"It's off," said the Feuler while looking over the rest of the portions. "They're all off. I include. We agree that they're all off."

"Uh... I didn't agree. But I set the machine to company standards."

Then, the Feuler glared up to the lad.

He was Xarchanzian, young and built with the likeness of man. His eyes clicked and glitched in different colors. His skin was computerized and full of dirty brown pixels. He wore a bloody brown apron and a Xarchanzian influenced outfit underneath. He was carefree and untainted by the currently brewing feud.

"May we?" The Feuler gestured while holding up the portion of alien meat.

"We who?" The young butcher responded, glancing about the shop.

The Feuler had already advanced behind the counter and over to the organic table.

"Sir! Sir! You can't come back here!" The young Xaris shouted as the Feuler stopped in front of the cutting table.

"We will show you this… one whole," the Feuler whispered.

"Sir… my boss will kill me!"

"Not before we kill him," the Feuler inserted as he reached around his belt, unsheathing that dastard, ungodly sharp butcher knife from its holster.

"Holy hell…" the young Xaris grumbled as he stared into the blade.

The Feuler gripped the knife's handle and lightly tapped the blade against the cutting board.

Full of inspiration, the young Xaris stepped over to the Feuler's side.

His cloak responded with ease as he lifted the knife quickly. Then, he sheathed the mighty butcher knife up into its holster. The heavy cloak fell back into place as he lowered his arm.

"There. We did it." The Feuler noted.

He high fived himself. Then, he turned slightly to the young learner as he stood watchfully, zoning into the alien meat.

"We'll have that wrapped in melathin," the Feuler acknowledged as he walked away.

The young lad stepped over to the table and slowly lifted the morsel up. A very thin sliver feathered back to the table. The young vendor picked up the slice of parillion with a farcical look in his eyes. The slice was way too thin to conceptually procure. Mainly because the young viewer had yet to see the Feuler cut the meat.

"Incredible," he spat, viewing through the slice.

He shook his head and smiled as he packed up the parillion.

Into the vast expanse of The Straitzs, the Feuler treaded as sluggish as his stride would allow.

He encountered several holograms that constantly displayed the slain dignitaries of Space Void. He watched, null and empty of any emotion as his tragic memories circled.

Moments later, the Feuler reached the outskirts of Garlken Tymus. He walked even slower as he finally neared the telepod.

The Feuler approached the large vacant pod with his bag in hand. He reached over to the control panel and typed a series of characters into the holographic screen. Then, the pod's circular door swiveled open. The Feuler stepped into the pod and the circular door closed shut. Then he sat into his seat, holding his bag in his lap.

The roomy telepod's interior was like none other.

It was full of mechanical buttons, transparent screens, maps, and dancing holograms, entertainment for the waiting occupants. The lighting about the inside of the pod flourished with derivatives of reds and blues. The average pod has four dense, uncomfortable seats within it, arranging from top to bottom.

The Feuler waited for only a moment before the Unitran approached, traveling beyond the speed of light and several thousand feet into the sky.

The telepod linked itself to the light speeding train. Joined by a highly advanced form of computerized interfacing, the pod detached itself from the ground port. It lifted high into the air and gravitated to the above Unitran.

The pod locked into its docking port and positioned itself aboard the corridors of the monorail.

As the mechanics secured to a locking, the mysterious Feuler sat with his eyes closed. He held his bag in his lap while laying back into the unbearable pod seat.

CHAPTER 5:

Vile Victory

Lenox Hill Hospital
New York City, New York

"*Gasp!*"

"And-", the doctor paused as he glimpsed over to me.
"Oh, my mother Mary. You're *alive?*" He whispered, as I glanced
about the emergency room.

My jaw was wrapped, and I was filled with stitches, casts,
and staples. Then, I was wearing an oxygen mask and tied to the
bed. There were two additional agents in the room. They were well
dressed and groomed.

"Don't get up, Lawson!" Said one of the agents.

"You need to rest." Said the other.

My pains were dull, and I could tell I wasn't supposed to
be talking. "They're coming." I grunted, breathing frantically.

"Well, *they* are gonna have to wait. Cause you're in no
position to be going out." The doctor blurted, staring at his
clipboard.

"You have four broken ribs. Both of your lungs collapsed.
Five shin fractures in your right leg. Your hands are crushed.
You've broken both forearms. Your left arm was cut to the bone.
Twice. We had to graft tissue. You have a huge laceration directly
in line with your back which shifted your spinal column two
centimeters in. Whatever cut you was very precise. It missed a vital

57

nerve… And to be exact, by one millimeter. The slightest move could paralyze you. Forever.

Your jawbone is beyond repair. That's something I am hoping will heal over time. But it will never be the same. I don't know how you're even able to talk. Perhaps your tongue will fall out.

Your right shoulder and bicep will have to be repaired in stages. Your large and small intestines and your stomach were cut in two. It took us forever to patch that up. You'll have to receive nourishment through injection.

You have a shattered nasal bone, frontal bone, and your nostrils were cut in half. There's a cut through your sternum, spine and back. You have about six more lacerations over your upper and lower back, forehead and shoulders, that were all cuts to the bone.

Oops, forgot to mention. You have three severe fractures in your skull. One's wide as a dime and long as the average pinky. But for some strange reason, your brain isn't swelling. The crater in the center of your fractured chest, shifted your heart to the left just shy of two millimeters. That readjustment could alter your balance and blood circulation. Let's hope that it moves back on its own. You could possibly suffer from a massive heart attack." The doctor lectured.

"That's over 2,000 staples, ten grafts, 900 something odd stitches and a hell of a lot of Fentanyl." The doctor exclaimed, looking harshly over to me.

"Mrs. Lawson… How are you not dead?" He marveled.

"The fact that you aren't is a mystery, an enigma if you ask me." Said one of the agents.

'Twas a mystery to me too…

"Looks like you got into a fight with Detroit." The other agent included.

With a smile, I grumbled, "My cousins' from Detroit."

Right then, a strong feeling overcame me. A telepathic reminder of some kind… "They're coming. You have to get me… Let me go!" I mumbled softly.

"Let you go?" The agent hollered, throwing up his hands. "I think your hearing is shot too."

"Lawson, you're fucked up." The doctor added. "Who's coming?" The other agent muttered.

With a face of terror, I glared over to him and grumbled, "…Hell's assassins. The end of humanity. Government takeover. The Aliens coming… They got a Hit List. It's on a drive."

"Aliens, huh?" Smirked the doctor.

"They. Are. **Real**."

"You said that they have a Hit List? On a drive? Where is the drive now?" The agent asked.

The pains in my jaw forced me to silence.

"You guys are seriously considering her rationale?" Jeered the doctor. "I mean… she is a bit… fucked!"

"She isn't that off. Just yesterday over a dozen agents died in Lotte Palace. Some kinda silent ambush. No leads or evidence. We lost a lot of good men and women," expressed one of the agents.

"You think this is linked?" The other agent implied.

"Could be… Lawson?" The agent asked. "Where was your briefing?"

Shaking my head, I groaned, "Can't remember."

"It's got to be the same incident. Gary, tell me this doesn't add up."

Gary dropped his head and put his hands on his hips.

"Well…" the doctor inserted, tapping the clipboard against his hand. "They'd be doing you a favor. Killing you, I mean… I'm joking."

We stared at each other with grave discord as I struggled to flip the doctor off. But my fingers were non-responsive, and I just couldn't say it like I wanted.

"AAAwwwww… I see it. A little." The doctor claimed.

"Don't worry, Lawson. You're safe here." Said Gary.

I shook my head with a demure, "No."

Ever since that bitch did her little telepathy trick, I've been somewhat... connected.

"Canieya... where is the drive?" Gary asked as I tried to get out of the bed.

"Mrs. Lawson! Stop moving." The doctor shouted. "You're going to tear something. I've got several patients to remedy." He added while glancing at his watch. "I'll be back in about an hour."

"They're here." I uttered with horror.

"Great!" The doctor shouted, holding the door handle.

The agents peeked over the room as my eyes locked open. "They're hereeeeee..." I whispered again.

The doctor cracked the door and turned to me, relishing in his departure, "Guest visitations are between eight and nine." He smirked as he opened the door.

Whisskk!

A flash of light cracked through the room.

The doctor's arm dropped from his body and a chunk of his face slapped the floor.

Sqwat!

Blood oozed as the male assassin shoved into the room, knocking the doctor's corpse to the floor. Then, came a terrifying hiss.

SSSsssssssssss...

The agents reached for their guns just as that bitch queen somersaulted over my bed, trapping the agents in the center.

Gary aimed as the male assassin rammed his sword down the gun, piercing through Gary's hand and forearm.

The female assassin kicked the other agent in his back, flicking the gun over the room. She whipped out her nunchucks. Knives sprung from the ends, as she stabbed the agent in the chest. She spun around, slinging the bladed nunchuck over her shoulder. And-

Ssszz!!

That flash emitted as she caught the nunchuck under her arm. The agent's head popped off his body, bouncing a smudge against the wall.

The head tumbled to my bedside as the male assassin yanked his sword out of Gary's arm. Kicking into his stomach, he lifted the agent off the floor. The merc spun and plunged his demonic blade meticulously through Gary's mouth and esophagus, crushing his spine to mulch. As the demonic ninja snatched his sword free, both agents fell to the floor.

With a whisk of devil hate, the knives retracted into the female assassin's nunchucks.

They timed their attacks with such horrific synchrony, I'd never seen anyone die so fast.

Standing in unison, the killing machines held their ground.

The male assassin sheathed his sword as the bitch queen placed her nunchucks into the rear holster of her belt.

Then, they turned and glared apathetically, quite soulless at me.

Infernally, I laughed out of anger. "You... Just couldn't stay away... I'm literally, anxiously bound to this, fatal attraction of yours. Yawl still think I'm sexy?" I beamed with sarcasm. "Huh?" I blurted.

They just kept staring.

My adrenaline started inching its way back into my system. My pains began to disappear, plus I was terribly doped up.

"What the fuck y'all staring at?" I asked bluntly.

"Why don't you untie me? Come over here. Untie me. So, I can beat... That. Ass! Please!" I begged as I lifted my arms as far as the constraints would allow.

But they just kept standing there, not budging at all. Then, I lowered my oxygen mask and said, "Is this some kinda joke? Oh, I get it. You just go stand there until I heal up. Until I can untie myself. *Then* I can beat that ass."

The two mercenaries looked at each other.

"I'm just saying though, y'all ain't doing nothing. Especially you!" I gawked over to the bitch queen. "Yeah, you!" I shouted.

The male assassin stared into the ceiling while the bitch queen glared sadistically at me.

63

"You mad cause I ran over yo' face? ...It's okay to cry. I cried when Willy died. Let's finish this! Tell your pimp to step outside so I can have my way with you."

With a sniff, I harked and rasped up a bloody loogie. Then, I spat it in her face. "Motherfucker!" I shouted.

The male assassin peeked to his counterpart as she wiped the glob away. She darted in, just as the male assassin seized her by the arm.

"Nawl!! Don't hold her! Let that bitch go!" I hollered as she stood to a casual rest, fixing her clothes.

"Man... what y'all got going on here?"

Then, I realized... They were waiting on something, or someone...

The male assassin put his hands on his hips. He stared up at the ceiling again, impatiently tapping his finger against his utility belt.

"They must be running late?" I quizzed. "Damn CPT. That's whatcha' get for dealing with niggas. Dey' ain't neva' on time."

Knock! Knock! Knock!

I snatched over to the door. And everything got quiet...

Fixed on the sound, my adversaries stood to attention.

I peeped over to them and-

Knock! Knock! Knock!

I snatched back over to the door as a degraded voice quizzed, "Anybody there?"

"Ain't nobody in here." I disclosed, just as the door cracked open.

"Is it safe to enter?" The voice asked.

"Man, damn!" I shouted. "Come in. Shit!"

The door creeped open and there stood a man.

He was African American and obviously mixed with another race. He must've been in his late thirties. He stood about 5' 7" or so with a head full of dreads. They stretched down a tad past his shoulders. He had a strong chin and a big nose, with light brown eyes.

He wore a gray and red pinstripe suit with a solid gray dress shirt, some light brown loafers, a red and white polka dotted tie, and a matching handkerchief; fluffed to bloom out of his coat pocket.

My eyes popped at his presence as he entered with a huge smile. He stopped, put his hands in his pockets and glared to the floor. The door closed slowly behind him. "Whoaaa... somebody had a boo-boo," he expressed, stepping over the bloody corpse.

"Teufel: Kalor. Ix Zhater. Did I miss the party?" He chuckled as he picked up the agent's head. He held it up in the air like a trophy. He took the head outside of the emergency room and sat it in the hallway as I spoke.

65

"Ix? "What the hell kinda name is that?"

The bitch queen rolled her eyes, mumbling, "Ix, in Xarchanzian, means the glory of beauty. I am the persona of appea-"

"-Sounds stupid. How do you even say that? Ix?"

"It sounds better than Canieya." She hissed as I tossed my oxygen mask to the side.

"Bitch I'll beat-cho' ass. With that shitty ass name!"

"Shut up!" Kalor pointed with interruption. "Why aren't you dead? I stabbed you repeatedly." He leered into my eyes while a soft steam arose from his shoulders. He folded his arms and hissed, "As the prince of darkness... Beelzebub will have your atman. The devil deals..."

Clap! ClaP!

CLAp!

clAp!

The man applauded. "Guysss!!" He chuckled while walking to the front of my bed. "Let's take a step back, Egh?"

As he continued to applaud, I followed this stranger with my explorative eyes.

claPp! Clap!

claP!

"Who are you?" I mumbled just as he stopped.

"You have something that belongs to us." He whispered, turning to me with his head down.

"What? What I got?"

"It's a small device, about… yay big." He gestured. "It's black, and full of alien information- an organized plan for galactic domination. You seen it?"

Who the hell is this cat?

"…C'mon, Lawson." He pleaded while sitting beside me.

"How do you know my name?"

"Really, Canieya?"

"Nawl. For real, man… Your friends nearly killed me. I'm having a hard time collecting."

"Take a guess." He indulged with a smile, and a weakening charm that enticed me to play.

The impractical idea, had me blushing.

"I'll give you a hint. Just one though." He inserted.

"Oooookkaayy…?"

"Your boss and a vast majority of the fuzz have been looking for me for a long time." He confessed with a mesmerizing tone.

A fascinating feeling brought everything together, connecting my puzzled thoughts. Then, I regretfully drew my mental picture as he leaned up to me, nodding his head.

"That's it…" he mumbled.

My disbelief turned my query into facts. But I was here, this close to the man I have longed to kill...

My body jolted as I started crying. From my lying position I observed, while hurt and furious, and in no shape to take him on. Let alone his assassins.

He sat on his hands, sighing as he turned away, kicking his feet in and out of the bloody puddle, which covered the tiles.

He looked to the floor as I cried.

The assassins stared on. No one was saying anything. It was just the sound of my sobbing.

"Kalor... would you pass me some tissue," he ordered.

The assassin huffed and then walked over to the sink, stepping over the dead bodies.

He picked up a pink box of tissues and walked back over to the dread headed man.

"Thank you, sir." He said as Kalor passed him the box. He took several tissues and scooted up to my head.

Teufel: Kalor walked back over to Ix, and stood to attention.

The dread headed man reached out to pamper me. "There. There." he muttered as he wiped my tears away.

The comment only made me cry worse as I yelled at the top of my lungs.

"Geez Lawson... you're just... God!" He shouted.

He threw the damp tissues to the floor, and he grabbed a couple more from the box.

"You figured it out?" He stated as he reached up to wipe my eyes.

"Horace Vaydin." I whined like a little child.

"Yes. It is." He sadly admitted. He slowed in my pampering and seductively asked, "You mad at me?"

Convulsively gasping, I whimpered, "Uh-huh."

"Poor thing. Must've had a rough day…" Horace mumbled just when Kalor stormed out of the room.

G-Sssekccccsss!

The door shut softly…

Ix stood in front of my death bed, with no emotion or feelings at all. Yet every essence of my miserable anguish, detailed my failure.

My torment came with exceptional timing…

CHAPTER 6:

Possession

In the medieval farmhouse, all was quiet as the empties of space. But the tarty stench of death came with Attica's time delay.

Suddenly, from the back wall of Archipus' stable, came a bright light.

Lowering quickly to the hay filled floor, was a one-sided, thin cast of air. But from this bright light, stepped a dark figure.

This figure approached Archipus while pulling out a bag of soil. It sprinkled the dirt over the horse, in the shape of a pentagram. Then, the entity kneeled and orated with a lowered head. A vile and disturbing message shook the stables as the specter muttered while rocking back and forth.

Just then, the bright window flashed.

The specter stalked over to the window and then back to the horse. But it whispered on, in this unknown tongue. Then, the being stood from the hay filled floor.

After gazing about the setting, the wicked entity walked over to the window. The portal closed quickly as the vile specter entered.

Then, Archipus' eye opened, burning red with hell's flame.

CHAPTER 7:

Unitran Trip

From one end to the other, hundreds of telepods rushed in and out of the monorail. The polluted noise from others boarding the congested cart became more than irritating. It openly divulged the Feuler's pulse of patience. Plus, the Feuler's destination was beyond Base: Trimmevel, which just so happened to be the last stop.

To gain some form of tolerance, the Feuler sat still as a rock in his uncomfortable seat. He glared lifelessly out of his pod window as the many beautiful, strange, and yet angelic settings passed. By far, the greatest of the settings to behold would be that of Markashuvu.

The flat land was full of wild plants that stretched high into the sky and over the distance. The vegetation flared up into glorious loops, forming remarkable shapes of floral developments. The godly arrangement came evenly placed with hundreds of planets and moons that cast thousands of unforeseen lights and colors. The sighting continued with daring creativity as the inventive grounds expressed themselves.

The Feuler captured a vast portion of this sublime, magnificent stretch of institution.

Eventually, the scenery and the pleasant sounds of the Unitran, traveling over the hyper rails, brought the Feuler to a humbled calm.

He finally dozed off, passing the moments with ease.

Lower Riaxon
Base: Trimmevel

The sign sat high into the atmosphere as the Unitran glided into the entrance. The station had only one large platform, which hovered high above the Layian ground.

"Welcome to Base: Trimmevel," the monorail spoke in Layian. *"This is your final stop aboard the Unitran division. Please secure all personal belongings and be sure to commute safely to your next destination. And as always, thank you for using The Unitran, the fastest means of public transit across the Layo Galaxy."*

The Unitran came to a stop as it finally approached the platform.

The Feuler opened his glowing eyes to an empty cart. He sat up to notice that none of the pods had detached from the monorail. He grabbed his bag just as his antennae erected slowly from the top of his head.

Then, the lights flickered, and all the screen displays, and holograms shut to a dark.

Without blinking his restless eyes, the Feuler stared out of the pod window. He sat back and placed his bag into the seat next to him. Placing his hands in his lap, he gaped continuously out the pod window.

The platform lights illuminated the alien surface with computerized holograms designed into the walls. The aberrant flickering aided the setting, but not the Feuler's sentiments. He finally glanced away from the window, dropping his head as if he regretted the ride home, in which he had yet to make.

"Phaldone Valeen! You are wanted for the irrational expiry of: Pias Grosine, Illian Cronz, Paymer Ijan, Qusar Gominis, Ordis Dant, Velleayan Fice, Straton Mage, Riva Aakush and A.P.A. Eliza." A voice announced over an intercom.

The Feuler sat his head back and glared into the monorail ceiling. "You are wanted dead. Or alive. Coaction is demanded." The voice sounded.

The Feuler looked out of the pod window, and at least twenty armed soldiers occupied the platform.

CHAPTER 8:

Archipus
Part 2

Dartmoor, England
Devon County SW

Collapsing stables and crumbling enclosures degraded with sparks of red lightning. The hay filled floor cracked with burning rifts as a mutilated pony toppled to the ground. This scene doubled with horror as all the steeds were smushed to their stables, foaming in a puddle of gore.

A path of destruction flowed through the medieval farmhouse. Ornaments and fixtures trashed the halls while hunks of flesh trimmed the floor. Red streaks of lighting zipped and zapped from the walls as this marred path covered the pasture.

But outside, and from a far, came the old stagecoach driver.

"Whoooaaa…" He whispered, slowing the rickety wagon to a halt. He stood slowly from his seat, in view of the disaster.

Blazing fires reached the sky as the farmhouse leveled to the ground.

The old coach driver's eyes noted the path of desolation, traveling off into the land. As the reins slipped from his hands, he mumbled in fear, "Greatime-ah-day in the morning…"

CHAPTER 9:

Triumphant Evil
Part 1

Early the next morning, I awoke to a banging jar of pain.

Peeping over the emergency room, I noticed it was clean, and the assassins were gone. But still, I was bound to the bed, and my space had shrunk. Tremendously...

There was a heaviness about the pillows. Something was lying next to me. Immediately, I turned into his face... He was lying so close that I could kiss him.

Shuffling and screaming, I awoke the Bomb King.

"Whoa!!!" He yelled. "How'd you get in here?" He asked as he sat up.

He was still fully dressed.

"Sorry. That couch is unforgiving." He yawned, walking over to the green couch as I grunted to free myself.

He picked up a magazine and plopped down, crossing his legs. "Ahhhh..." he sighed while sitting back and browsing through the magazine.

All I could do was stare as he turned through the pages.

The clock ticked as the occasional pages turned and every now and then the subtle sounds of traffic rumbled through the streets. But I was still staring at him.

He would glance into my eyes of unstable anger and childishly duck behind the magazine, pretending to be so immersed in reading.

"Horace. What were you doing lying next to me?"

He peeked up from behind the magazine, making eye contact.

I glared at him, turning my head sideways, anticipating his undignified response.

He ducked back behind the magazine. Like he was playing peek-a-boo.

"My love comes free, but the price is sky high for divorce. Prenups are the only true adversary in the uncertainties of failing loves." He said as I ogled with confusion.

"Anything that falls comes to an abrupt stop. Whereas, growing… Yes. Growing like a tree would be ideal. The only thing that could bring down such a love, would be a man with an axe. Or a lightning bolt. I'd rather grow in love like a tree, rather than fall in love like a brick." He stated as he finally closed the magazine, tossing it to the side.

"Henry Singuize." he quoted as he finally looked up to me.

"Man, why the hell fuck wuz' you lying next to me?"

"Why are you so mean? And you have a very foul mouth." Horace noted as he gripped the knee of his crossed leg, entangling his fingers.

"You were asleep for a long time," he disclosed as he stood up. "You like what I've done with the place?" He asked, putting one hand in his pocket and showcasing with the other. "I have an outstanding cleaning crew. Wouldn't you agree? We just got tired of stepping over that doctor. He was rude too."

"Mannn… why wuz' you lying next to me?" I asked again.

This was when things got scary, cause I didn't know what he was up to.

"The great Canieya Lawson. You were one of the most difficult, toughest, and resilient targets on the list. You just would not die. It was so bad that I had to meet you myself. In person. I even went about *'certain'* preparations for this occasion. I heard about your daughter. Quite tragic. No! Very tragic. And not my style by the way…" he hinted just as he stopped at the foot of my bed. "I love kids. You know, I have one myself."

Horace was a stranger and the agonizing reality of his company whaled over my accomplishments as a crime fighter. But here he was. The top of *my* list, roaming freely about this emergency room.

"How's that asshole? Crane?" He said, ogling out of the window.

Now, I can't stand Crane.

For real… I mean, I really can't.

But if it's one thing I hate worse than Crane, it's someone talking shit about Crane.

"Don't you dare talk about Crane like that. I will kick yo' muthafucking ass!" I screamed while wrestling for freedom.

Horace threw up his hands and turned to me. "I'm sorry, Lawson…" he paused as he braced himself up at the foot of the bed. "... But you're just not getting out of those restraints."

"I know that!" I shouted while trying to free myself.

He shook his head and put his hands back into his pockets.

"Let me tell you about myself. Lawson, I work for a very peculiar group of individuals. Here and there. A little bit of everywhere. If you can imagine a place in your mind, then they have already been there.

Anyway, twenty years ago, I graduated from Harvard, at the top of my class; with a major in chemistry. And even then, my brain was only using twenty percent of its capacity. I wanted more… A lot more." he lectured as he paced the floor.

"One day, we had a council. It utterly expanded my mental perception to something more than galactic. Now, I have a very special brain. It thinks ten times faster than the average human. Over time, bombs became my specialty. They are just so easy for me to… wield.

But I finally noticed how small I am, you are, we all are- to the voids in space.

How challenging would it be to own it all? The kudos. The reward sparked my interest. Then, Space Void happened. The Feuler, some crazed co-joined twin, put us on a fast track. And then… Then, you came… such a worthy adversary. So resilient that I just had to… Assass-A-nation." He said as he turned his back towards me.

He gazed out the window with his hands still in his pockets. "Lawson? There's a star in the sky with your name on it. All I ne-" he paused as he dug into his coat pocket. "-Sorry, gotta take this."

This thrilling soap opera drained me as I gestured with impatience.

"Attica! How are you, man? Oh no. Sorry to hear that." He said as he turned to face me, holding up his finger. "A stallion? I bet. What??? A Clydesdale? How tall is he? Get out of town. He fell? Oh, no. Don't you worry, man. I'll send him the other half now. Yes. It's automatic." He confirmed.

Horace put his hand over the phone and leaned over to me whispering, "This guy's long winded."

He sat up and put the phone to his ear.

"Yeah. No! I'm here. Guess who I'm with… Canieya Lawson." He chuckled.

"Don't you tell him 'bout me!" I hollered.

"Yeah, I slept with her. For real. She was kinda beat up. But… you know-"

"-No the hell you didn't! You a lie!"

"What's that, Lawson?"

"Motherfucker!!" I wailed while trying to get out of my restraints.

He turned to me and mumbled, "Attica says hi."

"Tell him I said hey."

"Lawson says hey!" He giggled, glancing down to his watch. "She keeps trying to get out of those straps."

"Oh, man… that's so sad. I'm so sorry to hear that. How's Capris taking it? Hey! Hey! Gotta go man. We're about to miss the fireworks." He said as he hung up.

Turning to face me, he put the phone into his coat pocket.

"Poor Yuely. He was something else. Folks died in a car wreck. Left the whole estate to him and his brothers. He's dead now." Said Horace. "Man…I just wired the other half of that money too."

Knock! Knock!

"Room service." Spoke a familiar voice.

"Ix! C'mon in!" Vaydin ordered.

In walked the bitch queen.

I threw my head back and howled, "Lawd. *This* bitch!"

She walked in holding a tray, with a bowl, a small carton of milk, a spoon, and a box of my favorite cereal.

"Why don't you like her? She worked really hard to kill you... I don't understand." Horace shrugged.

My head shook at this nonsense, psychotic situation. He was literally driving me crazy.

The bitch queen sat the tray on the rolling counter next to me. The Bomb King walked over and propped his hands up on the counter. "Lawson..." he whispered. "I know you're hungry."

The bitch queen glared over to me and smiled. Then, she glanced down and pulled out a really thin, transparent square.

"Hey!" Yelled Horace. "You want some cereal?" He asked, walking over to my bedside.

"I can't eat that."

"Why?"

"The doctor said I'd have to receive nourishment through a straw."

Blissshhh!!

He chunked the tray across the room.

Just then, Ix grabbed Horace by the shoulder. They turned away and ogled into that thin piece of glass.

"The hell yawl looking at?" I spoke as they whispered.

85

"I'll take care of it." Horace mumbled. He turned to me as Ix grabbed the remote from the counter. "Now! …Mrs. Lawson." Horace spoke just when the television came on.

Horace spun around as Ix pointed to the television. "That, is **not** Ultra Zach!" She shouted as the news blared with commotion. An aerial shot came into view. Then, a massive horse darted out of an exploding building. "I've seen the serum, and this is not the typical response." Ix spoke. "There's… something else, controlling that horse."

"What's wrong with that horse?" I grumbled.

"Do we have what we need?" Horace spoke as Ix held her hand up to her ear.

"Confirm code retrieval." Ix spoke. "The ruffian has the codes."

"Sweet." Horace answered as I sat glued to the television. This massive horse was mowing over cars and people… like it was nothing. "The fuck wrong with that horse?"

Horace whipped out his phone. "Attica." He whispered. "Pull the plug."

"I already did!!!" Attica shouted. "That's what I was trying to tell you!"

Horace hung up the phone, gulping as Ix spoke. "Tell me you have a contingency plan."

"I wouldn't be the king if I didn't." Horace said as he pulled out a small button. "Well, Mr. Archipus, it was nice knowing you." He pressed the button and we all glared up to the television.

But the massive horse responded with more anger. The steed had gone mad.

"That's strange…"

"What?" Said Ix.

"We added a group of nanobots into the vial. They're supposed to suppress the serum, but… nothing's… happening."

"Horace, if we don't put that thing down *now*, it will annihilate an entire region. He will spread like a virus. The Earth will resort to war."

"Yawl dumbass!!"

"**Shut UP!**" They hollered in unison.

Ix peered up to Horace and grumbled, "Fix this." She stormed out of the room as Horace lowered his head.

"Oh! … Almost forgot. Iiii… have something to show you." He coached as he released the locks on my bed. "Seriously, I was hoping you could eat some cereal and watch… But, due to the current circumstances…" Horace panted as he pushed me over to the window. He locked the wheels and opened the blinds. There came the beautiful sun, rising before me.

"Gorgeous. Isn't it?" He gloated.

87

The anger bubbled in my eyes as I laid there, speechless.

"Oh, wait!" He chuckled, rushing over to my bedside. He pressed the button on my bed and my upper body raised to the setting. "Forgot to sit you up."

"Agh!!!!" I screamed as all my injuries throbbed.

Then, something happened...

"I... I can't feel my legs. I can't feel my legs anymore."

"Huh? Did I just paralyze you?" He critically speculated. "I didn't know that was going to happen. Ha!" he roared. "Yes, I did."

Turning to him with tears in my eyes, I grumbled, "I'm gonna kill you!"

"That's what they all say. Sh! Shh.... You're gonna miss it." He interrupted.

He pointed to the far corner of the setting. "Isn't that Lotte Palace, the hotel you were staying in, wayyyy over there?"

A red bolt of lightning flashed through the clouds, then a ball of fire covered the scenery.

My eyes shut and opened to see the entire motel crumbling to the ground. Then, a very loud bang followed.

Ba-Booom!!!!!

The sound shook the room vigorously.

"You see that tall building over there? That high rise? There's a lot of important people over there." He mentioned while turning to glare in my eyes. "But they're in my way."

"No!" I shouted while turning away from it.

"Lawson, you're missing it!" He confirmed. "Look! Lawson! LOOK!!!" he screamed, darting up to my side. He grabbed me fiercely by the crown of my head, snatching my face over to the view. He took his fingers and forced my eyes open. "Look!!" He hollered.

Suddenly, another ballooning flash of destruction consumed the setting. Then, the bang followed.

KaBooooom!!

This explosion was twice as terrifying as it shattered the glass and the mounted television crashed to the ground.

Ga-Klliiiissshhhh!!!

The lights flickered as he walked to the edge of my bed. He put his hands in his pockets, just as several explosions mushroomed to the sky. One right behind the other.

The sound delay came to greet us, shaking the hospital's foundation again and again…

He turned around and unlocked the wheels on my gurney. Ruinous eruptions dazzled up behind him as he pushed me back into place. The destructive clamor shook my soul loose while my

89

perspective of Horace Vaydin became an instant classic, an epic mashallah of devastation.

He walked back over to the window and closed the blinds.

The sounds of hell, boiled up to the Earth's surface as I laid in anger. Not only was I paralyzed but I had just witnessed sheer evil. The complete mastery of Horace Vaydin. At that moment, I learned why they called him The Bomb King.

Vaydin walked across the room as I sobbed away in grief. He approached the door and stared at the floor. Then, he glanced over his shoulder and mumbled, "You lost..."

His proclamation drove me insane, as I gawked at the wall in front of me. Evil guzzled my attempt to protect and serve and Horace knew. I was only a useless advocate. He won by leaps and bounds, stepping and squashing me to a flat, pasty roadkill.

He opened the door. Then, he walked out of the room with no remorse.

Gggssssnk!

The door shut elegantly behind him.

There, I sat neglected, in a complete state of shock and with no plans to thwart his efforts. The fact that his assassins could do the things they did, it... it drove me insane. And then that horse was on the loose. That killing machine was spreading like a plague, and all I could do was stare...

CHAPTER 10:

The Blackline _ 101

We sprouted out of a reflective ground.

The room was massive. There were no windows and no way for light to enter. But the reflective shine from the surrounding walls gave us a sense of depth.

Just then, Guitussami materialized in front of us. "This room is made of antimatter, dark matter and Tierun particles. It is an unbreakable composite, allowing only a distinct class to sync through its walls. Cycles do not exist here. Time does not exist here. We have several eternities to master every technique. When I say dodge, you dodge. When I say strike, you strike. What I teach you, you will do proficiently and without haste. There is no room for question, because I teach with a definite, unmitigated sense of expertise. You will master the art of Astrodal Fist." He lectured.

"You will learn to punch and kick with the cosmos. You will deliver solid strikes with the moxie of a controlled asteroid, attacking at the speed of light. And before graduation, you will have the potential to single handedly eliminate an entire planet." He added while frankly tearing through my psyche.

Instantly, I understood him.

Guitussami didn't waste a single span of space. Our training began soon after he explained himself.

We, the anchors of the multiverse, learned how to punch with precision and with our entire bodies. We also learned every form of hand-to-hand combat- foreign and Layian. We must've thrown a single punch for an eternity. Everyone except Azix. She stood still as ever. In one spot.

Yet, we knew not of fatigue or pain. We became versatile in our movements. We studied the Wall of Ontology (the anchor). While the elements spawned quicker than light, we communicated with the septillions of Gastropods within our DNA. We learned to deliver a destructive channel of acidic slime. The uncharted pH level could decompose a surface forever or be reduced to a negative scale. But Azix... she just held her same position. Not moving at all.

We learned how to emit an extremely powerful jet-propelled blast of slime from our pores. Our hands, feet and bodies could adhere to any surface and then be used to propel us in any direction, and at an alarming rate. We caught on fast. Everyone except Azix. Finally, Guitussami coasted up to her side.

He glared into her eyes. She didn't budge or even acknowledge his presence. She simply stared straight ahead. At nothing... The Colonel didn't speak on this strange behavior. He politely dropped his head and floated off to continue the upskill.

Even I was being distracted by something. There were no answers for the delays... and I didn't want the Colonel to know.

Yet, the objective, and my place in this Layian equation came just as clear. I knew exactly why I was here.

First, there was REB (Radioactive Equating Biohazard) or Big-Bang, the head of M.O.S. He was ordered to devise fool proof plans to insure victory for the sake of the team.

While ultimately defined as the team strategist, REB is also a Biochemist and an Alchemist to the cosmos. This explained the random colors in his hands. He is the final step, this biohazard of total precision. His abilities stretched beyond me and the expanding voids.

Then there was me, Xon. Defined as the Regulator, the strong arm, engineered to equalize the battle, by absorbing and re-exerting emitted strengths and various forms of energy. This was ordered to ensure REB's plan for victory.

Finally, there was Infiltrate and Retrieve. This duo is always the first into battle. The aces in first wave attacks.

They share the same code because their duties are easily interchangeable, depending upon the strategy. The two are seldomly seen alone in a fight as they can so efficiently achieve any smidgen of information. From tissue samples, to pieces of matter, to technological instruments. Anything they can obtain is reported to REB, and later reviewed by the team. From there, a victorious plan of attack is devised.

Infiltrate and Retrieve's abilities are suitably different (via the infused learning matter).

Azix's skeletal structure is pervaded with Tierun. She can turn her infrastructure on and off, like switching a solid back into a liquid. She can flex and bend herself into a knot. She could flatten as thin as a sheet of paper. She can squeeze through cracks and still maintain her overall composition. But I had yet to see her do any of this. She may have turned off.

Rayefill, however... everything he did, he did it fast. His joints were infused with Tierun, allowing his speed to increase with even the slightest move. Then, his suit would glow with a faint green color that Guitussami referred to as 'Neon Speed.'

After our initial training, we were ordered to engage in hand-to-hand combat. The sparring matches would determine errors, if any, while yet sharpening our skills.

CHAPTER 11:

Platform Liquidation
Part 1

The Feuler turned away from the sea of men and stared lifelessly into the empty rail cart. It was evident that his mind was neither here nor there. He sat, just as still as before, without batting his hellish eyes.

"Feuler!" The Xaris sergeant shouted from outside the Unitran.

The Feuler had yet to respond as he continued to stare off into nothingness.

"That's it," the sergeant sassed as he lowered his megaphone. "Get em' outta there."

Four men rushed the cart's sliding door, loading their weapons. The door opened swiftly as the soldiers entered with caution.

The Feuler watched austerely from the rear of the cart as three of the men came, crouching close to the floor. They stopped nearly a dozen pods away, aiming their weapons about the Feuler's seat. Then, the corporal entered, stomping his feet.

With his oversized space gun resting on his shoulder, the corporal stopped in front of the small group. He stood about ten pods away from the Feuler when he began his placid speech.

97

"You know… when they told me that you killed Pias, I couldn't believe it. When they told me that Aakush was hacked into two equal halves, I was like… Nawl!" He chuckled while glancing down to his weapon. "I only hoped to meet the thing of a soul that could possibly conjecture the notion of escape- without trial by jury, council and verdict."

He advanced forward as he continued his monologue.

"The apprehension of such a devil would have to be swift and painful. But then I thought… this being killed nearly ten individuals. Not to mention, extremely important individuals. Politicians! Governors! Pias Grosine… That's major. This *should* cause for more of a prolonged, extensive, torturous death. I'm **hoping** you don't comply." The Xaris corporal smirked.

The Feuler just stared into the small group with those glowing eyes of secrecy.

"Just sit there… just like you're doing. Give us all a hard time. We'll be glad to assist you in your... enthusiastic quest for death. You know- I fail to comprehend, just what it is I'm looking at..." the corporal gabbled in observation.

He stopped about several pods away from the Feuler. Squinting his eyes, he whispered to himself, "What are you?"

"What's it gonna be?" Shouted another man from the rear. "You coming?"

"We're dying for an explanation here," affirmed another.

The Feuler had yet to budge as he stared into the men with an uncanny gaze of murdering gist.

ZZZZzsssaaakkkk!

Sparks of plasma rays blasted into the Feuler's seat.

Soft crackles graced the Xaris ears as the Feuler's pod melted to a fiery glow.

A haze of smoke lifted from the corporal's plasma gun as he stepped further into the monorail's eerie atmosphere.

He noticed the Feuler's cloak casually flung over in the other seat. He reached out to grasp the garment.

Chisz!

A savage cut came from under the seat.

"AAaaagghhhh!!!" The corporal screamed as his foot chucked off, scattering blood over the monorail.

He fired wildly, wobbling to the floor.

The Feuler stood out of nowhere, chopping into the corporal's head.

Bish!

He yanked his butcher knife out as the soldiers fired.

Sparks of death zinged by as the Feuler split in two.

The firing stopped when the soldiers lost sight of the butcher.

They advanced forward slowly, stopping about eight pods away from the Feuler's cloak.

The soldier standing in the rear reached for his intercom. But before he could relay the message, the Feuler popped up behind, fully reunited.

He chopped quick-

Shzz!

Cleansing the man's head from his body.

The vanquishing slice shook the soldiers as they turned simultaneously.

And there the butcher stood, holding his giant knives.

The men opened fire as the Feuler split in half, ducking the vicious lasers.

FL stood beside one soldier, juggling his knife into the air. As the man turned to blast, his hands fell from his body.

FL thrust his knife into the soldier's stomach.

Shlp!

And with an up and down motion, he cut across- until the blade cleared through.

At the same time, FR slid behind the other man. With a flick of his wrist, he aimed the butchering blade up, and -

Chup!

"Aaaghhhhh!!" The man screamed as FR chopped between his legs.

He pushed and pulled in an upward- sawing motion.

Yanking his knife out of the man's chest cavity, he twirled the blade back down, sloshing blood over the monorail windows.

Both of the Xaris soldiers dismantled into a plashing gore.

An instant death… As it should be. For the Feuler's knives cut before greeting a surface.

The Feuler rejoined, sheathing his mighty butcher knives in the rear of his utility belt. The oily gore coated him fast as he collected a few organs. Carrying the gobbets in his arms like gentle perishables, he strolled casually up to the railcar's entrance.

The men on the platform glared as the monorail doors opened. And there, the Feuler stood, with no emotion. For a moment, he gazed, lifelessly into the army of Xarchanzians.

Then, he dumped the mutilated lumps onto the platform.

And with that same disturbing face… He took a step back, and the monorail doors shut with haste, closing the mad man up inside.

The soldiers glanced in discord while perceiving the monstrous deeds. "Well! That's *definitely* our man," uttered one of the men.

The sergeant tweaked away in anger, clinching the intercom. "This whole time I thought we were shooting him." He sadly addressed as he lifted the intercom. "Feuler!!!!!" He screamed.

In the dark and gloomy cart, the Feuler stood with his back turned to the entry door. He looked at his chunky cloak and his bag of parillion.

"I was being nice!" The sergeant shouted from the platform.

The Feuler's antennae twitched as he tapped the side of the pod chair, motioning his head.

The cloak crashed through the pod window.

The men ducked as the garment soared over the platform and out of the base.

The sergeant glanced over and boomed with an urgent surge of hate, "You're a dead man, Phaldone!" He peeked viciously over to the men and muttered… "Light his ass up!"

CHAPTER 12:

Triumphant Evil
Part 2

The winds tapped lightly against the plastic blinds. Through the window came a dusty smell of death as a red bolt of lightning flashed across the sky.

As the helicopters and sirens brought me to, my adrenaline kicked in. Suddenly, my pains abated with haste as I wrestled for freedom, scrambling for my life.

Without warning, both of my knees shot up. Wiggling my toes with a smile, my squabble became chaotic as I curled my arm to snap the restraints.

Nothing.

Then, I tried again, scuffling with both arms to loosen the bands.

"Agh!!!"

Harder and harder did I scuffle. But still, nothing. Finally, I decided to struggle, or die. Hell, I was gonna die anyway if I just laid here.

Right then, a red bolt of lightning cracked across the sky. My eyes darted over to the occurrence. I ogled for a second because it looked like blood streaking through the clouds.

"Let's go Lawson!!" I cheered while tussling to no end.

My body fatigued as I grunted, pushing, and pulling again and again.

Then, the strap on my hand began to give. I focused on that one, pushing, pulling, jerking, and wiggling until-

Pap!

My hand was free!

Piz!

"AAGhhh!!" I shouted, glaring to a deadly shuriken, stabbing clean through my cast and into the mattress.

Piz!

Another bolted in, planting in my leg.

Screaming from the locking pain, I reached over to snatch the star out. Three more shurikens fastened to my stomach and shoulders.

Piz! Pat! Zig!

"Fuck!!"

My toil turned to hell as I worked to escape the room.

Then, an array of shurikens throttled down like plops of rain. The sharp stars painted over my body, planting violently into my legs, arms, and midsection.

My squirm for freedom came to a stop when the last star plunked in my forehead.

Patzzz!

Life began to slip away as my ability to baffle pain fleeted.

Suddenly, a woman dropped from the ceiling, crippling the bed.

Fwum!

Her feet landed beside my hips.

She was facing me as I glared into her pixelated emerald eyes. This was not the bitch queen… this was someone else. Her skin was caramel colored and it flashed like a popping soda. She wore a forest green blazer made of a crinkly fabric. Her thick, long sleeve shirt underneath, matched with an unnaturally large collar that covered her nose and mouth. She wore a faded green wrap around her hair, that held her snake textured dreads up. Then she wore a brown utility belt and a pair of skintight khaki pants that glistened like aluminum. She wore a pair of tall off white bicycle boots with dozens of sharp straps running up the front.

My screams failed as I coughed and gagged, drowning in my own blood. My sheets dripped with gore as the woman tugged the shuriken from my forehead.

Shkatz!

Her incredible weight jolted the bed as she kneeled over my chest. Then, she grabbed my hair with one hand and with the other hand, she sawed savagely through my neck.

CHk! Chak! CHk! Chak!

Every bit of her churning and tugging, trembled through my flesh as she raked the shuriken across. She sawed through my spine and blood splashed in her face as my head separated. And for some strange reason, I processed this. She stood to her feet and picked my head up with sophisticated grace.

That red bolt of lightning flashed again as she stepped over me. She hopped off the bed and landed softly to the floor. She walked to the front of the medical bed and sat my head between my twitching legs, with my eyes facing my vagina. Sadly, my brain caught this imagery, and my conscious decoded my fate. Then, the woman left the room.

For several minutes I watched my legs quiver from a view I never thought I would.

At last, my sight faded in exit of reality's bane.

Oh now. How triumphant.

Evil...

CHAPTER 13:

Platform Liquidation
Part 2

Zzzzzasskk!!

ZZZzzzzss!!!

ZZsss!!

Melting lasers trashed through the monorail, ripping the Unitran cart to shreds.

But with an unconcerned cool, the Feuler sat on the floor of the cart connector. He lounged with his head against the wall, his knees tucked into his chest and his elbows on his thighs. With his eyes closed, his antenna debugged the wild beams, even down to the smallest bolt.

The Feuler leaned his head over as a brutal laser seared through the connector's mechanics.

PPssszzzzzZZKk!!!!

"Hold your fire!!!" The sergeant screamed. "We need that body."

As the firing ceased, the Xaris sergeant rushed over to the cart, kicking the pile of gore out the way. He stuffed his fingers into the sliding door and pulled with all his might. "Ugh!!" He grunted. "The circuits are fried! Get over here and help!"

Two men rushed over to aid the sergeant. One man stood to the left while the other stood to his right. They dug their fingers into the split and tugged until the doors cracked.

Paxz!

The sergeant's head gaped open. His guts splashed to the platform.

Sqwappl!!

While heeding the gooey plop, the aiding men reached for the Feuler. This, of course, was another bad idea.

The Feuler chopped into the men barbarically, thrusting them yards away, leaving only their hands behind to grip the door.

"Rush him!!" The subordinate hollered.

The soldiers sprinted towards the demolished cart.

A couple of men attempted to enter through the broken window created by the Feuler's cloak. One man stood by, cupping his hands together. He heisted another man up as he approached. And through the window was he wrenched.

FR fed the man directly to FL, who stood beside, slicing up and down like an assembly line. A cutting factory if you will.

Gaduuushhhhhh!!!

The man standing on the platform was engulfed in gore. Portions of his comrade shot heedlessly from the broken window. Just as the man aimed to leave, FR snatched him in, feeding him into the same cutlery.

The man was hacked over twenty times before his corpse hit the floor. FL sliced like a sharp appliance, so keen that an electric saw was heard.

Five men came through the entrance firing. But FL slid in secret, and smoothly over to greet them.

As the men fired on FR, so boldly stood FL, directly in the midst, whacking their arms, heads, faces, and shoulders off into gory chunks.

Kisshhh!!

An explosive device smashed through the window.

FR caught the contraption in midair while gripping his knife by the mouth. He leapt out of the window and onto the platform. Only seven men remained to capture this horrific sighting- a half body, sliding awkwardly towards them.

The men opened fire as FR approached swiftly, grabbing one man by the collar, he planted the explosive device and tossed the man in the air.

CaFoouuum!

A bloody geyser launched into the ceiling.

Blood drenched the platform as three men rushed into the railcar, falling cloddishly into the doorway.

The other three men froze.

The sight of FR struck fear in their hearts as he slid towards them, taking the butcher knife from his mouth.

Inside the Unitran cart, FL cut one of the men in the midsection and shoved a large portion of his flesh off. The man fell quick as another soldier punched FL in the face.

Baq!

FL spun to parry the attack, wedging his butcher knife into the man's shoulder. He flipped the man head over heels, crashing him into the pod seat.

Plossh!

Blood sloshed in from the cart's entrance. One man fell to the floor as he entered. Two heads plopped in behind him, bumping against the walls as FR invaded.

FL hacked into the man that punched him, while another man approached him from the rear. But FL's arc, sliced the approaching man's face in two. He diced on like nothing happened. FR hopped over and stabbed the same man in the gut.

Cugz!

He raked the man's innards out, flaking them to the floor. The corpse fell as FL persistently hacked the man in the pod seat to clumps. Blood flowed with squirts of discharge running down the sides of the jagged seat.

FR turned and stood over the last man, squabbling on his knees. "Please... I have kids..." he said.

Thukk!

"Agh!" He hollered as FR planted the butcher knife beside him.

While the din of clang thrashed from the rear of the railcar, FR yanked the man by the shoulder, shaving his face across the knife.

SHkissz!

The merc's face sliced to a crooked segment.

FR stood, ogling at the face as it sloped to the floor. He snatched his butcher knife up with a grip of agitation. Mainly because the oddity of the angle troubled his logic. FR's reflexes remained peerless, but the sharpness of his blade could not be elucidated within the time allotted. Examination of the skewed chop waned, for his counterpart (FL) was *still* dicing.

The desecrated, mushy, and fragmented blob of a man was way beyond recognition. The mercenary had been gashed so much that he'd become more of a puree, with small cubes of flesh, draining into the aisle of the monorail.

"Hmmmm." FR grumbled as he watched his twin liquidate this… lifeless rival.

FR hopped over the slain bodies and out of the railcar. He glanced over the horrific setting as his antenna twitched. He skipped about the platform, and over to a corpse. Clenching his butcher knife by the mouth, he kneeled to grab a small localizer.

113

The device was still active. He immediately crushed the contraption and tossed it into the rear of the platform.

FR turned to notice his better half still chopping. In fact, FL had grown angrier. He had sped up, faster and more vicious than before.

FR entered the bloody cart again, spitting the knife into his hand.

As FL hacked through the pod seat, FR spoke in Layian. But FL responded with more aggression.

FR dropped his head and turned away.

Suddenly, FL stopped chopping into the slurp of gory froth. He breathed frantically as he held onto his bloody butcher knife. He stared into the puddle of minced merc as if the mound of filth was still aiming to punch him. And just like that, FL started back chopping. But at this moment, there was really nothing left to chop.

"Hey!!!" FR bellowed, turning to face his twin.

FL stopped and glanced up to him. "Huh?"

"The parillion thaws."

FL immediately sheathed his bloody butcher knife and rushed over to retrieve the parillion. "We leave." FL announced.

He hopped over the mutilated body parts only to stop and stare, momentarily into the bloody, remains of the man that punched him. And what started out as a brief glare, turned into a prolonged gaze of hate.

FL grew furious. His hand shook vibrantly, rattling the bag of parillion. This ushered FR to respond. "We leave!!" He shouted just as FL began to sit the bag down. "We agreed that we leave," FR urged with concern, sheathing his butcher knife.

FL glared over to his twin... He regretfully snatched away from the gory pile and skipped over to FR.

And with a sense of calm, the two demonic halves turned into each other. The many latches clicked and clacked the Feuler back into place; seamlessly, together... again. They stood as one organized twain of pitiless terror.

Harsh and desolate came the Layian environment, scourging with a staggering orange mist. Several suns accompanied the winds as they gust over the course grounds.

Leagues below Base: Trimmevel, the Feuler peered into the sky, to capture sight of his cloak. The shaggy garment floated above the base as it descended over, masking the maniac with fear.

Moments later, in the dry ambience of Lower Riaxon, the Feuler approached his Yueqatti, which had been concealed in an undisclosed location.

The Feuler double tapped a small grid on his belt buckle.

The Yueqatti Cycle materialized from the air like a smooth gust of flowing wind.

CHAPTER 14:

REB vs Rayefill

The black room glistened with a smooth glimmer.

We stood to attention in front of one wall while Colonel G stood in front of the wall adjacent to us.

"REB. Choose a wall. Rayefill. Choose a wall," the Colonel ordered. "If your opponent touches your wall first, then the match is over. The match is set. They will receive a point and you will have lost. You are allowed to use any of your abilities to stop your opponent from touching your wall. Do you understand?" He quizzed.

The two said nothing.

"On your walls," he demanded.

REB proceeded over to the wall on my right. Rayefill headed to the opposite wall. The span between the two was grand and Colonel G didn't care. His patience was overly impressive.

REB lifted his hand to a ninety-degree angle. He took his index finger and rubbed it in the center of his opened palm. A black fizz boiled up from his hand as he approached the wall. He turned to face his opponent and there in front of the far wall, stood Rayefill, still and silent…

REB kneeled to the coarse reflective ground, holding his hands over its surface. And in that position, he waited.

117

Colonel G floated in front of Azix and I, with his back facing the distant partition. To initiate the start of our meticulous drills, Guitussami would always shout- "-Ljaka!"

REB immediately shoved his hands into the ground, and it embraced him with open arms. And that fast, the alchemist owned the Blackline.

REB stood to his feet. Walking slowly over to Rayefill's wall, the alchemist studied his every move.

But Rayefill didn't budge. He only looked over the room for a short moment. Suddenly, he dashed off.

The room responded. Hundreds of cubes, small and large blocks emerged from the floor and walls.

Rayefill collided with a huge cube as it developed in front of him.

Boocck!

He landed on his back, sliding back to his feet. Rayefill bolted off again, ducking, dodging, and sliding over and under the blocks.

REB stopped and observed, quickly swirling his finger around in his palm. He shoved his hand in the ground again.

Suddenly, the blocks shifted from static to perceptive, detecting every one of Rayefill's moves.

Obviously reassured of his control over the room, REB stood back to his feet. Deducing that Rayefill couldn't best this obstruction, he strode with no concern as the room did the fighting for him.

True enough, Rayefill encountered a belly full of difficulties as the blocks knocked him around. He ran clean up a wall just as a massive cube dropped like an anvil from the ceiling. The brutal collision stopped Rayefill in his tracks.

He adhered to the block's surface and slid from under the mass as it plummeted to the floor.

Ckkkkrrrrrrrrooommmmmmm!

Suddenly, the cube jetted over to Rayefill's wall. Rayefill flipped from the block and dashed into a series of somersaults. His speed doubled in reaction time as he zapped through the obstacle course. He was moving so fast that the blocks couldn't detect him.

The Biohazard stopped, barely looking over his shoulder as Rayefill zapped by.

The neon blur persistently barged through the obstructions with ease. But REB heard everything. As the room spoke, the Alchemist slammed his hand into the floor again.

Ggiiizzzzzzzzzz!!!!

Rayefill stopped in front of REB's wall, reaching out to tap the barrier. But the wall backed away. Rayefill walked up to the wall afresh to touch it. But the wall replied again by backing away.

Rayefill peered over his shoulder and through the many cubes, to see REB shoving his hand into the ground. He turned

119

and sprinted as fast as he could to touch REB's wall. But the faster he ran, the faster the wall would flee. It was as if he had been placed on an invisible treadmill.

REB (kneeling in his current position) slid over the flooring, closer to Rayefill's wall, reaching out to grace the barrier.

Then, a fierce slap reigned through the black room.

Blaow!

-Striking REB's hand away from the wall.

The Biochemist looked at his hand as if it had malfunctioned. He peeked at his other hand (connecting him to the room) then over his shoulder to see Rayefill still dashing for the wall. But the wall escaped his grasp without delay.

REB turned to touch the wall again and that commensurate slap came with a thundering wham!

Blaow!

He turned quickly to see Rayefill in the same spot, sprinting for the wall. Then, REB chemically seduced the wall over to his reaching hand. He was inches away when that exact slap came twice as fast.

Swaat!

Suddenly, the Alchemist flipped in the air. He landed abruptly-

-*Kcccooooomm!!*

Squabbling back to his position, REB reclaimed the room, plunging his hand back into the floor. He snatched Rayefill's wall over to his grasp.

"Set!" Colonel G shouted.

Rayefill popped up next to the Alchemist, glaring in his face with those deep eyes of merit.

Guitussami gawked in awe…

This happened so fast that he couldn't tell who tapped the wall first. I assumed REB asserted his victory over Rayefill. That much was obvious to me.

"Great job, men," he exclaimed while floating between the blocks, marveling over REB's connection to the room.

The Alchemist stood to attention, glaring ahead as Guitussami floated to the center of the room with his mouth open. "Can you reset it?"

REB shook his hands vibrantly. He drew a line through the middle of his palm with his index finger and clapped his hands so loud that the entire room reformatted.

Guitussami batted his eyes as that same old plain black reflective room, glimmered to a crisp.

CHAPTER 15:

Chest Pain

BBBbbaaaaaaaaazzzzzzmmmmmmm!!!!!

Gaps between the lands of Lower Riaxon the Haylo Jet
zipped by, breaking sound barriers.

A giant rift tunneled into the Layian surface. The jet dove
into the fault at a supersonic speed, entering a low-rise tunnel that
soon leveled into a straight away. An array of dreary lights
established this crepuscular setting. And at the end of this sad
tunnel, came a dead end.

The huge wall opened and closed suddenly as the Haylo jet
cleared into a shorter corridor.

The hall widened to an underground parking deck.

The jet came to the center of the deck, revolving slowly to
face the gloomy hall.

The Feuler sat for a moment, reclined back into his seat.
He glared lifelessly out of the teal green windshield with his hands
behind his head. The cool purr of the engines pacified his
aggression, welcoming his granted kip. With no worries or
concerns, he had yet to recall any of his doings. His jumbled mind
was nothing but a scattered box … Well, two boxes of hostility-
mixed with the occasional disunion. Yet, the brains did agree… in
infinitesimal amounts.

Regardless of the many buttons, lights, and gauges within the Haylo Jet, one section triumphed over the rest and with a scintillate boom of significance. This section formed above the console.

In each corner of this section, sat two spheres (about the size of basketballs) flush within the overhead design.

The Feuler finally stood to his feet and placed his hands on the orbs overhead. The jet powered down and the cockpit chair flipped away into the floor.

He walked to the back of the jet and into a narrow hall. He tapped his hand against a hologram and a small storage bin opened from the wall. The Feuler grabbed the bag of parillion as the compartment closed.

He headed back to the jet's consoles. From the base of the windshield and over the consoles came a set of stairs. The solid panels of light vanished as he exited.

Gently waved the teal windshield as the Feuler walked through the transparent material. He stepped on the hood of the jet and down to the landing pad.

As he made contact, the entire deck illuminated.

The hover spheres revolved, levitating the jet off the ground as the assortment of parts began to rearrange.

Some parts shrunk and relocated while other parts transformed into another apparatus.

Within a matter of seconds, the Haylo Jet reconstructed into the Yueqatti Cycle. This sleek hover bike is nothing like the Haylo Jet, which is about the size of a small plane, and twice as fast as the Yueqatti. Yet, the compact hover bike's flexibility and multifaceted attributes flout even the toughest of terrains.

The converting vehicle is predominantly powered by light and is only awarded to a select group. Its industrial knowledge is irreplaceable, even for the Xaris.

The Feuler traveled through the landing pad as several monitors floated up around the area. Some screens displayed news alerts, while others played security recordings and missed calls. The Feuler spoke in Layian while walking off into a bisecting hall.

Just then, the Yueqatti Cycle lowered into a subsurface hangar.

Flashing lights established the dimmed stage of the Feuler's dreary butcher shop. A library of deadly knives swayed from the ceiling above. Sight of this collection could petrify the average being.

The walls of this butcher shop were grotesque and constructed with dozens of built-in compartments.

After, entering the room, he marched over to his massive cutting table. Behind this table sat an even larger group of shelves that were filled with books, skulls, and jars of random anatomical parts.

125

Now, the purpose of this room was extremely unclear, seeing that the Feuler wasn't operating a morgue or a hospital. Nor was he in the funeral business. He had absolutely no intentions of cooking anything, for the severed parts had been sitting for eons.

This could all merely be for the Feuler's dark infatuation for cutting. The constant reference of incisions could be used as a source of inspiration. To him, it was all about the cut.

To him, it was art...

He walked over to a refrigerator and sat the bag of parillion in a drawer. He shut the door and headed to the rear of this gloomy shop. While taking off his heavy cloak, he dropped it to the side and the thick fabric levitated from the floor.

He stopped in front of a set of drawers, built into the walls. He squatted to one of the lower compartments and pulled out a large alien carcass that had been wrapped in a concealer. He lifted the meaty hide and closed the drawer with his foot.

He hauled the cadaver over to the cutting table and slammed the carcass on the rugged surface.

He walked over to another cabinet and pulled out a dingy apron. While heading back to the cutting table, he put the neck of the apron over his head and tied it into a knot about his back.

Upon reaching the filthy table, the Feuler grabbed his ultra-sharp butcher knives from the rear of his belt. He sat the knives on the cutting table and began to unwrap the mass of gory remains.

He gathered up the concealment and pushed it to the corner of the table.

The corner glowed red and the concealment evaporated.

The Feuler took his butcher knives, one in each hand, and placed them on the sides of the cadaver.

The Feuler looped in thought as he turned the alien carcass over, deciding on where to start.

But first, the ultimate dilemma…

The Feuler (as one may have already concluded) has a major issue with verdict. Both halves must agree before an action could ever occur. Simple acts are easily resolved. But in this instance, the decision of, 'who would cut first' effervesced in their detested souls.

The issue had been solved once by the point system.

Every cut that FL and FR made, had to be counted. If one side excelled in points, then the other side would have the rest of the Layian day to equal his score. Then, the count would reset.

Preferably, the Feuler would remedy this craze in a cut-by-cut fashion. An easy method?

Of course, not…

The twins are malign, stirring, deadly and titillating.

127

FL is very blunt, always angry, eager to detach, and even quicker to cut without reasoning or style. Especially if the two halves disagree.

But FR is clean. He appreciates the art of cutlery. His tastebuds are divine. He is more controlled, mindful, sane, witty, logical, and savvy.

And with that in mind(s)...

"You've excelled in cuts. No... You propose?" Rambled the Feuler. He looked up from the carcass and put his hands by his side.

"You cut one man nearly twenty times. And the other you cut repeatedly until he liquified. Did I? Yes. You did. I fed him to you. Remember?" The Feuler hinted.

"'Tis true. Cut away. We concur," he answered.

The Feuler grabbed his butcher knife and hung it up into the library of knives above. Then, he lifted the other butcher knife from the table.

He tapped the blade against the cutting board gently, scooting the corpse over.

"Easy..." He softly expressed.

Precision and exactness housed his cut, shepherding the Feuler's urge to a burning flame.

Schuk!

"Beautiful!" He announced as he lanced through the carcass.

The blood flowed from the alien meat quickly.

He slid the slices over while preparing for the next cut.

Chup!

A chop of total accuracy overwhelmed his desire for more.

"That was thinner than your previous. Intentionally done," he stated while lifting his right hand.

Then, the Feuler cut again with so much grace and focus.

The slice fell smoothly to the table.

He again pushed the remains over to the right with his butcher knife in hand.

"Fine. Wonderful sliver." He admitted as the blood ran down the sides of the table, staining the floor.

"That was pretty impressive. Breathtaking. I would say more, but that would only pump your pride. Talking just to talk… speaking to be heard? I'm serious, and jealous at the same time."

"Bash!" He blurted.

"Can you cut as fast as me and still be accurate? No. To part with the art of cutlery is against me. But not me. I love to see chunks fly!" He bellowed, chopping into the alien flesh.

"Who's counting here? I am. What's your numeric? I'm a long way off. What numeric are you thinking?" The Feuler asked.

"All of them …" he noted while scraping the slices over.

129

He grabbed the alien integument and turned the meaty substance over to inspect the dead weight of brawn.

"Hmmm… so pristine. I like that spot. I don't. Well, it's not up to you now, is it? What's your numeric?" Quizzed the Feuler as he repositioned the meat again.

"No response, eh?"

He studied the meat carefully.

Suddenly, his entire body snatched away from the table.

Reaching for his knife as it flipped to the floor, he flew through the air, slamming into the shelf behind him.

Crroooom!!

The shelf shattered into pieces, trashing all his jars and containers across the room.

The Feuler rolled over to his stomach and lifted to his feet.

"It's not me!!" He screamed.

The jerk was too fast for him to unravel.

"What was that? I…" the Feuler mumbled as he lost mobility.

He jetted forward into the cutting table, breaking it in half.

CaFloom!

The cadaver and all the slices scattered through the air.

The Feuler crushed into the wall in front of him.

He attempted to force himself out, but his body fastened to the depression.

Debris fell as he slid abruptly to the floor.

"What is this cowardice?" He mumbled, glancing over the room as he stood to his feet.

"Convey your privacy!" He ordered just when FL attempted to detach.

A pain wrecked through him so fierce that it knocked him to the floor.

"AAhahhh!!" He yelled, falling to his back.

He scrambled over the bloody floor and rested on his knees. He glared in anger, grabbing his head as his antenna raised with a pulsating discomfort.

"I see it!" The Feuler said just as FL attempted to detach again.

The clasp released and quickly reattached.

CLik! Clack! Click! Clack!

"Ahhhhhhh!!! Stop that!" He cried, squabbling over the nauseating floor.

"I have never witnessed an arrangement such as this," uttered a rough voice.

The Feuler froze ...

"There's two of every organ, completely identical in size and position. You are indeed a rarity."

"Too bad I have to do this." The rugged voice continued.

The Feuler had yet to turn around as the voice sounded from the shop's entrance.

"There's so much to say, but I just can't find the words. My anger has locked my compassion. The hurt will never portray itself through your demise. I'd have to kill you three times before receiving satisfaction." The voice cried.

"You can only die once. Or maybe… Maybe I'll torture you. I don't know yet." The voice growled as the Feuler crawled away and over to one of his cabinets.

"But how? How in the lands of sand are you able to function? How is it that your innards are not colliding from muscular strain? Why aren't these organs dropping out of you?" The voice quizzed.

The Feuler reached out for the cabinet's handle.

But then-

ZZaaszz!

-A ray of light slashed through the room, slinging FL's forearm across the way.

"Agh!" cried the Feuler as he stared down to his severed arm. "Brother…"

Blood fell from the laceration as the Feuler mumbled in agony. He bled from the mouth, bracing himself up with his right arm. Using his elbow, the Feuler dragged scantily over the floor.

The voice whispered as the Feuler finally reached the wall. "I have decided."

The Feuler turned around and sat against the wall, clenching his nub as the blood pumped away.

"I feel this… Do you?" He babbled while gripping his stub even tighter.

The Feuler lifted his head and stared into the eyes of Simma Fice, who now stood within arm's reach.

"Ugk!!" the Feuler grunted as Simma grabbed him by the throat, yanking the butcher into the air.

"I'm just gonna beat you until I devise a way to kill you." Simma painfully scowled.

He was in such a rage that he cried tears of blood.

"Can't you see… The devil in my eyes," he whined with a grimace tone just as he bashed the Feuler's head into the wall, dismantling the partition.

Simma struck repeatedly, fracturing the Feuler's skull until brain tissue seeped from the cracks.

"Oooo," Simma whispered, waving his hand over the Feuler's skull.

"Aaaaaghhhghhh!!" The Feuler screamed as a tiny portion of his brain snatched from his skull and into Simmas' fist.

"I've got an idea…" he said with a look of sagacity. Simma opened his fist and glanced down to the brain tissue.

"Ugh…" he grumbled, puffing the speck of brains to the floor. "It just… *slipped* my mind."

Simma chuckled as he punched the butcher to death. Just when the Feuler began to faint, Simma cried, "Nooo!!! Not yet!"

He hoisted the Feuler higher, placing his hand up to his chest.

"You took my heart. Now, I will take yours."

Simma ripped the organ out of the Feuler's chest.

"AAAaaagggggghhhhhhhh!!!!!"

is

CHAPTER 16:

Archipus
Part 3

"Lemme get twenty on pump one."

CLk! Kp! Clp! Kc!

"Twenty even." Said the cashier as the customer lifted his hat to scratch his head. The clerk opened the register as the patron paid.

"Be safe out there." The clerk uttered, closing the register.

"You too." The man spoke as he walked out of the station, tugging his hat.

The patron trekked with ease to his car. He opened the gas cap and removed the pump from the machine. He placed the pump into the gas slot just as a vicious nicker puffed his hat off. The man turned slowly, and his eyes lifted in horror.

The gas clerk squinted through the window and took off.

Caw!

Caw!!! Caw!

Crows fluttered from the treetops as a bulge of red lightning coated the sky.

BbbZZZzaaacccc!!!!

A reputable gentleman shinned his spoon and placed it back on the white covered table.

The simmering sound of succulent steaks misted across the eatery, as a waitress passed with delectable dishes. She trucked quickly to a waiting couple who sat eagerly outside.

"But though, you can't say Bruce will kick everybody's ass. When Bane broke his back."

"Yea but look what happened after that." The man said as his wife looked over his head.

"Oh! That's us!" She shouted.

"Bout time." The man replied as the waitress sat their food on the table.

"Can I get you guys anything else?" The waitress asked as she tucked the tray under her arm.

"That's all for now. Thank you." The woman pureed.

As the waitress marched off into the restaurant, the man stabbed his fork into a spear of asparagus. Then, his eyes fixed over his wife's head.

The woman tasted her steak, glancing up to her gawking husband. "Man... that's tender." She whispered. "What?" She mumbled, shaking her head. "...What is it?"

CHAPTER 17:

Bloody Chariot

Simma shoved the heart back into the Feuler's chest. He released his grip about the Feuler's neck, suspending the butcher in midair. He mentally thrusted the butcher into the wall.

Kccroom!

Cupping his hands behind him, Simma walked to the rear of the shop. Chunks of debris flurried to the ground as Simma dragged the Feuler beside him- telepathically.

"Never have I ever thought to embrace your kind. You... Mollusk. Even those that we can't readily locate. You all are artifacts. Bits and pieces being defragmented from our system's database. It is a must that you all are deleted from our motherboards. It's really nothing personal. Our coverage requires expansion. To expand, we must reformat the entire makeup of living things. Be it fiction or nonfiction in design." Simma lectured, while walking and dragging the Feuler along through the partition.

A speck of dust landed in his clothes.

"So..." He paused, and so did the Feuler.

Simma brushed the debris from his shoulders just as the Feuler reached feebly out to grab him.

He kindly tapped the Feuler's hand away. "Where was I?" He asked.

"Oh!" he shouted as he started back walking.

Just as he took his step, so carried on the destructive lugging of the Feuler, ripping the coarse wall to shreds.

"Had it been left up to me, I would've had Pias **xute** the entire galaxy, cycles and cycles over until there were none of you left." Fice exclaimed as he walked slowly, dragging the Feuler on within the wall.

"But circumstances would have it as such… coincidence, moirai… You killed Pias. And Velleayan Fice. You remember him?"

"Yea."

"You made this personal." Simma yelled, snatching over to the Feuler. "Irrational! What you did in Space Void…"

His eyes twitched from a rumpus combination of thinking. He dropped his head and the Feuler's body heaved out of the wall.

Floomm!

A clobbering close line slung the Feuler over.

Krrooomm!

Cracking the floor, as he landed.

"Poor thing of an excuse. You freak of classified nature." Simma growled.

As the Feuler braced up from the desecrated ground, a piece of the floor hurled to his face.

Brackkk!

"Ah!" he shouted as the portion exploded. "Even the floor attacks us." The Feuler stumbled to his feet, bleeding roughly.

"We could've been enemies." Simma mumbled as he glanced over the butcher shop. "Now… we have become something, much worse."

At a devastating speed, all the cadavers sprung from the compartments. They welded to the walls, crashed through the amenities, and bashed into the Feuler. The repulsive gore forced the butcher to the rear of the shop. He dropped lifelessly under the pile of carnage.

Simma stood boldly behind the Feuler, staring into the mound of filth. He stretched out his hand, with his palm facing down. And with a subtle swipe, the pile of chunks brushed to one side of the room.

Shhusccsss!

The Feuler laid face down and from a sickening view.

"You're not dead. I can still feel your hearts beating. One's a bit slower than the other. I think… Yes! It's the left one." Simma informed as he lifted his hand.

"What's wrong with that one?" He asked while beckoning for the organ.

141

The heart tugged and jerked slowly as the Feuler braced himself.

"I thought I put it in correctly…" Simma noted.

Blosh!

"Aaaaggghhh!!!" The butcher wailed as his heart gushed out of his back.

"Why… Would you look at that." Fice chuckled as the thumping organ floated over to him. "I put it in backwards."

The Feuler closed his eyes as his face smacked the floor.

"Your death serves me no purpose. I'd rather take you home and pick you apart, one tiny pieces at a time… Then, if you do die, I'd keep you as a trophy. Oh! I forgot my promise. To bury you next to my brother." Simma mumbled as the Feuler's heart floated over to him.

"How about I keep this heart? And every time his day of death should cycle, I'll take a small bite. I'll stretch the rationings as far as I can… then…" Simma paused. "Feuler?"

The butcher didn't respond.

"Did you die? Where… is it?" Simma whispered.

As he searched for vitals, the Feuler's heart froze still.

"It's not here." Simma stood in anger.

Ka-FllllooMmmmmmm!

A dingy vest dropped in, crushing Simma to the ground.

Plaqk!

The Feuler's heart smacked the floor.

Then, from the ceiling came a male, Gastropada: Tritokis, slug.

He stood about 6 feet with bright yellow glowing eyes. His face was sleek, no ears or a nose, but a pair of antennae erected from the top of his head. He was completely hairless with a grayish green skin tone filled with black speckles. He was younger, very muscular and at the moment, shirtless.

He wore a pair of khaki cargo pants tucked into a pair of Timbs, a pair of brown fingerless gloves and a large necklace for accessories. A strange medallion hung from the necklace. It bore the shape of two exclamation points, one upside down and right side up. Then, he stood with a toothpick dangling from the corner of his mouth.

"Damn bih!"

He dapped over to the Feuler shouting, "Jake!"

The Feuler laid silently.

The slug turned about the room and walked over to the Feuler's heart.

"Jake!!" he shouted even louder as he picked up the organ. "Yo' flicted ass bet-not be dead. If you iz'… I'ma kill yo' ass."

The slug gently placed the heart back into the Feuler's cavity. Then, he yanked the toothpick from his mouth and flicked it across the room.

143

"C'mon." He urged as he stood over the Feuler.

"Jake!"

The slug reached down and slapped the Feuler in the face.

Swac!

"We need you, homie."

"..." mumbled the Feuler.

"My man," whispered the slug.

He glanced over the Feuler, while snatching various organs out of him. "Man, you lost an arm too? Damn!!"

"You got folk's eyes and legs all in you. Why you keep all dis' shit in here anyway?" He protested while yanking a hand from the Feuler's leg. "Look at all dat shit ova there!" He gestured with the severed hand.

The grotesque mound of body parts bled over the Feuler's floor. "That's some nasty ass shit." He blurted. "…Is that a dick?"

"What took you so long? You… source. Pathetic pusher…" the Feuler mumbled as he rolled over to his back.

"I hate you too," the slug replied while tossing the lanced hand over to the pile of gore. "That's why you fucked up now."

The Feuler stared into the face of the slug as he began to smirk. "You… backstabbing caitiff," the Feuler uttered.

"Uh huh. I dun' tol' you 'bout using big words round me. Maybe I should put my vest back on. Crazy ass!"

"We have a code to keep. And what are you doing to the English language? It sounds ridiculous and absurd." the Feuler inserted.

The slug put his hands on his hips. He stood for a moment then he walked over to Simma Fice. "Just a lil' summ I been studying. It's called Ebonics…summ you don't know nut'n, bout." the slug mumbled as he lifted his vest out of the rubble.

"And what is that damaging odor?" The Feuler snarled.

"Wait a minute…" The slug paused while putting on his horrid vest. "I know dis' fool."

"It smells like piercing daggers of, doo-doo." The Feuler continued. "Why didn't you amp the Plyka? You could've killed him easily. Are you using your own pharmaceuticals?"

"I could've, but I didn't. Cause I can't," the slug replied.

The Feuler grunted as he sat up, looking confused as ever. "You're as mad as I am. Me, too," the Feuler noted.

The slug tapped his fingers against the medallion about his necklace. He walked over and stopped just in front of the Feuler.

"Holy Shit!" The Feuler gagged. "It is that vest!!!"

"To always stand against the odds. Never to die alone. To forever fuel the anarchy. Bloody Chariot." The slug reported, stretching out his hand.

The Feuler sat with his lips buckled. He planted his foot and rested his arm on his knee. He rolled his eyes away from the slug, peering to the right of the room. "I need my arm," cried the Feuler.

"Shit! I need a million quotoms. We gotta code to keep."

The Feuler glanced up to the slug and down to his extended hand.

"Your derogatory help quashes my consolation," bleated the Feuler.

"What?" The slug inquired as the Feuler gripped his hand.

"Ugh," The Feuler grunted as the slug pulled him to his feet.

"Say it."

The Feuler dropped his head and sighed, "...Bloody Chariot."

"Now. That wasn't so bad." The slug wandered as the Feuler limped over to obtain his arm. His stride was crooked and awfully unbalanced.

"You flicted!" the slug shouted. "That damn Simma, still kicking ass. Whoa!" the slug shouted just as the Feuler toppled to the ground. He rushed over, bracing himself under the Feuler's shoulder. Then, he wrapped his arm around the Feuler's waist. "Why the hell he after you?" The slug quizzed.

"I don't know… I think I do." The Feuler speculated while picking up his arm. "I'm infirm… going to need some succor."

"I got somebody…" the slug stated out of qualm. He hoisted the Feuler up and scolded, "Yo. You can't come back here. And how come I feel like we forgetting something?"

"Because we are," the Feuler replied as they exited through the hall.

The slug stopped. "What? What we miss?" He queried, looking down to the Feuler.

The Feuler hung to a droop as he began to separate.

"Jake!" The slug shouted in Layian, shaking the Feuler back together. "What we forget?"

"My…" the Feuler mumbled weakly, gesturing with his severed arm.

"Huh? What the hell is… OOOoohhh!!! Your knives!" the slug yelled.

"I'll get them," he said while lowering the Feuler. "What they look like?"

"No!" Roared the Feuler.

"No?" The slug yelled, ditching the Feuler to the floor. *Fumm!*

"First off, that answer don't make any sense. Secondly, you're half dead. Literally!"

"Bifurcate, the weaker fraction. You'll move faster," the Feuler ordered as he sat up from the ground.

"What?"

147

"He wasn't talking to you," the Feuler blurted.

The slug bated his eyes with confusion.

"It's far enough to nullify," said the Feuler.

The slug threw his hands up and shouted, "What!"

Just then the Feuler split in half.

"Aw that's nasty," the slug gagged.

FR stood up and handed the severed arm to the slug. "Hold this," he hissed.

"Just gimme it." The slug huffed, snatching the arm away.

FR limped to the wall and glanced over to the slug, who only stared with disgust. Without blinking did he ogle, into FL's vertical split, the gel casing trapping the Feuler's organs in place. He cringed to a retching jerk.

FR adhered to the wall's surface. "Watch over him," he demanded as a powerful excretion shot from his hand and foot.

"Um supposed to just stand here and look at this!!" The slug shouted as FR wiped against the wall, in an antithetical motion, zapping him down the hall.

"You know I- Ugk! Gotta week stomach..." The slug gagged.

FR entered his shop, flipping from the wall, landing briefly to the floor.

He slowed to moderate hops while searching over the pigsty of parts.

"Man, hurry yo' ass up!" The slug shouted from afar.

FR glared to the broken cut table and beneath the rubble, he found his butcher knife. He kneeled to obtain the weapon while glancing over to Simma laying beneath the wreckage.

FR sheathed the knife into the rear belt holster. He hopped a few feet away and reached up into the library of blades.

"Man. Brang! Yo! Ass!!" The slug shouted from the hall. "I got people trying to get fucked up!"

FR's antennae twitched. He spun quickly, glimpsing over the decimated surface. Simma had vanished.

FR snatched the knife from the collection.

Meanwhile, the slug repositioned FL's heart as it creeped out of the bloody opening.

"Man whatchu' doin in there?" The slug hollered as he attempted to remedy FL's limb. He pressed the severed end up to the bloody nub. The appendage held for a moment, then it dropped crudely to the ground.

"Damn," he chuckled just as FR propelled into the hallway. "'Bout damn time. Got six quadrants to visit."

FR approached with haste, grumbling, "He left."

"I know," the slug replied as he picked up FL's forearm.

The slug shook his head in distress. "Man, you need to do something. He ain't looking so hot. I mean, both of y'all ugly. But… he **real** ugly."

149

FR glared towards his butcher shop, staring as if he detected something. "Sit him up," he mumbled.

The slug laid the severed forearm down. He gripped FL by the shoulder and gradually sat him up against the partition.

FR waved the knife in front of FL and he followed the blade slowly.

"Yo, hurry up. He coming!" The slug hollered.

FR sheathed the butcher knife into FL's rear holster right as the slug chuckled, "Just kidding."

FR sat next to his half and the many clasps joined them together.

"Ugk!" The slug heaved, turning away from the occurrence.

The butcher stood and nodded. His cloak swooped into the hall, shrouding the twins in mystery.

The slug gave the Feuler his severed forearm, then he braced himself under the butcher's shoulder. "Ugk! You know I snort coke whenever you do that?" The slug gagged while guiding the Feuler to safety.

"What is this... coke?" The Feuler asked as they trekked leisurely down the hall.

The slug grinned as he spoke with culpability, "It's a long story..."

CHAPTER 18:

Kontriss Quiaussuss

****

Shit started when I was about eight, Layian periods. Right? This shit was over a hundred cycles ago. Back when L-boots were in.

I had on a full body gorshiff with a brand-new pair of brown Locin boots. I was heading to Kiepeson. Taking up Earth Studies. I know everything about that planet. From politics to Jordans, global trade, food stamps, you name it. But I was running late, right? And so was Chip Byton, a fellow classmate from Gastana.

Oratorically speaking, I got into a fight with this cat. Well, it started out as a fight…

Anyway, we in class studying trig and English. But I had been having problems out of this Xaris cat ever since we were in Kiepeson.

Cycle after cycle he had been rambling on about social classes, race and lineages, right? Talkin' bout Tritos this and Tritos that. He said some crap about us not being mathematically equated into the laws of universal modes. Some crazy Xaris shit! I'on know.

But I was getting upset...

So, he got up in my face, right? And I didn't flinch.

Then the teacher ran over to break it up. And just when she did, Chip decked me in the face.

Blap!

He hit me so hard that the teacher and I both fell.

Did I mention he was bigger than me?

Who cares though, right?

So anyway, we're fighting, right? On the ground, rolling round, tearing shit up. I'm getting my ass kicked, while my don't giva' shit ass cousin, Spee (Xzta Spaceshock), sat in the back of the classroom chewing on gum.

But then, the teacher runs over to the wall, slams the panic button. In charged the principal. He was heated. He snatched us apart and hauled us out the classroom. While Spee just sat there, chewing on her gum and staring off in the ceiling.

Anyways, I got my ass kicked by the school bully, and in front of everyone. Then I got suspended, but Chip didn't.

Now how dat' add up?

My parents were pissed, because I spent the rest of my term at home, but not Chip. Chip stayed in school. His folks didn't give a damn. They let him do whatever he wanted. He was pulling all the girls, free lunches, everything.

Man, I was so pissed that I learned his schedule, watching this cat go and come.

One day, I caught Chip walking to da' house. The timing was exact. Right when he turned the corner, I struck his ass in the face with a Bolter Bat.

Bam!

He dropped like an anvil.

Now, I hadn't realized it, but Chip was walking with a little kid. Dis' bitch started crying and shit.

I took off and hid behind a large wall.

Peering back down the crescent, I saw that Chip hadn't moved, at all.

People came out of their homes to aid the poor kid, and I just knew that I knocked Chip out.

Later that night I was lying in bed, just chilling, right? Minding my own business.

Knowhatumtalmbout?

Moms bust in the room, like-

"What'd you do?"

She tossed an info gram over as I sat up and caught it with one hand. Cause I'm tight like that, right? But I opened the holographic newspaper. I scrolled through the digital displays and there was some kinda media craze playing some shit 'bout a Xaris man dying on the corner.

Mom was like, "What'd you do?"

Boom! Boom! Boom! Blared from the front door.

Mom whirled around suddenly. Then, she turned to face me. "What'd you *do?*" She hissed with fear just as I stood to my feet.

She stormed off through the pod maze and I stood quietly behind as she approached the door.

"Who is it?"

Some kid was like, "Is Altizma home?"

Mom was like, "Oh! It's Chesqe-"

Boom!

-The Xaris kicked in with that same little kid, pointing his finger at me yelling, "That's him! That's the guy who killed my daddy!"

Stupid ass bitch, I was already sprinting through the pod maze.

The Xaris trampled over my mother, firing Para Rays through the house, searing the walls to magma mush.

The rays ripped the furniture to shreds.

Bloozzzk!!!!!

The frig exploded as I bolted through the kitchen.

Kicking into my room, I tossed my bedding off its frame, shoved my stash of dirty magazines to the side and snatched up the floorboard. There sat my coded safe box.

Before the Xaris unraveled the maze, running throughout my mom's pod, I cycled the dial over the box briefly.

155

Blazing Para Rays scorched through the walls as I failed to enter the code.

"C'mon, C'mon!"

Pzzzaaassszz!!!!!

In crashed another Para Ray melting right into my room!

"Shit!" I squatted, barely missing the deadly stream.

The safe popped open. I yanked out my TPD and immediately programmed the device.

Pzzzaaassszz!!!!!

A Para Ray grazed my arm, flinging me across the room.

Faloomm!!

My TPD fell in front of the bedroom door as my right side went limp.

"He's in here!" the merc shouted as I glanced through the cracks in the wall.

Bungling over to my TPD, I entered random coordinates into the device as the Xaris rushed in.

Just as I pressed send-

Crasssh!

Pzzzaaassszz!!!!!

A Para Ray grazed my back when a portal opened over the floor. The window dissipated swiftly as I fell in, landing on my back. The TPD dropped on my stomach.

This all happened so fast cause it was stupid... I panicked; you know? Cause I didn't secure my location and I had no idea where this gateway would take me...

Man, it was so black when I woke, I couldn't tell if my eyes were open or closed. But I knew I was somewhere, and it smelled like shit.

Very small ticks, tacks and squeals surrounded me quickly. While stuck in my paralyzed state, I noticed that the sounds were growing in volume. They tripled with every moment that passed. Could've been Savalliens... but Savalliens didn't sound like that.

"That tickles..." I whispered, realizing that my short-term paralysis had ended.

"What the hell?" I asked.

Covered in tiny critters, I sat up fast, brushing over myself. They scuttled away as I grabbed my TPD. Then, a host of noises followed... With no lighting, I struggled for visual clarity. Lifting the TPD overhead, I stood as the device illuminated the cavernous ceiling above.

I turned slowly... and the TPD brightened my doom. I found myself on a hill... A hill of sleeping Pokidods. Everywhere I looked, from the top of the mound and down to the ground, was nothing but Pokidods. Thousands and thousands of Pokidods.

I was smack in the middle of a nest....

"Fuck. Me." I whispered while lowering my TPD.

If it's anything I hate, in all the Layian lands, it's Pokidods. Their bodies were made like monoliths with evil faces. They had over twenty eyes strayed over their body and a complex mouth located on their underbelly. Their teeth were jagged and black. Their legs sprouted from the sides of their hideous body in pairs of two, four, and sometimes eight. And they were like segmented prongs that came to a very keen point. And that's where all the danger lies… at the very tip of their legs.

While recalling my Kiepeson classes, I started shaking. Cause Pokidods are attracted to constricting arteries, fast paced heart beats and heavy perspiration. And if you know like I know, Pokidods are extremely deadly. One sting from the tip of their legs, could level a Bealbriean in a second.

The good thing was that the nest was asleep.

My goal came clear as day. Get out of here! Without disturbing this nest. But the more I thought about how deadly these things are, the more I began to panic.

"Stay cool Kontriss… Stay cool," I coached, typing quietly into my TPD.

Now, I couldn't go back home. It was swarming with Xarchanzians.

Suddenly, one of the Pokidods moved at the base of the mound.

"Ma- maybe it's having a… dream?" I gulped to a standstill.

Glancing over my setting again and as far as I could tell, I was staring into an endless vault- an ocean of acerbic Pokidods. If I woke one of them, I woke all of them.

Then, as I backed up, the Pokidod under my feet started to move. I stood as still as possible while dimming the light on my TPD.

There was nowhere to go. Shit, I couldn't tell if I was heading deeper into the nest or out to freedom. There was no escape, or any less of the Pokidods.

Suddenly-

Aaaaaaaaaaarrrghhhhhhhhhhhhha!!!!!!!

-A roar sounded, waking every Pokidod.

"Shit!"

Shaking like crazy, I tried to enter a set of coordinates. But my heartbeat revved up like a motor. The Pokidods squirmed over each other as I typed into the TPD. Right then, the mound of Pokidods scrambled.

"Fuck!!" I wailed, leaping off the hill, I landed on the side of the collapsing mound.

They struck as I took off.

That roar sounded again and this time, the whole cave shook.

A huge boulder fell from the ceiling as I leapt into a forward roll.

159

Kooommmmmmmbb!

The solid fractals decimated a herd of Pokidods behind me. That didn't faze them at all.

While searching for a clearing to set up my TPD, I noticed a glimmer of light from the ceiling where the huge mineral had fallen. Shoving the TPD into my pocket, I scaled to the top of the boulder.

The Pokidods followed behind- stinging me like they didn't have any damn sense.

The first sting caught me in the leg.

And I was like, "Aggh!!"

Youknowhatumtalmbout?

Another stung me in my other leg. Another followed in my arm and another in my back. By the time I reached the top of the boulder I was so weak I could barely stand.

The Pokidods were so eager to sting me, they were attacking each other.

I took out my TPD and tapped the send button. The window of light opened in front of me just when a pack of Pokidods topped the boulder.

Their stings swamped me from the rear.

With my TPD in hand, I fainted into the window and the bright portal vanished....

The poison traveled like a wildfire.

A fuming smoke and a shambling shake bolted through my skin as my organs and muscles ignited.

Plopping face first onto a rugged ground, I lifted my head to see a blinding, yellow blur.

There came a glimpse of a woman approaching from a distance. It looked like she just stepped out of TPD.

Man, I couldn't tell, cause the struggle to keep my visual was so severe, that my eyes shut like a motion censored hell door.

CHAPTER 19:

Cocaine Theory
Part 1

A sweet odor flowed as I awoke. There I lay, in a strange jacuzzi, shaped into the floor. The tub was filled with leaves and some kinda' diluted Tierun.

An array of white and pink lights established this setting. The floor's majestic tiling flowed unexpectedly with the gold and marble walls.

This space was shaped like a large cylinder. And all over the walls were these tubes and cords- flasks and filters running everywhere. It resembled something of an angelic-driven lab.

Sitting up slowly, I noticed a couple of IVs running into my wrists. And boy did I feel drunk, drugged, and high all at the same time. Oh, I felt so, so… unstoppable.

Peering into the IVs, I trailed a white liquid running into my system.

"You cheat death efficiently," spoke a melodious voice.

"Who's that?" I asked as my antennae grew out of my head.

No one responded as I glanced over the room's splendor.

Sitting patiently for an answer, I finally closed my eyes and laid back into the bath.

When I opened my eyes, I was staring directly into a woman's crotch.

"Whoa!" I shouted sitting up to attention. In more ways than one… Knowhatumtalmbout?

The woman beamed into my face.

She was dressed to kill.

She had on a gorgeous long-sleeved black and blue speckled dress that stopped at her ankles. The top of the dress blossomed at her shoulders and formed into a choke chain. There was an opening in the chest region that revealed a small portion of her cleavage. Then, an elegant formation of expensive jewelry covered her neck. The midsection of the dress was form fitting and it came with a wide black belt, pronouncing her curves. She wore a pair of light blue fishnets and a pair of seven-inch light blue and coral peep toe stiletto heels. Her shoes were so hypnotically seasoned with priceless trinkets and treasures.

Her face was equally beguiling. Her eyes were orange with yellow pupils. Her skin was light gray with lime green blotches here and there. Her jawline was so smooth…

But the oddest thing about this female slug, unlike a lot of slugs, nearly all the slugs, was that she had a head full of hair. Solid black, bouncy and full of volume hair, which stopped evenly at her shoulders.

She finally stepped away from me and over to the wall of tubes. My eyes followed her 'slow walking', child-bearing curves.

"If hips could kill." I mumbled while glaring at her ass.

"I am Vykra Dane-Flats."

"I bet you are."

She approached the wall of laboratory devices and reached out to make a few adjustments to the knobs.

"What is this bath?"

"They are cocoa leaves, mixed with an oil-based form of Tierun called Opily. The mix came from my own Harshapa."

"It feels good."

"You were attacked by a legion of Pokidods. One of these creatures possesses enough toxins to level an entire population. You were stung over twenty different times… and you did not die. How did you stumble upon such a nest? And how are you not dead?" She asked while gazing into the wall of tubes.

"You got me there…. What's the white stuff?"

She peered over her shoulder and uttered, "Its a liquid composite of Erythroxylon, in its purest of forms."

"Did you say you're a virgin?"

"The process is simple." She gushed as if I hadn't said a thing.

"The leaves are hand-picked and dried to a crumble and often cooled to contain its potency. We have a light slicer that's used to grind the leaves into microscopic shreds. The bits of leaves are held in a small pit, laced with Milafilme. Opily is then poured over the leaves. The concoction is stirred even slower for half of a Layian cycle or until total maceration.

165

Afterwards, the solution is hauled off in small preservers and then slowly mixed again in my factory of light blenders. We have at least sixty.

After this thorough mixing, the extraction begins.

The mush is trajected and drained into a vast system of self-cleansing microscopic pipelines. The system of strainers is laced with Nieleyaian, which strips the substance of Opily and any other additives. This removal is repeated several times over and the ending containers are filled with the solution. The compound is later vaporized by oxidizers that effectively convert the puree into a very fluffy-crystal clear, white cloud of powder called, cocaine." She lectured.

The madam walked about the room in her explanation of this tedious process. Best believe, I was watching her every step. This hoe was hypnotizing.

"It is a lengthy undertaking that I have grown quite knowledgeable of." She expressed as she stood beside the tub, staring into my eyes.

The buttery leafy soup, bubbled and popped, sounding softly about the room's elegance.

And right as I began to speak, she boomed, "That nest you found has been dormant for light ages."

"...Soo?"

"They have your scent. They know you and they will find you."

She walked away, sadly adding, "And so will the queen."

"Queen? What queen?"

"Temple."

A grave silence came as she walked over to the wall behind me. She looked into the ceiling for a moment, right?

"Your family is in danger. You must take them far away. You must destroy all your belongings. Everything!" She bellowed.

I was like, "Even my dirty magazines?"

"Yes!"

"Why?"

"You've awakened a nest. By doing so, you have revived the celebration."

While laying back into the bubbling bath, I smirked. "Celebration. It's like a party! That's good, right?"

"No. Be assured, The Celebration in definition...

Every 1,000 cycles Temple would arise to devour the lands and all its inhabitants until she is satisfied. It has been over a billion cycles since the queen has surfaced. It would appear that the queen was dead. But no. Her minions run wild under Layian lands." She announced.

"Let's just kill it."

167

"Temple is an unstoppable force of nature. She is larger than several suns. This is why her day is referred to as a celebration. Her day is considered to be supreme in horrific liberation. A beautiful tragedy designed to bring stability to the Layian Universe. We are powerless against it. Even 7-Dial," she declared.

"When you say, '7-Dial', you mean you want to give me your number?"

The gorgeous slug dropped her head. "But if you leave now, you may delay and maybe even stop her coming all together."

"Naa... I'ma kill it. It's just a bug. Fuck dat bug!"

"All the lands will suffer from this choice. We all will comply on that day. It is when we pertain to the periphery of extinction." She fretted.

"The Pokidod's poison runs rich. But you, somehow you have survived the onslaught." She added.

"Yeah. Its only cause you saved me."

"No. Pantis Jann saved you," she interjected. "She traveled a great distance."

"Oh," I uttered while standing to my feet.

The concoction drenched down my body slowly.

"Sir!" She shouted, rushing over to me.

"Damn, Vykra," I replied as she approached, rubbing her hand against my chest.

"You took all of my clothes?" I asked with humor.

"The process required complete exposure." She whispered while looking me up and down, blushing with the minutest of grins.

"Do-it!"

"Do-it!"

"Do-it!" I cheered, pumping my fist.

She snatched away and stomped behind me.

"Just kidding." I said as she walked over, wrapping a towel about my waist.

"Go. Do as I have told. Or doom the entire galaxy." She ordered, taking the IVs from my arms.

"Uma kill it." I blasted. "Fuck dat' bug."

She shook her head while traveling over to a small container. She took out my TPD and turned to face me, gripping the device firmly.

"Never return here. Never return to that nest. You should erase such coordinates." She disclosed, tossing the device over to me.

"Wait!" I hollered, catching the device with ease. "How can I get some of this?"

"Some of what?"

169

Glancing about the room as if someone else was listening, I whispered in secrecy, "The white stuff..."

Vykra turned to retrieve my clothing from a nearby cabinet, and uttered, "It's not for your facsimile."

"Facsimile...? What dat' mean?"

"It means no." She sassed, while walking over to me, holding my clothes.

"Is 'no' your favorite word?"

"No!!"

Then, my mind flipped. In confusion I stood for a good minute. Cause I was trying to figure out if she was answering the question, or if she was, *answering* the question.

"...It's circumference," she added, handing me my clothes as I placed my TPD on top of them, caressing her hand in our little exchange.

Stepping out of the tub, I shouted, "Let's make a deal!"

The gorgeous creation folded her arms.

"I'll leave. I mean, all the way leave. But only if you show me how to replicate this. I'll burn my shit, take my family away from here. Whatever! But I know this, cocaine is the remedy. And maybe the only remedy. You don't want these Pokidods to resurface. You don't want me to die, do you?" I wailed with conviction.

She glanced over her shoulder.

And I was like, "Say?"

She dropped her head as I continued my spill. "You don't even have to-"

"- Okay!" She interrupted. "But you must promise to leave the galaxy before the third sun sets."

And another face of confusion chanced my fret. Cause I thought the sun was already setting.

"Deal!"

She whirled around holding up her finger. "I will give you one cycle of supply and one drive of informative procedures."

"Baby, that's more than enough."

"And I will need a sample of your blood." She included.

"I'll give you more than that." I giggled.

"That won't be unnecessary."

Immediately, I threw my hands up, dropping my clothes and my TPD.

The towel slipped from my waist and into the bubbly tub.

She glared reluctantly onto my nakedness as I stood there silently. Right?

She gushed, from what I thought to be a burning infatuation. But then, she started gagging.

I rushed over to help her, but she held up her hand, stopping me in my quest.

She kneeled over and heaved up a clod of vomit.

171

Puwatt!

She sifted through the barf and took out a black capsule.

The gorgeous woman walked over with this pill in hand.

I started backing up, shaking my head.

"You take this," she ordered.

"Nu uh!" I chortled. My jaws inflated as I ralphed in my mouth, swallowing the lumpy acidic warmth, hoping that she didn't notice.

"<Gulp!> Whew!"

She bit the tip of the capsule and proceeded to feed it to me. Finally, I agreed while embracing her soft lips.

The kiss was immaculate, sexy, and completely arousing. However, the beauty spot of life, Vykra, used her persona as an illusion just for the purpose of distraction. You mirror of lust!

She served in duty when she shoved her tongue into my mouth- ensuring that the pill went in.

She reached down and groped me passionately...

"God! Your breath could turn off stars." She sneered. "Did you, barf? In your mouth? What is that? Chicken juice?"

I nodded my head as we kissed briefly.

"Swallow it," she demanded with a grimace tone.

Just as she stopped caressing me, I swallowed the pill. She pricked my finger with a needle and dabbed my blood on a sterile gauze. Then she folded the pad up and stuffed it into her boobies.

"Now. Get dressed. We move expeditiously." She urged as she backed away from me, stepping over her puddle of puke.

"Can you clean that shit up? I can't stop looking at it. And how am I going to get all this stuff away from here?" I asked, while putting on my pants.

The woman of elegance reached the room's entry door. She turned around to acknowledge my questioning. "We have an aircraft."

"Aircraft? I can't fly!" I retorted with a hint of frustration just when the entry doors slid open.

"Then I have a pilot. Now hurry!" She insisted.

I truncated my TPD and tucked it into my pocket. Right?

Moments later, we stepped out into a massive Harshapa full of thickets and shrubs that grew neatly together.

The angelic landscape soared high as we entered a passage of majestically colored feathers. They never seemed to fall, but sway and flutter with no end.

Up ahead, right? It was a dude, a big, massive, wide creature that stood about 8ft tall. The monster was covered in a decrepit brown poncho that dragged over the ground. His skin was ragged, and his face was unclear. He stood over a large pit, with a big stick in his hands. He was stirring up this goop really slow. He seemed to be completely engulfed in his duty.

"This way," said Vykra as she grabbed me by my hand.

173

She stirred me off into the thickets and pulled on a branch behind her. The wall of shrubs shuffled and slid back into each other, opening a path within the woodlands.

Then, from the ground multiplied a flight of solid gold stairs. They were filled with chunks of diamond, embroideries, and luscious engravings. Dust and other leaves fell as the steps redefined themselves, lifting up into the top of the trees.

My eyes followed the stairs as I gathered myself in amazement. But Vykra, she must've seen this shit a million times. She tugged me up the stairs with a hurried pace of importance.

Looking back down the golden stairs, I captured a breathtaking view of the flowy feathers. The unification could dose as a long-deserved vacation. But at the top of the stairs…

Ooohh this here top!

"Oh. My! Fucking! A!" I bellowed as we topped the stairs, thinking that we stepped into the clouds.

This must've been an alternate universe or dimension or something… I mean, everywhere I turned were these white, fluffy hills and valleys of ultraclean, crystal pure and unspoiled spreads of cocaine. The fluff was so abundant and so unbelievable. This stretch of angelic clouds continued in every direction and as far as my eyes could see.

I immediately began to stuff my pockets.

But then, from the angelic dust, lifted a grand spaceship. It was shaped like a big ass can turned sideways. The craft was sleek and full of connecting parts, with a massive window on the endcap.

"Time doesn't exist here." Vykra hummed as I turned to face her. "But, the third sun does." She pointed into the sky.

And way up in the clouds, were three suns, tripling the settings' effective toll.

"It sits high, but they all will set in ascending order. And when that happens, this location will become public to the Xaris. Then, this place, this Nirvana, will momentarily cease to exist. As I will have to relocate this entire planet to maintain its privacy."

I stood with blow sifting out from my clenched fist, cajoled by the whole thing. My belief in magic sat firmly in this founding moment.

"Am I... hallucinating?"

"No." She promptly assured.

"Which one is the third sun?"

"The yellow one."

"But they all yellow…"

Seconds later, four large crates floated in. They were black and shaped like coffins, with Layian engravings infused over them.

Vykra introduced each crate as they strolled to a stop. She was kinda like one of them game show presenter girls. You know, holding out her hand...

"The first crate is untampered Opily. The second container is 100% Milafilme. And the third container is Nieleyaian. And the final crate is thinly diced cocoa leaves and seeds for planting." She said as she turned to see me filling my pockets.

"I will not repeat myself." Vykra retorted as I scooped a handful and sprinkled it over my antennae.

And man... Oh man, I inhaled like a savage. "Huh?"

She gestured behind me, in a presentable manner.

While turning around, I smiled from cheek to cheek.

Then, I saw him... and for the first time, as he floated down from the ship's loading dock.

My smile diminished slowly as he emerged.

A thin smoke followed from behind him. The lights from the inside of the ship gave this man an eerie, or more of a ghostly feel. Never have I ever seen a dude without arms or legs float in the air like that.

"Yo! This shit got me trippin'."

"No. It does not. Cocaine is not a hallucinogen." Vykra responded.

"You sure?"

"This is Guitussami. He is my pilot." She explained while handing me an all-black drive.

"How *he* go fly a ship?"

"This drive contains all of the procedures as promised. The crates will follow you aboard the spacecraft."

While taking the drive from her and tucking it in my boot, I scooped up a tad more of the of the angelic, cloudy fluff.

"Do not abuse this," Vykra coached as I sprinkled the coke over my antennae again.

This time, I breathed in slowly, cherishing every taxing feel that came with the angel's cloud of elation.

"I'm leaving. For real." I boomed as I glared over to her, stuffing the rest of the coke into my shirt pocket. "Are you sure you don't wanna-"

"-No."

"Yo' loss." I bragged as I turned to face the ship and the floating man who waited by the lowered door.

"Hey man! How you go fly dis shit with no arms?" I hollered as bits of coke trailed from my pockets.

He didn't say a word. He just glared lifelessly into the distance as I boarded the ship.

The closer I got to the man the more I realized that he was a little more than just a man. His skin was so old that it was cracking. It looked like fleshy tree bark and wood mixed together.

177

"Skip the lotion?"

The man didn't respond.

"How you go put lotion on anyway? You aint got no arms or legs. You must was in a bad accident? Like Clayface."

He still didn't respond.

"Oh! You got that hard water in yo' shower."

"The sun sets!" Vykra shouted from the distance.

"I'm going!" I yelled as I turned to catch a glimpse of her.

She stood boldly in the same position as before. She kept her hands behind her with agitation in her eyes. She lowered her head as I entered the ship.

The loading door started to close when I noticed this so-called, 'pilot' hadn't even boarded the ship. His wooden, floatin' ass was still outside.

"This dude…" I whispered. "Hey! I ain't flying this shit by myself. What the hell, man?" I shouted as the last of the floating crates entered.

The loading door shut.

Kclooommm!!

CHAPTER 20:

Mechanism

A dimmed lighting settled, in midst of my turn.

"Aaaahhhh!" I screamed as the Wooden Man stood behind me.

"Man, you ugly."

He just looked at me without blinking.

It was terrifying, close up on him. His skin was dirty brown, and it wasn't cracking at all. It was millions of engravings, or ancient symbols of some kind. His muscle structure bled over into multiple layers. And he was nearly naked, if not for the dingy loincloth, wrapped about his pelvic area. Then, there was the no arms, no legs, floaty thingy that kept me backing away.

"Follow me," he hissed as he hovered down the corridor.

Klooom!

The four large crates crashed to the floor, jolting my body. But my eyes were still glued on the Wooden Man. Following cautiously behind him, I remained at a neat distance. That's just cause he was floating so damn slow.

Anywho… right?

The dark ship hummed like a smooth sewing machine. The sound was so melodious it could rock a baby to sleep.

A few minutes later… I saw a gorgeous light ahead.

With an eager zing I neared the cockpit's unique design. Then, from the circular entrance, I heard an annoying voice, increasing in volume with every step I took. It was bad, yo'. Like, real bad.

You ever heard pigs squealing, a knife raking over a stainless-steel table and ice cubes scraping out of an ice tray?

Okay...

Now combine all those sounds together and that's how this voice sounded.

Guitussami entered the immaculate light. He drifted over to the control desk as the annoying voice blabbered on.

Finally, I entered the cockpit, which opened up to a very large bridge.

The room was shaped in a half circle and from wall to wall it flourished with buttons, switches, levers, cords, and light drives.

At the front of the flight deck sat an extremely large window that circulated along with the overall shape of the room.

My eyes fixed on to the window as I stopped in place.

We were already among the stars, the solar systems...

What a view of zipping fast beauty th-

"-Damn Chobe!" Shouted that high pitch aggravating voice.

Glancing to my side, I saw this young lady, sitting in the pilot seat, still talking.

"Gimme one night with you. That's all I need. Just one. And you can have you back. I'll make you forget all about what's her name."

"What?!" I retorted.

"You got that, let's do it face. Lemme sit on yo' face!"

"Who?"

"Where yo' mamma at?" She blurted, unbuckling herself from the pilot seat. "I'll slap her face in for making your face look like that!"

She jumped out of the seat and rushed over to me.

Now, I hate when people talk shit about my momma. But I couldn't tell if this was a compliment or not. And, I'm all about one-night stands. I'm the man for that. And usually, I'm the aggressor. But this? This???

Na man...

"Aren't you like twelve? What the fuck!"

"You got a dirty mouth too." She beamed as she began to caress my arms. "Your mamma teach your face to talk like that?"

"Yo! Stop talking about my momma!"

"This is my pilot. And she is not twelve. She's actually pretty old." Guitussami inserted.

"Hush!" The woman bellowed as she turned to shush the Wooden Man.

I began to hug myself, right? Shaking my head and stuff when she turned back around, glaring into my eyes.

"Let's go. Me and you. Right now." She hissed, tapping me on the shoulder.

"Man, what the hell?" I boomed with reproach as she licked her lips.

She drooled like an uncouth animal, smacking me around here and there.

"Boundaries! Ugh… Boundaries?" I retorted as bits of coke pitched from my pockets.

"Huh?" She replied, slapping me softly in the face and on the arm.

Bip! Bap!

"I'm ready." She mumbled, while looking me over. "I'll do anything."

"Can you shut the fuck up?"

And just like that, she shut up.

But the crazed woman kept tapping me, pinching me and shit. She punched me softly in the stomach. Then she smacked me in the neck and in the face again.

Wak!

"Hey!" I screamed. "Ugk!"

She dug her fingers in my throat.

183

I swatted her hand away, hollering, "Yo, I'm bout' to clock dis' bitch!"

"Please adjust yourselves," ordered Guitussami.

"You better come get her." I demanded.

The woman stopped her simple assault and put her hands in her pockets. She rocked childishly back and forth on her heels, while staring in my face with those twinkling gray eyes.

She kicked me lightly in the shins, snickering and gushing as if she found love at last.

Mind you, this woman wasn't ugly by no means, right?

She wore a short sleeved thick skin corporal sweater. She had on a thick zip up vest that seemed to be made from Bealbriean hide. She had on some dingy brown work gloves, some khaki booty shorts with a very thick and wide utility belt. And she had these bulky white socks that stopped just at the brink of her boots.

She was a rare Gray Garden slug. Her body was extremely curvy. She had a flat stomach, smashing thighs, big knockers, a nice ass, and a pleasant face. Her skin was so smooth and full of tiny dark green speckles with white blotches to blend.

She was an easy ten. But her demeanor, her basic personality, the way she carried herself, cost her dearly.

She became a two. Real quick!

"Merge the Transportal Device into the light drive correlative plane." The Wooden Man ordered.

The crazed woman smiled at me and held out her hand.

I just kept standing there looking shot-out.

She slapped me on the arm again, holding her hand out as if she was waiting to receive something.

"What?" I asked.

She beckoned even firmer for the collection of such, I didn't know.

"What woman?" I shouted.

"Give her your Transportal Device." The Wooden Man directed.

She rolled and batted her beautiful eyes while still holding out her hand.

Reaching carefully into my sleeve pocket, I gave her the device.

She shifted her hips and grunted, "Hmp."

Then she spun around like she knew ballet or something, skipping over to the control desk. She typed into the TPD and into a separate floating panel. A transparent window lifted up beside her and a series of coordinates scrolled within the panel.

Venturing over to the Wooden Man, I watched this woman diligently as I couldn't recognize her duty.

"What dat' crazy bitch doing?" I whispered without taking my eyes off her.

"She's decrypting your TPD and downloading all of your portal inceptions." Said the Wooden Man.

"I thought that took life cycles to decipher."

"Not for Mechanism." Guitussami replied while looking over to me.

"Holy shit… that's crazy." I confirmed while ogling at the phenomenon.

Then, that crazy bitch raised her hand like a student or sum shit.

I glanced over to the Wooden Man.

"Don't look at me. You're the one who told her to shut up." He protested.

While gazing on to the crazy woman, I walked over to her and uttered, "What bitch?"

"Permission to speak, sir!"

"Okay."

"I've found the coordinates for Kontriss base. Should we proceed with course destination?"

"Proceed." said the Wooden Man.

"Kontriss…? Wait! Y'all going to my mom's spot?" I asked while turning to face the Wooden Man.

"Yes. We made a deal," he answered.

"I know. I know… but that place is covered with Xarchanzians."

"We can readjust the landing zone. If that's okay?" The crazy woman asked as she turned to face me.

With a face of unrest, I pled. "Yes. Please do."

The Mechanism smiled.

She turned to type into the control desk.

Then, the entire vessel reconfigured into its own orbit. And just that fast we came to a stationary hoover.

"Hey… I recognize that high rise," I mumbled while squinting through the large window ahead.

Pondering the event over and over, I stepped closer to the window and uttered. "How'd we get here? So… fast?"

"This ship is like a giant TPD. It's great for short, light year distances." The Wooden Man announced. "It's not Anarqkis though."

"You better go get your family," the crazy woman said.

She typed quickly into the controls and a small tray opened from under the counter.

"How many?" She asked.

"How many what?"

"How many times you go make me cum?" She chuckled. "Ha! Naaa… How many family members do you have?"

"Just my mom and dad."

187

"Then here. Take these," she ordered as she reached into the compartment and pulled out two microspots. She grabbed my TPD and walked over to me as the tray closed into the control desk.

"Give one to each parent," she demanded while giving me the microspots. "Once you have them all together, tap the send button on your TPD. The microspots will serve as instant displacements. They'll be safe here. I suggest grabbing whatever you can."

She gave me my TPD and headed out from the main bridge.

"What about everything else?" I quizzed with a voice of urgency.

"We'll take care of that." said Guitussami as I turned to face him, stuffing the microspots in my pocket.

The Mechanism stopped just at the bridge's circular entrance. "We gotta go, Chobe... I'll show you down."

"Man... y'all for real," I huffed, rushing over to join the Mechanism.

But then, I caught a glimpse of another man. Apparently, he had been sitting on the other side of the bridge the whole time. He was reading a black book and he was sipping from a small white cup.

He had eyes like tiny balls of flame. His skin was like an untarnished brass and his hair was thick and nappy. He sat right in front of a sign that had been mounted on to the cockpit's wall. I've never seen him before. He was a total enigma.

"Who the hell is that?" I asked as the Mechanism, and I exited.

She answered with no enthusiasm, "Oh, that's just another co-pilot."

We came to a Teledeck, and I boarded with no hesitation.

The Mechanism patted me down quickly. She tightened up my boots and my clothes.

"Let's go." She yelled.

"Alright."

"You are approximately 20,000 feet above your domain. You must have a supreme sense of urgency. Remember-"

"- Wait!"

"..." She paused.

"My niece. Her name's Altizma."

"Shit!" Boomed the crazy woman. She lifted her head to the ceiling and lowered it. "Where is she?"

"About two sectors east. XVN-Waqn Misz." I responded.

"Don't worry." She exclaimed. "I'll get her."

She typed into the Teledeck and noted, "Don't change any of the integers on your TPD. You grab your folks and your things. Do this fast. Really fast. You understand?"

"Got it."

"Give them the microspots and click send on the TPD. And come back to me, Chobe… Simple. Right?" She voiced with sincerity as I tucked my TPD back up into my sleeve pocket.

"I'll set a course for Altizma now. But once I love you, I meant- move you, this vessel will appear on Xaris radars. You gotta act fast, to limit their response time."

Zipping up my sleeve pocket, I glared at the Teledeck floor and smirked, "Let's do it."

Just as she pushed the teleport button-

CHAPTER 21:

Observing T-Day

Materializing in front of my favorite model's poster, I heard giggling behind me.

As the portal dissipated, I turned to see my niece sitting on the bed, staring into my face. She still had on her sleeping gown and her antennae bonnet.

"Altizma?"

"Uncle Kontriss, how you get in here like that in all that light like that?"

"No time, ma!" I shouted

Suddenly, a harsh rumble shook the pod.

Debris fell from the ceiling as I grabbed her off the bed, hoisting her up to my waist.

"Where's everybody?"

"They're all outside." She replied as I hurried over to the chest of drawers to grab another pair of pants, some socks, and a chan-

"- Aaaaaarrrrgrgggggghhhh!!!!!" Came a horrible roar.

I dropped everything. Including Altizma.

Fwlom!

"Da' fuck?" She mumbled from the floor.

My eyes shook with anxiety as I glared up to collect this. "What the hell…" I grumbled as various objects fell from the walls.

Dropping my head, I froze for a second. Then, I recognized the roar as it finally died away. But I was still in disbelief. Well, I wanted to be in disbelief...

"That was loud, uncle. What was that?"

"I'm not sure..."

But I knew exactly what it was. A nigga just didn't want to accept it. Not that fast.

"I gotta get outta here." I declared while grabbing my nearest duffle bag.

"Momma!!" I shouted, rushing out of my room.

"They're outside, uncle K."

Damn, I forgot about Altizma...

As I peered into her gleaming face, her poor little eyes teared up to a glimmer.

"They're all outside. Everybody. There's a big celebration going on and they said I couldn't come." She cried as she gazed up at me.

"Climb on to my back, ma. And hold on tight!"

"Ok." She whined as I lifted her up.

She wrapped her legs around my waist and clasped her hands about my neck, bracing her stomach against my back.

The ground shook and quivered as I dashed through my mom's pod.

The racket, the screams of the celebration intensified as I started to sweat. Then, that smell returned.

After entering the living room, I sprinted towards the annular door.

"Hang on ma!" I hollered as I reached for the exit panel.

FaBoom!

Three Pokidods crashed through the hatch door.

They crowded the space attacking viciously with their solid bodies wrecking the room.

"Fuck!" I hollered, shaking, and dodging their prongs of poison, I jumped on the table.

AAaaghh!" Altizma screamed as I hopped over the furniture.

Landing on the couch in front of the pod's glass, I hollered, "Hold on, ma!"

A Pokidod rammed me through the window.

Cllaasssssshhh!!!

In the Layain streets I fell, and right into an uproar, spilling my coke everywhere.

It was an upheaval of universal cataclysms.

Then, a severe pain throbbed in my neck. "Agh…" I whispered as I stood to my feet, rubbing the area.

One of the Pokidods got me and I seemed to be unphased. But the one that stung me fell back into the pod.

The other Pokidods circled around, watching as smoke seeped from the monster's pores. Then, it fell on its back, kicking and squirming.

Still rubbing my neck, I gawked from the streets and-

Blop!

The monster popped like a balloon, swashing a thick pus over the pod.

"Euw," I frowned as Altizma tucked from the carnage.

The other Pokidods glared at me with such hate, I could see it in their eyes.

We took off!

Turning down a corner, I viewed out to a scape of pure destruction.

There were several massive craters all throughout the Layian lands. The gaps were so deep that I couldn't grasp the perception. All the craters looked the same, with rigid marks around the edges. The one I was standing in front of was fresh, as massive boulders were still dropping into the cavity.

Just then, I heard small little tinkles, whispers coming from an abandoned structure nearby. And out of the corner of my eye I saw a legion of Pokidods behind me.

While, slowly backing away, I turned with caution.

They were all just standing there with an unmatched urge of hatred boiling over in their gravy souls. It looked like every

Pokidod that existed was in attendance of this sanctimonious occasion.

A fog lifted into the air as I reached the edge of the crater. Then, from the abandoned building came a shout.

"Hey! Hey! Over here! Over here!"

"Aw man." I whispered, glancing over to see my mom and dad.

"Auntie!" Altizma shouted as she lowered from my shoulders.

"Don't go over there!" I scolded, snatching her back.

She spun behind me as she finally noticed the herd of Pokidods.

"What are they?"

"Pokidods…"

Suddenly, a group of them rushed over to my parents while the rest of them stayed in front of me.

Turning to face Altizma, I took one microspot from my pocket and instructed, "Take this. Don't let it go. You run to the center of this crater, and you stay there until I come back."

She looked at me and started huffing and puffing.

"I can't… uncle. I can't. Please don't make me. I'm scared. Don't leave me… please don't leave me, unc-"

"-Listen! If you don't go, they're gonna kill us. Both of us! You wanna die, ma?"

She shook her head.

"You remember what happened to mommy?"

She nodded and started crying even harder.

"Ok... that's not about to happen today. But you gotta trust me. Go, ma! Now!"

She took the microspot and trailed cautiously into the crater.

When I turned around, all the Pokidods were up on me. Eavesdropping?

Reaching into my boot, I took the little coke that I had left and sprinkled it over my antennae.

My parents had been backed into a corner.

"I'm coming over there!" I shouted. "Don't move!"

And right then, all the Pokidods backed away from me and my parents. They literally cleared a path...

We were all defenseless and I didn't know what to do.

So many thoughts ran through my mind. Maybe I could rush the herd, let them sting me, and snatch my family away. If I could just get everyone to the center of the crater, with the microspots and my TPD, I could teleport us all at once.

I'd probably die in the process, but that would be cool.

"Run, son!" My dad yelled.

"Don't. Fucking! Move!" I bellowed while pointing sternly.

He looked at me like I was crazy. "Maybe we should listen to him, Hun," mom persuaded.

"Yea, but he just cursed me."

"Ima' getchall outa' here!" I shouted.

The Pokidods and I stared at each other. It was like they were thinking and communicating. Obviously, they were waiting on something, but I had to check on Altizma.

She stood safely in the middle of the crater, clenching her microspot.

"Don't move, ma!" I shouted.

She lifted her thumb and nodded.

With every moment that passed, the Pokidods became more and more motionless. It was then when I understood that they were simply waiting on me.

Suddenly, an elevated voice shouted from a speaker.

"Kontriss Quiaussuss! You are wanted for the blatant expiry of said father and corporate, Chip Byton."

A shuttle or a spacecraft hovered above.

"Damn."

The Xaris heat.

You know, I still wonder to this day if the Xaris and the Pokidods were working together...

Anyhow... Right?

"Stand down Kontriss. You will be killed if not processed for trial." The voice carried.

From the sky came a group of Xerc Mercs, lowering from the aircraft.

The roar from hell's womb quacked again as they landed between me and the Pokidods.

My hands lifted and suddenly, the herd of Pokidods swarmed my parents.

"Noooo!!!" I hollered, attempting to intervene just as the Xaris restrained me.

My parents were torn to shreds.

The Xaris latched a cord about my waist that yanked me up into the air.

This intergalactic clatter was a traumatizing instance that I thought couldn't get any worse.

But then...

A group of Pokidods gathered in the center of the massive crater. A terrorizing cloud of gore bubbled into the sky.

The Xaris tugged me on into the ship as the Pokidods ripped my niece apart- like plucking grapes from a vine. They lugged her pieces out of the crater, as I screamed to the top of my lungs.

"Altizmaaaaa!!!!"

Aboard the Xaris vessel, they shoved me to my knees, kicking and punching me around like a ragdoll, speaking in their ancient dialect.

"Serves you right. You killed that poor kid's dad."

"Yeah! We got your ass now. I hope they put you in a Plyka Vest for an eternity!" Another shouted.

They burst out laughing hysterically as I laid on my side, staring over to the blinking lights at the base of the ships' flooring. Whatever I was getting, I must've deserved.

"Setting a course for Karisya Olayak." The pilot announced over the intercom.

The spacecraft shifted into another gear as we lifted higher into the voids. Then, I heard her… The roar of all roars. It was so loud that it shook me out of my depression. My soul was somehow tied to her. This queen.

The dreaded consternations of the day. Everything. Everything was my fault.

My deal with Vykra flopped. And where were they anyways? The Mechanism. The Wooden Man. They all just left me.

And how did the Pokidods know I would be here? At this exact moment. My thinking quivered as the queen's roar finally ceased.

The Xaris weren't worried at all. It was like they couldn't even hear the queen's cry. They acted like it was just another day. They had no feelings, no remorse, no nothing. They only worked to rid the galaxy of any threat. I know because I've seen them do this shit before.

I'd just like to know if I could hate them any worse than the Pokidods? Or maybe I should hate the Wooden Man and the Mechanism for sending me on this dummy, stupid ass mission. Or maybe I should hate myself for not acting fast. For not responding first. Yeah! That's it. That's who to hate...

Myself.

Wishing, deservedly for my rapid death, I shut my weeping eyes, hoping that this all would go away. But this was a real-life nightmare of unexpected melancholy. Agony. Hatred. Horrendous evils and now...

Nothing.

CHAPTER 22:

Hang Tight

Upper Riaxon: Karisya Olayak

My eyes opened to the sound of the ship landing.

The Xaris held me under my arms in front of the loading door, which had just lowered.

They dragged me out into the Layian environment. And there it stood. The one place I never thought I would see. Karisya Olayak. The biggest, escape proof prison in all existence.

With an engulfing odor, and a constant sound of horror did this enormous prison float, in midair. KO was constructed out of Layian composites too baffling for me to interpret. The tarnished tan prison had no windows, no openings for ventilation of any kind. The structure towered so high that it curved into the air.

Man, I was bending over so hard, trying to grasp the top of this building. But anyways, right- I started panicking, struggling for life as the fear of this stockade set in.

The Xaris hauled me like a mutilated calf, skipping the whole intake.

We came to an arena called Cebora. This massive half circled room was filled with computer lights. The walls where platinum, high, and packed with thousands of balcony boxes. There wasn't an empty seat in the house.

This was where I would deliver my plea, which didn't matter. Cause the Xaris didn't give a fuck. They held no justice, no liberty for any other than their own.

They dropped me to the floor right in front of a massive podium made out of a sleek dark and shiny material. The front of the stand bore several Layain symbols that translated into the phrase:

'Symbassy Rule.'

"How do you plead?" Announced a deep and degraded voice from behind the podium.

Staring lifelessly to the ground, I lifted my head to this voice of judgment and chimed, "Does it matter?"

From the podium stood a man in a blue suit. His hair was fluorescent as its colors would change every so often. But this guy stood in his power as his presence humbled me.

"Submit your plea."

At this moment, I wasn't mad anymore and I didn't want to live either.

"Guilty. Guilty as charged." I grumbled bowing my head to the floor as the man spoke on.

"I, Pias, Governor of Zenickdale, pass this judgment to Judge Supreme Hanto."

Far up into the ceiling of this great room sat another podium. There stood another man typing fast into a transparent floating plain. Then, another monitor popped up next to Pias. The governor of Zenickdale double tapped the plane.

He glared at me with a grin so evil, that I snatched away, just as the transparent monitor vanished.

Honestly, I wanted to see what he was reading, but I couldn't stand the eye contact.

"Death!" He shouted. "By Plyka Vesting."

The tears rolled down my face as he uttered, "Come. Gather your trash."

Several Xarchanzians came from behind and dragged me out of Cebora.

Moments later, we came to the end of an extremely long hallway. They took me through the sliding doors and left me there in a dark, browbeating room.

"Good riddance," said the Xaris merc as they exited the room.

The sliding doors shut behind me. And as soon as the doors closed, the entire floor of this room elevated up to a larger space.

An eerie feeling conquered me quickly. This room was six sizes larger than the floor below.

My senses left, and I couldn't see anything either... But. Wait...

A glimmering blue light emitted from the ceiling above.

205

Squinting my eyes to capture this sight, I assumed this glare was lowering down to me.

Then, came a snicker, just as I whirled around. There stood two men, off in the distance.

They were gawking at me from a small control station.

One of the men lifted a Pararay gun from the floor. He loaded it briefly as they walked over.

"We do have your cooperation. True?" Asked one of the men just as the other aimed his gun directly in my face.

"Yes." I grunted, glaring at the ground, struggling for comfort. "Just finish me off already. I don't wanna anymore. I can't any- What is that smell?"

"That's the smell of a thousand deaths," the guard uttered as they finally approached.

This smell was so horrible that I began to gag, turning to and fro, trying to figure out where it was coming from.

"Jeez! That's so bad!" I cried. Literally... "What in the world?"

Then, I finally looked up, and there, that blue flicker was actually a very long cord with a hook at the end of it. And hanging from this hook was a garment. A foul vest, the appalling origin of such a smell, with the word 'PRISONER' stitched into the back.

It was a dingy rust orange bubble vest, overly stained with blood. The spots must've sat in marination for so long that they changed the vest's pigmentation. Then, I realized that these stains and this smell, came from previous wearers.

The vest lowered in and the smell increased.

The revolting garment stopped right by my head, toppling me to the floor.

As the Xaris soldiers stood over me, one man freed me of my constraints.

Wallowing in anguish, I covered my face, and lowered my antenna to reduce the smell.

The other guard held out his hand and smiled.

"Come. Let's die," he bellowed as I glanced up to him and over to the repulsive stomach-churning vest.

"Might as well." I replied, reaching out for his hand.

They were so persuasive.

He lifted me up and guided me over to the vest.

"Why y'all hate us so much?" I asked.

They didn't say a word. They just carried on without any emotion.

"Can't we all just get along?" I reasoned- but no, they acted like I wasn't even talking.

There was no reasoning with these cats.

The horrid odor quelled my stability as they snatched me out of my t-shirt.

"Not many get this fate. It's actually one of the worst ways to die," the guard said as they both fitted me into the disgusting fashion.

"I'm gonna die by the smell."

"Plyka defines itself as a weight expansion." He explained while tucking my arms into the vest of damnation.

"The vest will lift into the atmosphere. The higher the vest travels the more gravity the vest will simulate. The longer the sentence, the heavier the weight."

"Mr. Kontriss, you have been sentenced to death. You don't have a set cycle. This means that we will elevate you to the highest height possible. And as you can see... the ceilings here are pretty high." He lectured.

Glaring up into the ceiling, I couldn't see the top. All I saw was a pit of upward woes.

One of the men stood in front of me. And right then, a transparent monitor opened next to him. He began typing into the hologram. The other man finally zipped the vest up. He locked the zipper in place and put the key in his pocket.

The stench and the weight of the vest came quickly. My knees buckled as I attempted to stand. This was about to get nasty.

The hologram vanished right when the Xaris soldier finished typing. "There, Mr. Kontriss. I've set the weight of the vest to unlimited for Plyka simulation."

"Oh. We trying something new?" Quizzed the other guard.

"Oh yeah?" I growled.

"This means that the weight of the vest would probably force you to implode. You'll more than likely die before you hit the ground. In theory. You'd barely even leave a mark as your body will burst into flames and disintegrate during your rapid drop." He assured me.

"Aw thanks." I blurted as the guard took the butt of his gun and bashed me in the face.

Baf!

"Agh!" I hollered, rocking to the side. "Fucking, dick in a can!"

The other man violently tapped the panel on his wrist, and I shot up into the Zions.

"AAAAaaaggghhhhhhh!!!!"

"Hang tight!" Shouted the Xarchanzian as I raced into the air.

The winding wire zipped into the pulley as I screamed myself hoarse. Pretty soon, everything turned to a black, empty area of thin air.

Eventually, my will power crushed. Anxiety crippled my desire.

CHAPTER 23:

Archipus
Part 4

From the starting gate came neighs and nickers, mixed
with clangs of the stall dividers. Jockeys sat on their steeds, eagerly
facing the door modules. With their feet stuffed in stirrups,
clenching their reins and whips, they eyed the starter through the
spring-powered barriers.

RRRrrrrrrriiinngggggg!!!!

Ka-Boufffff!

The gates sprung open and down the stretch they came,
galloping through the cuppy lanes. Thousands went wild as the
harass made the clubhouse turn. Swiftly approaching the straight
away, number seven slowed to a canter. The jockey responded
with haste, cracking his whip over the steed.

Kihs!

Kihs!

"Ya!" He scolded as the horse slowed to a trot, then to a
full stop. The jockey searched over the steed as several other
horses began to slow. With a showy neigh, number seven reared
up.

"Whooaaa!!!" Shouted the jockey as the steed lowered.
With its eyes fixed on the grandstands, number seven began to
back away. The jockey again, searched over his steed while the

entire harass came to still, ogling in the grandstands. That's when every rider cheered on, urging their stallions to safety. It was then when the jockey of number seven, dismounted his steed. His eyes fixed on to the grandstands ahead. As the jockey dropped his reigns, his steed galloped away. But he advanced slowly, stalking with a squint… "The fuck is that?" He asked.

"Aaagggggggggghhh!!!!!!" A woman hollered as a freak of nature stood beside her.

Screams filled the stands as the audience scattered for the exit. The riot trampled over each other as the jockey cleared the tracks.

A savage nicker blared through the field. The monstrosity vanished and a red lightning bolt blazed across the seats, leveling every human to slop.

Bbbzzzzzaaaaasssssskccc!!!

A massive cavity covered the arena as the gory blast dissipated. A dense fog of blood lifted from the wreaka-

"-Egh, Yo! Fuck dat' damn horse!!!"

CHAPTER 24:

Hang Tight cont…

"Stupid ass horse fucking up my flashback."

"Horse? What horse?"

"Shut the fuck up Feuler and listen."

"Oookkaayy…"

****

So right…

Shit felt like a million cycles had passed, I lost track. On several occasions, I went in my clothes. It was bad, but not as bad as that stankin' ass vest.

The anticipation of my dramatic doom manifested as I gazed down into the dark, bottomless chasm of death. By this time, the weight of the vest had already begun its foolishness. The wire began to slow. The hoisting came to a creeping delay. Then came a click, and I stopped.

Now, I didn't know for sure… but the Plyka vest was getting heavier. It was subtle, cause I could still feel it. But if the hook would hold long enough; I could possibly ponder a way of escape. Right?

While peeping behind me, I saw the ceiling and the pulley responsible for this lifting. It was a pretty pulley, and the wire was smooth and legible. What type of material was this string made of? It had to be strong, to compensate for the weight of this vest.

"Did you take that pill?" A voice sounded.

My eyes opened as I peeked over the emptiness, looking vividly to my right, and left. No one was there. Just the darks.

"Who's dat'?"

"Did. You. Take. That. Pill?" The voice sounded again.

"Man! C'mon with the games!" I cried while batting my eyes. "Are my eyes even open? Yes! Yes, they are!" I babbled in lunacy. "I'm going crazy. That's it! I've lost it all!!"

Then, from the ceiling, floated a being, at a slow menacing speed. He had the silhouette of a man, but he didn't have any feet.

I'm seeing shit...

He had on an all-brown trench coat that concealed every bit of his physical makeup. The coat was full of pockets and brown buttons, with a brown belt about the waistline. He wore a pair of brown work gloves and a brown brim hat. His eyes were completely white. But his face was a total abyss. The more I looked, the more it began to resemble a night sky.

"I'm dead, right?"

The being glimpsed up to the pulley. He tucked his hands in his pockets and answered, "Not yet. But you bout' to be."

"Shit!" I hollered as the being floated.

"I'm just trying to see if I teleported to the right place." He wondered as he glanced about the room. "Vykra told me a pill was here. But since you didn't take one, I guess I'll be moseying on al-"

215

"-Vykra? Wait! Don't go. Don't go! I took a pill. I took a pill!" My soul erupted when the being looked into my eyes.

"I did. I swear it."

"Oh yeah?"

"Yeah!"

"Uh huh… What color was it?"

"It was black. A black pill."

"Nope!!! It was orange." He bellowed as he lifted to the ceiling.

"HHHhhheeeyyyyy!!! Da' fuck, man! Hey!!" I whaled as the being giggled.

"Aw man… you should've seen your face." He chuckled, lowering back in front of me. "I'm glad you didn't throw up. You would've been straight outta LoCash."

"LoCash? Man, what the hell!" I hollered. "Who is you?"

"I'm a pill tracker. I redefine low stratums of Layian Telepathy to further nourish such weaknesses. And I just so happen to be a walking portal, serving Vykra by way of Symbassy, venal disposition."

"What nie?"

"I'm your escape plan."

"Fuck!" I screamed just as the Plyka Vest tripled in weight.

"Don't panic." The being said as he placed his hand over my stomach. "Something smells like poo!"

Glancing frantically over the darks, I bellowed, "I'm bout to die!"

"Hold on." He grumbled while slipping his hand under my vest. He closed his fist and a vast understanding of weight, mass, gravity, objects in motion, equations and formulas, flooded my brain. My reality and my every physical composition changed.

"What happened?"

"There," he stated, tapping me on my shoulder.

Bik!

"Aaaagggghhhhh SHHhhhiiitttttttt!!" I screamed as the winds beat against my face. I hurtled to the floor like an asteroid.

A wheezing sound thundered through the room. My skin heated up. Tiny flames sparked about me as the heavy vest flapped in the wind. Right before I combust into flames, I thought of decreasing the weight of the vest. And just like that, the flames vanished, and I fell at a slower rate.

Was this vest defying gravity? As my thoughts faded, so did my attention to the vest. It immediately increased in weight again.

Without notice, the floor came plain in sight as I thought to decrease the weight again. The deadly garment responded just as fast. Then, I floated like a feather.

Turning my back to the floor, I crossed my arms and tucked my knees into my chest. Over sixty feet from the surface, I increased the weight of the vest again.

Booom!!

A mammoth crater crushed into the ground.

The vest lightened in weight as I relaxed my body. With massive chunks of rubble covering me, I gazed up into the dark gap above, awaiting death's untimely visit. Just then, the door to this torturous chamber opened. A Xaris officer walked over to the crater and stood.

I played, 'dead' still, daydreaming about my pathetic life as the officer glared. "Dummy!" He chuckled as he walked off.

The officer shut the door behind him, leaving me to rot in my errored ways.

If I had just punched Chip Byton in the face, none of this would've ever happened.

That poor kid…

Shit, if I make it out of here alive, I'll find that poor little kid and I'd punch him in the face too! Poor kid. Then I'd buy him some sour ice cream. I'll apologize... years later.

That entity…?

He must've been a fragment of my imagination. But if he was, then how did he do what he did to my stomach? It must be that pill, it got me seeing shit.

After deciding to move, I finally pushed the debris off me, only to notice how enormous the hole was. The crater was so deep, I had to climb out of it.

Rolling clumsily out of the hole and onto my back, I heard his voice again, "My name is Core. You know. Like the center of most significant things."

His brown and heavy trench coat flopped gracefully as he descended, floating right before me as I gazed.

"Kontriss Quiaussuss," I whispered, dropping my head back to the floor.

"This polar bear walks into a bar-"

"-Aw shit. Egh man!"

"Ssshhhh!" He hissed. "The Xaris think you're dead. They won't come until your corpse decays or until someone else receives the same sentence. And don't worry about the surveillance cameras. I rigged those too." He lectured.

"If you my escape plan, then why is we aint escaping?"

"The Plyka and the Gravitol are linked to this room." He pointed to the console. "This moment will change you forever. It'll take another cycle before you digest the pill in its entirety. You will consume the pill through service of intellect, brain power and superb understanding. This will assure the development of your Layian telepathy." The being neared as I lifted my head.

219

"You will hone your skills and turn this death backing vest into a weapon. Your weapon. And we will use this room to do it." He concluded.

"How? I can't hardly move. Ugck!" I gasped as my breaths shortened from the weight of the vest.

"Lesson number one. Never use the word can't," he bellowed.

The weight of the vest decreased substantially, and I inhaled with a gasp.

"The pill will unlock your true ability while I expedite your training. You will master the knowledge base given to you, which in turn, holds not even a microcosm of contrast to the full practicability of Layian thought transference." He asserted as he tugged on his gloves.

"So, you're not a fragment of my imagination?"

"No. I'm not a *figment* of your imagination." He added while looking in my eyes. "Can you move?"

Wiggling my legs, I lifted my arms, and sat up straight. "Yea."

"Good. Make the vest heavy."

"What?" I retorted as the being floated over to me.

He pointed to my forehead and said, "This, encased within your skull, tells your limbs what to do, how to perform, how to act. It gives you ideas. It gives you strength when you need it because it's a muscle. A mental muscle. Now... *this* outside of your brain is only inanimate objects that possess no mental functionality at all. The trick is to put your brain in that inanimate object of voided immaterial. The possibilities could be endless, just as your own imagination. I'm not asking you to go after all the objects in this room. No. Just that." He noted while pointing to the filthy vest. "Just this one, lifeless object."

The vest suddenly increased in weight, forcing me back to the ground.

"There. Don't kill yourself. Control it." He commented. "Use that pill. There's plenty of it left."

While focusing on the garment, the vest became lighter as I fell back, exhaling with relief.

"Sit up." He ordered and I responded. "Keep it up. I need to do something about that smell."

Right then, I sat back and when I sat up, Core had vanished. Seconds later, he floated from the sky, tossing a change of clothes over to me.

For at least a full cycle, increasing, and decreasing the weight of the vest, I did over a million crunches.

Core had been with me in my confinement for an extended period. He would fold into himself and unfold back out, moments later, with different foods for me to eat. And this torture chamber didn't have a bath stall, I'd just go in the corner.

221

The vest and I soon reached an ultimate equipoise when I learned to adjust the weight without even wearing it. The vest could be light as air as I held it and then heavy as a planet as I dropped it. Man, I was so attuned with the vest that I could even trounce Core's authority over it.

We had been training for so long, I didn't notice that I became a hunk. My mind could crank out trillions of references and facts about weight, mass and gravity. They all came fully vouchsafe and at my complete exposure. And just like Core said, the possibilities were endless.

The Plyka Vest was mine, in mind. All mines. Thus, the establishment of my Layain Telepathy…

"You're ready." Core noted as he floated over, retrieving a blue card from his coat pocket. "I can tell." He revealed as I continued my pushups.

"Better be. All this damn shit!"

Core waved the card over the vest's zipper lock. The clasp chunked to the floor.

THck!

"You got a foul mouth. Too bad Layian Telepathy can't fix that."

"I'll fix yo' ass." I grumbled as he tucked the card away.

Then, he glared behind me.

I stopped in the middle of a push-up. "What?"

While sitting on my knees, I glimpsed at a light reflecting off the floor. With my hand cupped over my forehead, I turned around. And out of the window egress a figure. A shapely figure...

"Chobe!"

Immediately, I turned back around, dropping my head in sorrow. "Mutha fucka." I bawled with hate.

"Chobe?" She whispered as she approached my side.

Man, I was so pissed I couldn't look at her. She had let me down.

Core just kept looking spaced out.

"You hear someone talking?" I asked rhetorically.

Core threw up his hands and chuckled, "Hey man, I ain't got nothing to do with this. I put that on Trump."

"Could've sworn I heard someone talking to me."

"I'm sorry, Chobe!" She blurted.

"Oh!!" I shouted. "That's just the wind blowing. Thought I was hearing shit."

With my back turned to her, I stood slowly to my feet

She dropped to the floor just as Core snatched over. "Oh my! You, ok?" He asked.

"Stop this." She sniffled and sobbed despotically. "As soon as I moved you the Xaris boarded the ship. We didn't make it to Altizma. We didn't have a chance. If it wasn't for Tissami-"

"-Tissami?" Jeered Core.

223

"Yea…?"

"That's my best friend. How's he doing?" Core asked.

"He's doing fine." She answered.

"Is he still floating around?"

"Yeap. You know him."

They giggled as I interrupted. "Man hold the fuck up! I'm pissed as hell right now! And y'all in here, *laughing?*"

"Wait, I Just gotta ask. Did he talk the Xaris to death?" Core asked, deliberately ignoring me.

"He did. He's quite effective with his words, as always." She giggled.

"Man hey!!!" I screamed. "Am I not standing here?"

"Apologies… I got a little excited," Core smirked.

"It's gone, Chobe. They took the crates and the ship. In return they spared our lives for information on your location. It was planned, Chobe. The whole thing was. But we didn't expect the Pokidods. No one did… I'm so sorry." She dribbled in tears.

"You know they're dead right," I bleated.

"Who?"

"My mom. My dad. Altizma…"

"Sorry for your lost." Core chimed.

A grave silence grew as her eyes wandered aimlessly about.

"But don't worry about that. Just pop up whenever you feel like it! And how the hell did you know I was here?"

"A guy on the inside told me."

"Do you know how long I've been in here?"

"No Ch-"

"-Me either!" I bleated. "Do you know how many push-ups I've done, how many times I've gone to sleep?"

"Ugh...I-"

"-Shut up! I'm pissed!"

She dropped her head and started sobbing, "Chobe. You look so good. What have you been doing?"

"Bitch! Didn't I just say push-ups?"

"Clearly the two of you have some problems." Core inserted.

"I'm sorry Chobe. I didn't think the Xaris would act so fast."

With my hands on my hips, I glared up to the empty abyss. "Thank you." I countered with arrogance.

"Even as I gravel..." She cried. "I'll dedicate my allegiance, my life, the rest of it that I possess, as an avenging angel, until my debt for the death of your loved ones is paid in full."

While peering down to her, I held out my hand. "Hey!" I shouted just as she peeked up.

"Yes, Chobe?"

"Kiss my hand, bitch!"

She leaned over and kissed my hand ever so gently.

"Now get up. You're starting to look good down there."

She stood up slowly, dusting herself off. She glanced behind her as if she heard something.

"Where did they take the crates?" I asked.

"We don't know. But I do have this." She added as she reached into her vest pocket.

She pulled out Vykra's black thumb drive.

"I found it in your boot just before you loaded the Teledeck. It had some white glittery stuff on it… I brushed it off. It looked important. We couldn't risk the chance of you losing it. The Xaris would have the upper hand with it in their possession"

"Good call." I exclaimed.

"The Xaris can't unlock the crates without this drive. And I know Vykra. She encrypts everything."

"Cool. See if you can use the drive to locate the crates. It's our only chance to combat the Pokidods."

Just then, her antennae lifted from her head.

She bowed, well, it was more of a wobbly curtsy.

Then, she loaded her TPD and bolted off into the window of light. The portal vanished swiftly, leaving me and Core in this pit of dark.

"What was that all about?" Core asked.

"That's another story."

And I'll be damned if I do two flashbacks in one.

Don't even think about it... Stupid ass author!

Back to the ground I dropped, cranking out these push-ups, and-

Hooooommmmm!!!

A quake came so fierce that it shook the entire foundation of KO.

"Now what?" I quizzed while stopping amid a push-up.

"Well now…" Core calmly expelled. "This is the moment that you and I depart."

He began to unbutton his coat and I didn't notice, cause another boom immediately followed.

"Man, what the fuck?" I shouted as large particles fell from the ceiling.

"My friend, that is a man that not even I would dare to face. He is the last of his kind. Ever." Core bellowed.

"Yeah right. I'd kick his ass!"

"This man can punch you and mistakenly level a galaxy." Core advised while floating over to me. "You are more important than the quarrel. Come now."

And that's when I saw what he was doing… unbuttoning his coat.

"Man, whatchu' doin? I ain't with that shit!" I yelled.

"I know it looks strange-"

227

"-You damn right!"

Suddenly, all the lights came on as well as a blaring siren.

Then, another quake followed.

KaFlooom!!!

This time the foundation cracked wide with large rifts and disastrous gaps.

"Holy shit…" I grumbled, staring at the door to my oversized cell. It was thick, with a very small window within the design.

More particles plunged from the ceiling. Including the pulley and the incredibly long wire.

Then, I sensed something… something grand.

My antennae eased out of my head slowly. Whoever this was, became spiritually apparent. It was beyond my competence to amass such power.

A small quake started rumbling and throbbing with consistency.

"Man… what's going on?" I quizzed, glancing over the devastated room.

"You wouldn't believe me if I told you."

"Try me."

"That's a heartbeat. This being has so much control over every muscle in his body even until his Layian Telepathy falls victim. The vibrations of his heart can travel with very destructive evaluations and without causing him harm. Trust me, he will end us both and at a fraction of light's speed.

Do not attempt this, disputation you have fabricated in your imagination… It is but a fairytale. It will not happen as you have so discreetly plotted." Core answered assuredly as he finished unbuttoning his coat. "You are more important than you know."

Suddenly, the rumblings stopped.

We gazed over to the oversized cell door as turmoil spawned from behind the barrier. Yells and screams bellowed from the depths of hell's hallway, followed by the crunch of a million bodies.

Glancing over to Core, and as dark as his face was, I could see a glint of a tear, forming in his eye.

The cell door stripped off its hinges.

Ka-Plunc!

It shrunk to the size of a pebble and trickled to the floor like a grain of salt.

Blood sloshed into my cell like a wave of water.

Behind this bloody entrance came a slug, standing shirtless in the doorway. His skin was a smooth hue of perfect tonality, a solid black of unflawed etch. His eyes were just as black as his skin. And from the top of his eyes, ran two red lines that continued over his head and onto his back. His wrists were swathed with hand wraps and filled with bloody stains. He wore a

pair of gray and red fighter trunks with bronze and yellow symbols
running down the sides. The shorts had an elastic band at the top
with a white drawstring tied in several knots. His muscle structure
was extremely defined. He looked denser than the entire Layo
Galaxy. His legs were big as columns. His arms, chest and abs
were everything but scrawny. Shiiddd, I thought I was ripped, but
this shit was uncalled for... His sense of muscular definition gave
me a lifelong image of terror. And yet, puzzling tears dropped
from the being's eyes. As he softly wept, I noticed more gore
trailing off like tumbleweeds in the hallway behind him.

He held two decapitated domes, one in each hand, while
standing amongst a pile of more severed heads. He gently kicked
out of the bloody mound and the noggins spilled over as if they
were being poured from a cauldron. The heads thudded
gracelessly into each other, spreading out into my stygian cell.

He stared with a blank face.

Spellbound... I could not turn away from this.

Man, I was so mesmerized that I failed to notice the being
heading straight for me, holding those facially painful heads.

"My acumen... has yet to recriminate me. I knew... there
was... something else *here*." He uttered.

In a supreme pose of dictation, did this being stand.

"We are light leagues- quantum expanses beneath you. We
pose no threat, defiance, or remonstrance. Nor do we seek to food

any altercation. Such vitiating wouldn't be arduous and not even the least bit formidable. Depleting peasants would denounce your eclectic cultus, obsession for the arts. You are way beyond our first thought of attack. We have sworn to never strike one of our own- Not that we could, at any estimated scale." Core lectured convincingly.

The being glared into me even firmer.

And I had yet to end my bore of eye halting grit.

"Kontriss…" Core whispered. "I can't force you in. You have to…" Core paused in speech as the being progressed over to us. Core had become extremely worried, like he knew something was about to happen. He glanced back and forth, in a fast and edgy manner.

"Why so many heads?" Core asked.

"They are adversaries. Those who had the audacity to lift a finger against me. Some did. Some didn't. Some thought about it and suffered a horrible bleach death. I had them follow me here, rolling like small minerals, behind my feet."

"Kontriss," Core whispered as the black slug monologued.

But I was still affixed, with the loss of self-control. The being was too overwhelming.

He started crying again as he walked over to us in a slow and alluring style.

"If I force you in, the void will eradicate you. Kontriss?" Core grumbled.

Inclusively subjugated, I still couldn't respond or move a muscle. The being's eminence had me.

"He means nothing Dak'r." Core suddenly boomed.

"Oh... I beg to differ," he responded while plaguing my every molecule.

"His death shall profit you nothing but the organization of prodigality. Where is she?" Core asked while glaring over to the being.

The smooth-skinned slug stopped in his tracks and stood with an aborted face.

"Your search has landed you nothing but death and an unyielding desire for untamable violence. But I can help you."

Dak'r batted his eyes and dropped his head in sorrow.

"I'll help you find her. You have my word." Core spluttered. "But only if you can spell Racecar, backwards."

Dak'r smirked with arrogance, "Hmp. You moron. That's easy. R-A-C... E... Waaait a minute."

Right then, I awoke from a deep trance. Dak'r stood in front of me, holding those severed heads, he grumbled, "... It spells the same thing."

"Kontriss," Core whispered as Dak'r dropped the severed heads.

Pwuftt!

I snatched over to Core, standing with his coat open. There was a starry sky, traveling off into an unparalleled distance. The space within this, 'Core' did not fit his uniform area at all. It was like he embodied the entire universe, in his coat. "Come now, Kontriss." He whispered as Dak'r walked over to the wall, mumbling, "What the hell...?"

Now, I didn't know what was happening. But it seemed like Dak'r was distracted.

"Just step in. It isn't as bad as it looks," Core uttered as I frowned with distaste.

Dak'r slumped to the floor with a ponderous look in his eyes. He said, "How, does it spell... the same, *thing?*"

"Go!!" Core shouted as I closed my eyes and stumbled into the black void.

CHAPTER 25:

Trailblazer

Tumbling on a wooden floor, I opened my eyes to a wooden ceiling. Then, directly in front of me was a bisecting hall, full of patrons of all types of species and races.

"Gets em' every time." Core spoke as he folded out of himself. As his trench coat flopped to the ground, I found myself in some type of convenience store, full of gadgets and weapons.

"Man, I hate when you just pop up like that. I'll never get over it." Howled a gurgling voice.

"Camper Spain!" Core yelled. "How goes it?"

"*It-* is just fine. Who, is *that?*" He pointed.

Standing slowly, I turned to see a marvelous counter in the shape of a rectangle. The stand was clear and full of weapons.

Behind this large counter stood another slug.

He was massive, on the obese side. He was a two-toned Flavius with a light gray and orange blend. He was covered with small dark orange spots. His mouth was wide, and his eyes were white. His antennae were short and stubby. He had on a dark gray t-shirt with an odd logo design on it. The image looked like an old archaic anchor, but I couldn't see past his waist. The counter covered his lower half.

"This is Kontriss Quiaussuss." Core answered as he floated over.

235

"So." Camper inserted.

"Where am I?"

"This is beyond you Kontriss. But I will say, welcome to Wavemaker." Core announced. He held out his hand and we shook firmly.

"Seems like you just joined the rebellion kid," Camper added as he reached out to shake my hand. "Any crony of Core is a crony of mine."

"That's great…," said Core. "Cause I need access to your weaponry. And-"

"-And what?" Camper quizzed, dropping my hand.

Core stood quietly.

"And what?" Camper addressed.

"Yeah! Core."

Camper and I, ogled over to Core as he stammered in his speech. "… We need a ship," Core admitted with shame.

"A ship?!" Camper yelled.

"He made a deal with Vykra. The deal went south when the Xaris confiscated his vessel."

"Yeah, and now we don't know where it is."

"A ship!?" Camper repeated.

"C'mon Spain. You owe me this one. Besides, I know you got something."

"Yeah… I do. But I cleared that last favor. This one's coming out of pocket. How you gonna pay?" Spain asked, folding his arms.

"Agh… I don't have any quotoms," Core answered with a lowered head.

"I'll pay for it!" I shouted.

"How?" Camper asked.

"You take payments?"

"No. I don't kid."

"What about a down payment?"

"That's the same thing."

"Camper! C'mon man," Core interrupted.

"How much you got?" Camper asked.

"How much do I need?"

"Six and a half."

"Whhhoo Weee! You steep!" Core inserted.

"I got five kids to feed." Camper added as I walked over to Core.

"So how do you work?"

"Come again," Core sassed.

"Like, I mean… You're a portal, right?"

"Yea."

"What if I had a stash of quotoms, how would I get to them from here?"

"OOhhh! Okay. Just think of the place, wherever they are, and I can take you there through a mental link."

"Okay. I'm mentally looking at them right now." I said as Core began to open his coat.

And there it was, the space of all spaces...

"Close your eyes. Keep that image in your head and reach in."

"Just like that?"

"Yes. It's that simple." He proclaimed while holding his coat open.

I stepped over to the void and I reached all the way in.

"There it is. I see it now." Core said as I rummaged about the dark space.

Suddenly, I felt the corners of my bookshelf. Patting down the side and then to the bottom shelf, I reached for my golden safe box. Grabbing it by the handle, I snatched it out of the void.

Mysteriously, the box came directly from Core's abyss.

Ogling with amazement, I held the box up. "Holy shit..."

"Let me see what you got, kid," Camper gestured. He wasn't the least bit impressed. He must've seen this over a thousand times. "How do you open it?" He asked, sitting the box on the counter as I walked over.

"It's rhythm coded." I tapped on the counter, with a distinctive pattern, and the box popped open.

Spain pulled the box over to him, mumbling, "Let's see."

"Is that enough?" I asked.

"This is more than enough," He quickly replied as he closed the box.

"Not bad, Kontriss," included Core. "How'd you come up with so much?"

"Oh, I used to sell pharmaceuticals. That was before I showed up on Xaris radars." I noted. "And I can have the rest for you in three cycles."

"One cycle and we got a deal."

"Damn." I cooed.

Camper, aggressively folded his arms again just as Core shouted, "We'll do it!"

Glancing over to Core, I inserted, "We will?"

"Yes," he whispered.

Peeking up to Spain, I convincingly shouted, "One cycle!"

"Then we have a deal," gurgled Spain as he shook my hand.

"You can have Trailblazer. She's fast, versatile, and easy to navigate. A child could fly that ship." He boasted with a smile.

"That's good. Cause I can't fly shit."

"Ha!!" Laughed Camper as he placed my safe box into a built-in drawer. He closed the drawer up into the counter, then he stepped over to the wall. And that's when I noticed a brilliant black glass located within the wall behind him.

There was a gun encased within this glass. The handheld weapon shined bright. It was thin, white and sleek in design. The grip was clean, and the trigger was crisp. The gun was beautiful, sharp, and flagrantly perfect. Quite costly looking if you ask me. It seemed that it had been crafted by several gods.

"What is that?" I pointed firmly.

"Huh?" Camper paused while looking over to the gun, just as he gripped a lever on the wall. "Oh! DayArni? That... is t*he* last Light Gun. One cartridge and an unlimited supply of ultra-thin sheets of solid light. She'll cut through anything. And it's not for sale," he shouted as he pulled the lever.

Just then, the massive counter split in half and retracted into the side walls. And there underneath the counter, sat a flight of stairs.

"Come fellas!" Camper gestured while heading down the stairwell.

Core and I looked at each other. He floated to the side as I walked over to the stairs.

"Now don't you screw up this deal. Camper is a great friend of mine and I-"

"-Man fuck you, Core." I said with a smile.

"... After you," he replied.

That had to be the largest flight of stairs in the history of stairs. But the whole time- Spain was raving on and on about how many ships he had. My mind was elsewhere, thinking about how I was going to come up with the rest of Camper's quotoms.

We finally came to the bottom of the stairwell, stepping into a larger hall. This corridor was massive, and I was in complete shock. From one end of the hall, in the air and back, ran nothing but small, medium, and large spacecrafts.

And with all the ships in this underground bunker, there was one that stood out among the rest.

This ship sat in its own massive room. It (the room I mean) seemed to be empty. That was until I saw a quick refraction of light bouncing off the ship's surface.

It was about 320ft wide and nearly 720ft in length, and very basic in structure. The ship was very smooth and clean. You could see through it plainly. It was only a unique parallelogram with no controls, no wires, no engines, no nothing. Just an empty enormous rectangular shape of astonishing, unobscured shine. I found it hard to fathom how a ship could function without any controls.

Staring from the entry door, and into this 'empty' room, I pondered. "What in the Layain flames is this thing?"

"Oh… yes sir! That is one of a kind as well. The mother of all spacecrafts." Said Spain as he stopped behind me.

Core floated to a still as well and mumbled, "Is that-"

"-Yes, it is," Camper heckled.

"It's what? It's no ship… It's empty." I exclaimed. "You can see right through it."

"That's because it's off, kid." Camper announced while folding his arms. "You're not ready for that beast of space conquering speed. We're talking solid light powered by Inphions, dark matter, God particles, protons, and a vast length of Inatech advancements. This ship removes time and placement by forming a connection between radio waves and light refractions. Instead of hyper-driving, she snaps to a distinct position in space. The teleportation flouts the space-time continuum, making it impossible to land the ship upon advent. Slowing the craft down, at its' moment of arrival, will speed a timed planet into the future, or back into the past. We just installed a chronometer to alter the time alteration. Kink's a bit testy though." Camper said. "But really, what's better than a TPD conveying system? The reality folding-"

"-Anarqkis," Core concluded with a menacing tone.

"You'd break this ship out, only if your aim was to trounce the multiverse theory." Camper said as he and Core trailed off.

"No one could ever afford such a ship though." Core spoke.

"Ha!" Camper laughed hysterically. "It's already sold!"

While ogling at the awesomeness of this spacecraft, I dropped my head in disappointment and grumbled, "I want…"

Later, we entered a shorter corridor and from there, the hall opened to another hanger of ships.

"Man, how many ships you got?" I asked just as Camper pointed ahead.

"There she is!"

"Where?"

"There!" He shouted, pointing up into the corner.

There sat an awful red spaceship. It stuck out like a sore thumb. It was full of dents and hundreds of scuff marks.

"Oh, hell nawl, man. Let me get dem' Q's back."

"Nope!" Spain shouted. "A deal's a deal."

The craft had about four engines and two turbines, on each side. It was in the shape of an oval, laying horizontally. At the rear of this ship, just in front of the vents and right below, sat a yellow decal saying, 'Trailblazer'.

"Besides, this is more of your speed. You'll love her, I promise." Camper said while tapping on the side of the ship. "How about this. You fly her until your cycle is up. If you don't like her, I'll give you your quotoms back. Otherwise, I'd be expecting your final payment." He offered with a serious face.

Camper meant business too, cause he had his arms folded.

Placing my hands on my hips, I glared over to Core.

243

"I like her." Core said, "Red attracts the ladies."

"Alright! I'll take it."

"Ha!" Camper chuckled as he lowered the ship's loading door. "Let me show you around."

We boarded the ship and Camper Spain walked us through the many levels. Within a few moments I knew exactly where everything was, well almost everything.

The ship came with hundreds of projectile weapons, TPD(s), display monitors, a fridge, and even a coffee machine with over three cycles of grounded coffee beans.

What really got me was the large den. It came with a huge circular bed, sitting in the center of the room, and a fully functioning bar. To the left and the right of the den sat a flight of stairs that lead up to the main bridge.

"This ship was built by Inatechs and Xarchanzians which explains the homo sapien features. Trailblazer has been around for an extremely long time. You couldn't tear this ship up if you wanted to." Camper said as we climbed the stairs. "One of the unique things about this ship is the autosave feature."

"Autosave?" I gushed with puzzlement.

"You'll see…" Camper giggled.

As we reached the top of the stairs, Camper turned to us and reported, "Fellas, I've got another matter to tend. My pilot will show you the ropes. And be careful kid. She'll get away from you."

We then entered the main bridge, which opened up to a great space of controls. There came a bunch of buttons clicking and switches flipping. Then a low running engine began to purr, sending a fumy exhaust over the space around us.

"Alright, guys. I'll leave it to you," Spain shouted from the rear of the bridge. "And remember kid. One cycle!"

"One cycle!" I hollered as Camper exited into the hall.

See now, I hadn't looked at the pilot yet. Hell, I was too busy trying to figure out how I was going to pay Camper.

Then... I heard it.

"Chobe?"

Immediately, I closed my eyes and lifted my head to the ceiling.

"God, no."

"Oh! Hello again," Core shouted as he floated over to her.

She hopped joyfully out of the pilot seat and hugged him shouting, "Hi!"

Then, she started crying.

"There, there," pampered Core as she sniffled and sobbed.

She deliberately glared over to me while Core's back was turned. But I could see this- her fraud of a performance with obvious clarity.

"The sum of a bitch," I bellowed.

"I thought I lost you guys. Oh, I've missed you so much." She chattered and snorted, sniffling- fighting to catch her fake ass breath.

She passionately rubbed Core's back as I shook my head.

"Yadda, Yadda! Kill that shit, the Mechanism!"

Core peeped over his shoulder as he embraced her. "Now, Kontriss... that's no way to treat a lady." He beamed.

"What the fuck is she doing here?" I boomed as she sobbed and sniffed.

"I'm sorry you have to hear this," Core whispered as he caressed her. She folded her arms like she was cold or something.

Core glanced at me then back to the Mechanism, he mumbled, "I'll talk to him."

She nodded her head and whipped her fake ass tears away while Core continued his gentle brushing. "It's just that I'm so in love with him," she grumbled wiping her face.

"I -I know..." Core said. "Why do you treat her like that?" He asked while floating slowly over to me.

But then, that Jezebel of a woman started groping herself, grabbing her breast and shit, while Core's back was turned. I've never seen a woman stop crying so fast.

I pointed over to her and hollered, "Core! She's making faces."

"That's fine," he gently inserted.

"What?"

The mobile void didn't even turn around to acknowledge her deception.

Snatching away from them, I bit my bottom lip and gritted my teeth.

"You've got to forgive her, Kontriss. There was nothing she could do about the situation. Let it go man. Let it go."

Putting my hands on my hips, I stared into the rafters above cause I wasn't ready to forgive her. Not even a little.

"Chobe…"

I didn't respond.

"I've got something for you," she said.

"Nope. Not looking. I'm pissed."

"C'mon, Kontriss. Just turn around and look at her."

"Quit interesting, Core."

"We got them," she giggled as Core looked confused.

"No! The answer is no!" I shouted.

"But she didn't ask you a question, Kontriss."

"Core!!!" I yelled.

"Don't be like that," he responded.

With a huff, I finally turned carefully, no, reluctantly over to the Mechanism.

She was holding Vykra's black drive.

"Huh?" she laughed as she placed the drive on the console.

She had my attention as I turned around even slower.

She picked up a TPD from the console and immediately typed into it.

Just then, about several feet from the rear of the bridge, a bright window emerged.

She punched the TPD, and the window flipped over with a flash and a flicker. Then, four large crates dropped from the portal, slamming to the floor.

Crammmm!!!

My jaw dropped.

A soft smoke lifted from the speedy transference just when the window squandered away.

As I walked over, she quizzed with desperation, "You gon' fuck me in the ass, right?"

In my stride, I mushed her in the face. She toppled over the control desk, landing in the fiddliest pose.

Laying on top of the crates, I rolled onto my back and gazed up into the ceiling. Then, a vision of quotoms rained down from the sky. In total bliss did I smile, with a devilish grin pasted on my face.

"You guys ready for a test run?" Camper announced over the intercom as the Mechanism lolled in the same spot.

Thwak!!

She hurtled her TPD on the control desk. Then, she flopped with anger into the pilot seat and strapped herself in, shouting, "We ready!"

She started flipping on all the switches and the ship lit up.

"Good. I'm clearing the airway." Camper announced.

The Mechanism may have just redeemed herself, but I was still in dreamland.

"Unlocking counter brackets," she replied while flipping more switches. "Chobe, you may wanna watch me. Maybe not like that. But you know… Exactly like that."

Core floated over to my side as I lay on top of the crates. He prompted, "You've got one cycle to come up with the rest of those quotoms, Kontriss."

"I've got it!" I hollered, sitting up from the crates.

Core and the Mechanism stared over to me.

"I'll replicate it."

"Replicate what?' Core wondered.

Scooting to the edge of the crates, I hopped down to the floor. "This…" I gestured. "And I'll sell it. Just like I sold the others."

The room got so quiet; all I could hear was the engines purring.

The Mechanism smiled and spouted, "That could work."

249

"Damn right it'll work. This some good shit," I exclaimed while rubbing the crates.

Dashing over to the control desk, I snatched up the black drive and kissed it. Then, I tucked the drive into my cargo pocket while glancing over to the Mechanism.

She was in the pilot seat puckering her lips up to me.

"Quick! Show me how to fly this thing." I demanded.

She stopped in her urge of affection and smacked me on the arm.

"Hey!"

"Sit on my face- I meant, in the seat, so I can walk you through the controls," she insisted as I grabbed the co-pilot chair.

With a deep focus I put on the seat braces. Then, I realized we were staring at a blank wall. Suddenly, the wall converted into tiny pixels that vanished away, only to reveal a smashing scenery which developed right before our eyes.

It was a long stretch of grassland, a clear airspace along with a sunny morning of yellowish omni lights. My eyes squinted as the beams of beauty bounced about the ship's controls.

The Mechanism took me through every step of the flight process. We practiced landing the ship and taking off repeatedly until I got it down. And to be honest, the Mechanism was actually a pretty good teacher. She would still try to cop a feel whenever I'd flip a control switch. Then get mad at me for slapping her hand out the way.

Anyways, right?

I'm a fast learner.

Retaining the knowledge of Trailblazer, I learned how to access the Z plane mirrors for target shooting. And I learned how to access the 'Trailblazer' feature.

This feature would allow the ship to enter a hyperdrive then convert into a light drive. Trailblazer could stay in this state for an eternity and not lose any power, ultimately saving on fuel consumption. The phenomenon was confusing, but I didn't question it.

Not even a half cycle later, I mastered the dinged up red blaze. She was mine now. And I fell in love with her... Trailblazer.

The training session came to an end when Core finally left us. Alone. In the bridge. Together. The decision troubled me, but the horny woman held her composure.

While switching the ship to copilot, I sat back in the seat as the Mechanism stood behind me.

"Where to now, Chobe?"

"I need one last favor."

"Just one?" She asked.

"We need to reproduce this."

"Thought you'd never ask. I know a few people in Basma Folld. About six systems north of here. They'd gladly help with the process. With payment, of course."

"Okay. So that's for mass production. But I need your help with a small batch."

"Let's do it, Chobe."

"First, I need a Marsha."

"No, you don't," she chimed. "You need some good climate."

She typed into the control deck and smiled, "Here. I'll take you there."

Moments later, we landed on a planet named Malcron-V. This planet had been overlooked for several reasons, mainly because it had no technology, it was purely off the radar, completely vegetated and it remained the same temperature every day. All day. Forever.

We unloaded the crates and ventured off towards a small yard. We didn't waste any time. The Mechanism opened the crates and we pieced together this somewhat lengthy procedure. My first batch was small, but it was 99.97% pure cocaine. A total success in my eyes. And I knew exactly who to sell it to... Ju Felvin.

CHAPTER 26:

The Aerial Counselor

Instances later, we flew into Nappassiss. This brilliant
planet of peace and accord floated unsoiled and tranquil. That is,
as long as you didn't upset the king, who pretty much ran the
entire planet. But still, the king's son and I were good friends.

We landed near the outskirts of a vacant island called
Zaclmin. And that's when I saw Ju standing in front of his
hovercraft with a huge smile on his face.

"Wait here."

"You got it, Chobe."

Instantly, I unbuckled the safety straps and grabbed a kilo
of coke (sealed tight with Milafilme) from my stash.

Stepping from the loading door of Trailblazer, I jogged
over to Ju laughing.

Ju wasn't a Xarchanzian or an Inatech. He wasn't of slug
descent either. He was Nappassian. And Nappassians have
features similar to that of Inatechs, except their skin came in very
odd colors.

Ju's skin glowed with a coral blue. His eyes were yellow
and green. His hair was winter white. He had on a wealthy long
sleeve thick fuchsia shirt full of costly ornaments that were built
into the design. He had on a pair of black gloves, some black
pants, and some black high-top boots.

255

"Sup!"

"Man… I got something for you."

"Is it drugs? You know I love drugs!" He chuckled as I approached.

"Aw man…" I giggled as we hugged briefly. "Dis' nothing like you've ever had before."

"Jeez, you stink." He scowled as I held the brick up to him.

His eyes locked in as he spoke with salivation. "Man. That is crystal, super clean and clear right there. It looks like tiny, shiny angels."

"You wanna taste angels?"

Ju beckoned for the product.

"Hold up," I bellowed as I flicked out my pocket razor. "I'll give you a sample."

Slitting the Milafilme open, I scooped up a small portion with the razor.

He held out his hand and chuckled, "That's for you, right?"

"No. This shit potent, Ju." I blasted while sprinkling the coke into his hand.

He looked down at it and drooled, "What I do? Eat it?"

"You inhale it. If you want. Now don't-" I stammered, as Ju sniffed the whole thing. "…Sniff it all."

"Kontriss, I don't see anything," he thoughtlessly muttered. "What's it supposed to do? Cause it ain't doin' it."

"Ju?"

"Yea. You need to take that one back."

"You sniffed too much, man."

"That's garbage, mate!" He shouted. "You know I was in the middle of a-"

He froze and his face went blank in the silence. A real silence... His eyes shut.

"Ju?" I whispered.

He didn't say a word. He just rocked back and forth, batting his eyes uncontrollably. He stood speechless for a moment, rocking slower and slower.

"Ju!" I hollered.

Suddenly, his eyes popped open.

"Fuuuuccccckinggg AAaaaaa..." he grumbled.

He leaned over to me and braced himself on my shoulder. I struggled to keep him from falling to the ground. He stood up right and looked at me with those displaced eyes. "Dude, do you know? How many people...?" he babbled.

"Yes, Ju."

He started swaying and rocking again.

"That's why I brought it to you." I said, cupping the kilo into my arm.

257

"That's not enough." He proclaimed as he rocked and swayed, sniffing, and spitting.

"This all I got for now, Ju."

"How much?"

Now, mind you, Ju Felvin is filthy rich. His father is the king of this entire planet. Needless to say, Ju swims in currency. Literally.

"Name your price, Ju. You know we go way back."

"UUgggghh… six, maybe seven. Eight quotoms at best. And that's best right there."

And then, I knew it. Six quotoms was all I needed to pay for Trailblazer.

"Give me six, Ju." I nodded with confidence.

Instantly, Ju reached into his garment and pulled out a solid Gollith, eight score Quotom. He placed it in my hand and gestured for the cocaine. "Keep the change."

I eased the brick over to him and he snatched it out of my hand.

"I need more, Kontriss. You call me when you're ready to do business," he ordered as he turned away.

He didn't say anything else. He headed up to his hovercraft. Turned it on. And left…

I bolted back up to Trailblazer.

Upon my entrance to the main bridge, I found the Mechanism in the pilot seat with her legs propped up on the control desk. She swiveled around, crossing her legs, and slinging some kinda toy away.

"What! Happened?" she huffed with intensity.

With a smile, I pulled out the Gollith Quotom while she shuffled in her seat, biting her lip. She shut her eyes and huffed again, catching her breath and clenching her legs even tighter. She looked at me and rolled her eyes closed, shaking her head. She clenched the armrest as her body jerked and jolted. She opened her eyes and rolled them closed again.

I was still smiling, holding up the Quotom.

She expired to a calm and inhaled to a steady, slowly lifting her eyes... her legs remained firmly closed while they yet jolted and jittered.

"No... way..." she faintly huffed.

We hurried back to Camper Spain, and I paid him in full.

He was shocked at the Gollith and how fast we came up with the payment, seeing that my cycle had nearly just begun.

And just like that, I was in the massive reproduction stage. Man, I was supplying universes with ultra, high grade blow. A veteran in the juncture, and I didn't have to make it anymore. We paid the guys in Basma Folld to crank that shit out.

It was like, as soon as we made a sale another batch was already being sold. We're talking galactic portions here. But I still kept the crates as a backup.

Shit, I tried to buy Anarqkis from Camper. He wouldn't budge though. Instead, I got Trailblazer fixed up. We got the dents out and made some other major repairs.

In the end, I kept my word with Vykra. Leaving everything behind, I moved far from Layian lands. Then I put the Mechanism on call and her crazy ass was cool with me becoming a lone wolf.

With all that power and control, I got quiet. It turned me into something else...

They started calling me Maeyick- The Aerial Counselor.

Everybody knows me... I'm somewhat of a necessary evil.

Shit came even easier with that Triple Beam. We could spread the drug faster. Soon, we'll all be immune to the Pokidod's sting.

No slug should have to experience the same fate as Altizma, and my parents. Cause, for real, my desire to avenge my folks burns as bright as the nearest supernova. And I won't be satisfied until I take her and all her little minions out.

Maybe I'll just build a big ass weapon, or buy a big ass can of bug spray or something...

But anyways ... It's been what... Six cycles now?

No! Ten.

Ten cycles I've been Trailblazin' from planet to planet, galaxy to galaxy, supplying every being, foreign and domestic with high quality blow.

****

CHAPTER 27:

The Antidote: Radula

"Did you mate with her?" the Feuler asked as he laid on the bed in Trailblazer's den.

Kontriss, sat on a nearby couch with his feet propped up on a coffee table. He glared at the Feuler with an odd face and retorted, "What?"

"Did you make babies with the Mechanism?" The Feuler restated.

"You mean to tell me, outta all that shit I just said-"

"-You either did or you didn't, Chobe," the Feuler giggled.

"Oh, you think that shit funny huh?" Kontriss sassed. "You lucky I saved yo' ass!"

He stood abruptly from the couch and hurried to the bar behind him.

The Feuler continued to lay on his back, staring up to his cloak as it floated high above the bed.

BaDuth!

Kontriss snatched his TPD from the counter.

The Feuler sat up, holding his wounded arm in place. "What are you doing?"

"I'm calling Chest Pain to come finish yo' ass off!"

FL detached as FR fell gently back to the bed.

"You wouldn't dare!" Wailed FL.

Kontriss typed violently into his TPD. He then carried on in conversation, walking and laughing, with his hand on his hip.

263

"Who is that?" FL cried just as Kontriss stared into his halfhearted face.

Kontriss rolled his eyes, laughing hysterically into his TPD, he bellowed, "Oh yea!"

FL turned to FR and mumbled with a trembling voice, "Who is that?"

"Oh… He's here. Right now," Kontriss added just as he stopped walking. He propped himself up on the counter and stared at FL again.

FL glanced down to FR and shook him as much as he could. "My arm isn't well…," cried FL.

Kontriss smirked with a mumble, "I'm moving you right now." He tapped into his TPD with his eyes fixed on the half bodied Feuler.

Suddenly, a bright window opened next to Kontriss.

FL squinted his eyes while shaking FR. "Come! We've been compromised. Betrayed!" He shouted.

Right then, the Mechanism walked out of the window holding two duffle bags. The window of light closed quickly behind her.

FL stood up in the bed, scowling at the Mechanism with a twisted face. She ogled back at the butcher.

Fump!

His injured forearm fell off into the bed.

Studying the Feuler's handicap, Mechanism glanced over to Kontriss and noted, "I can't fix that."

"You can't?"

"Naa… I don't do ugly."

"Ha!" Kontriss chuckled while tossing the TPD on to the bar. "Now *that's* funny!" he pointed.

FL glanced about, appearing lost as ever. "Why? I don't understand. I do," replied FR as he finally sat up from the bed. "You were pranked." FR stood next to his counterpart and the many clasps fastened them back into one unit of terror.

"Whooooaaa…. That's cool." the Mechanism whispered.

"That shit ain't cool." Yelled Kontriss. "That shit nasty!"

The Feuler kneeled to pick up his severed forearm and his eyes locked in with the Mechanism's. It was as if some type of chemistry was forming.

The Mechanism walked over to the Feuler's bedside while Kontriss grew bitter with the slight of eyes.

She sat her bags on the bed and held out her hand. "I'm Mechanism. Pleasure to meet you, sirs."

While gripping his severed forearm, the Feuler held it over to the Mechanism. The dead hand closed its grip, and they shook hands, modestly. "The pleasure is all mine. Mine too."

"Hey!!!!" shouted Kontriss from afar.

The two stopped shaking hands. The Feuler turned to face Kontriss while Mechanism kept her eyes on the maniacal butcher.

"None of that."

"But I am hurt," the Feuler whined.

"I'on giva fuck!" Kontriss wailed from behind the bar. He noticed Mechanism gawking the Feuler up and down. "Why you keep looking at him like that?" He asked.

Mechanism reached out to touch the Feuler's leg.

Startled, the Feuler snatched over to her as she seductively caressed him.

"Egh! Hey! Eghhh!" Shouted Kontriss. "You take him somewhere and you get him fixed up. That's all."

Mechanism gestured for the Feuler to get down from the bed as if he was a little baby. "C'mon baby. Mommas got you." She mumbled as the Feuler stepped from the bed.

She lifted him up into her arms as if it were their wedding night. "Hm. Hm. Chobe number two," she mumbled as they continued to stare into each other's eyes.

Kontriss grew even more irritated with the clouded chemistry forming between the butcher and the Mechanism. He showed every sign of jealousy.

"Come on. Let me take you to my... *Infirmary*." She chuckled while hauling the Feuler over to the bar.

She stood the Feuler to his feet and he leaned carefully on the bar, placing his severed forearm across the countertop.

Fump!

"Wait! Let me grab my supplies," Mechanism said as she rushed back to the bed.

"She called us Chobe number two." The Feuler feebly whispered.

Kontriss looked straight ahead at Mechanism in a wild and zany manner.

The Feuler looked down to the counter and softly stated, "You know, we have two of everything…"

With a shifted face Kontriss snapped, "So!"

"Okay!" Shouted Mechanism as she approached the bar, dropping her medical bags to the floor. "We're going to my place."

She picked up the TPD and started typing. "I'll have you fixed up in minor measures." She declared while handing the TPD to Kontriss.

He snatched the device from her as she lifted her bags from the floor.

"Don't you do nuthin' else," demanded Kontriss.

"I can't promise you that."

"For I am hurt," the Feuler added sympathetically.

Kontriss wagged his finger at them and shouted, "Fuck outta here!!"

He violently punched the TPD, and a bright window of light opened right behind the bar.

The Feuler grabbed his forearm from the countertop and proceeded over to the portal. He stopped and softly gestured his head. In swooped his heavy cloak, covering the Feuler in that ghostly silence. "Would you be so kind to fetch my service belt behind you," the Feuler asked kindly. "It's actually mine."

"Oh!" Mechanism shouted.

She dropped one of her bags and turned to the base of the bar. She grabbed the Feuler's belt with the massive butcher knives sheathed in the rear holster. She hoisted the belt over her shoulder. Then she turned her back to Kontriss and purposely bent over to pick up her duffle bag.

"Thank you." Hissed the Feuler.

"Don't mention it," she confessed as she stood upright. "After you."

The Feuler looked down to the ground and cautiously entered the window. Mechanism followed behind him. Just before entering the portal, she stopped momentarily to wink her eye at Kontriss. Then, the window depleted. Kontriss's company vanished without a trace as he lifted his head in anger. He cholerically chunked the TPD on the counter.

Klumm!!

Meanwhile, several thousand light cycles into the Layo Galaxy, a group of Xarchanzians discovered hundreds of illegal drug trades. This Intergalactic Task Force (known as the ITF) eventually cracked the center of drug traffic and supply.

An exploration for pursuit developed. Yet, the ITF wouldn't dare send an entire fleet, just for the apprehension of one slug. Preferably, the Xaris sought to forward another. A being of the same family.

This species was of snail descent, found in the outlands of Akaramm. This specific genealogy of primitive snail is neither male nor female. The mollusk lacked the ability to figure and or deliberate a thought process besides that of its own self-preservation. The air head simply performed out of routine. It had no soul or no desire to feel.

The mollusk sat at an even six feet tall, while smoothly gliding on its under belly. Its eyes sat at the end of its antenna which sat on top of its head. The snail has over a thousand rows of razor-sharp teeth in its mouth. Its grayish skin is filled with yellow and blue spots running down its back. Then, protected by an impenetrable golden shell, the mollusk remained dormant and highly toxic. The slithering creature could produce an acidic solvent strong enough to melt through the center of a sun.

269

The snail was perfect, in the eyes of the Xaris. And not because of its appearance or its towering pH levels. But simply because the snail could naturally detect other mollusks, regardless of their lineage or Layian telepathy. These attributes made the Xarchanzian findings even more remarkable.

The Xaris studied this specific snail for over a decade of cycles.

At the dawn of day, the mollusk would visit a small marsh located near the purlieus of Akaramm. The apparent routine made this mollusk a prime candidate for further experimental testing.

The Xaris created a tranquilizing gas that was dispersed over the small marsh of Akaramm. And just as they predicted, at the crack of dawn, the large snail returned to the same marsh.

The gas acted swiftly. After several seconds of exposure, the snail fell into a deep sleep.

The ITF transported the massive snail back to Xarchanzian labs and by the time the snail came to, it had been completely revamped.

The now fully functioning cyborg had mechanical arms, legs, hands and feet, all constructed out of Razor Blach. The limbs fitted to assist the snail in standing. Walking, however, became something of a different matter, seeing that the snail didn't think.

A speedy solution was devised when the Xaris forged the snail's brain with a lightning-fast computer. The link could instantaneously interact with the hydraulic implants. The limbs were then remotely controlled by the service station sequestered by Xarchanzian terminal engines. The embedded computer became the brain for the species as it assisted the toxic monster in combat decisions.

The circumstantial division of duty gave the air head snail a host of weapons. Plasma lasers and pulse seeking missiles were but a few additions, as well as advanced strength and speed.

The snail's decorative shell was redefined into a motion sensor cannon. A systematic durable conduit was constructed in the shoulder of the golden shell. The cannon could now project the devastating stream of acidic sludge, reaching up to 1,000 yards of accurate transmission.

The archaic mollusk also inherited a massive carrying case called an Anehk. This large (pearl white with black polka dots) housing unit is strangely shaped like an egg. When summoned by the snail, it can materialize out of nowhere and inches away from its' host. Then, the Anehk can voluntarily generate projectile weapons. And because of the Xaris' unfathomable reach, the Anehks' assortment of arms, became just as endless.

The snail's threat grew in reticence when the scholarly Xaris activated their influence. Eventually, the monster was promoted into the ITF and prepensely codenamed, 'Radula'- For its many rows of teeth.

271

The monster's initial duty was simple.

Obtain, or fully discontinue the Tritokis Gastropoda Slug: Kontriss Quiaussuss.

CHAPTER 28:

Archipus
Part 5

San Bernardino, California
Regional District 43: Little League Baseball Complex

Fhum!

"Strike one!" The umpire yelled as the young catcher hurled the ball back to the pitchers' mound.

Paff!

The pitcher caught the ball, while the crowd roared with applause. A woman stood in the stands, screaming, "Strike him out, Blake!"

Blake grinned as he tugged on his baseball cap. He stared over the field and into the catcher's signals. Blake shook his head. He shook his head again while the batter repositioned his stance. Then, Blake nodded. He gathered into his windup position and stared quietly over home base. With his feet aiming to the third, Blake shifted his weight, and lifted his leg as his throwing arm leveled into its' sweet spot. Then came the pitch-

-ZzBlllooiiiissssssshhhhh!!!!

Blakes body scatter into a shower of gore that sprayed by the fences and into the stands.

Screams consumed the field, as a massive Clydesdale developed on the pitcher's mound. The monstrosity stood, soaked in bloody chunks of tissue that flipped and flopped slothfully down the steed's structure. Then, came a violent whicker…

CHAPTER 29:

The Carbon Event

Concurrently, trillions of light years away from Layian lands, the drug lord Kontriss sat on a couch, in the den of Trailblazer.

In front of the couch sat an old-fashioned coffee table. The table was clean, all but for the lines of coke evenly spaced across the surface. He'd been sniffing the drug for a moment before he grew just as spaced out as his unconquerable profession.

He slouched back into the couch and propped his foot up on the coffee table. Suddenly, tiny spots of mist, fluffed over the large circular bed. Kontriss stared absently as Core folded out of himself and into reality.

The moving portal landed gracefully in the center of the bed while buttoning up his coat. "We got a problem," he announced.

Kontriss stared with an absent look. He took his foot down and laid his head on the coffee table. His antennae reached out and violently sniffed two lines of cocaine.

The drug lord echoed with a sigh as he slouched back into the couch, closing his eyes.

Core put his hands in his pockets and floated down from the bed. He glided over to the opposite side of the coffee table and keeked down to Kontriss.

The drug lord rested soundly, listening to the hums of Trailblazer's engines.

"I'm just chilling, waiting on this Super Red connect. You hear that?" Kontriss whispered with a grin. "They, *'high-bernating'*..."

"Can I join you?"

Kontriss propped his foot back up on the tabletop and politely gestured, "Help yourself. I don't know how you would do it but-"

"-I have my ways." Core answered. "It'll take a whole planet of this stuff before I could feel anything."

"I've seen a whole planet."

"There's a couple of things I need to tell you."

The drug lord ran his hand through his antennae, taking his foot down from the coffee table. He leaned over and snorted another line.

"Geez man."

"You fucking up my high, Core!"

Instantly, a gust of wind rushed over the table, skittishly blowing the cocaine about the room.

Kontriss sniffed and smirked, wrapping his hands behind his head. Laying back into the couch, he chuckled, "I've got tons more."

"The Xaris have created a beast. A mindless monster designed for the assured destruction of criminals."

"Core!" yelled Kontriss. "I am a drug lord. Dddrrrruggg. Lllooorrrd! I'm in the midst of nowhere. I've got goons from one end of the Galaxy to the next. Hired killers, Core! They come after me- Wait! Before they could even find me, I'd know it."

"Kontriss?"

"I'm untouchable, Core."

"The monster is of the same family. It is of snail descent."

"Ha!" Kontriss chuckled while propping his foot back up on the coffee table. "A snail? …Really?"

"The beast is naturally designed to locate other mollusks. Plus, it was specifically programmed to capture or kill, Gastropoda: Tritokis. It knows your name, Kontriss."

"Yeah? How you know dis' shit?"

"Guitussami. The Xaris reach is forever. But not even the Xaris can locate every mollusk. This thing can." Core urged as he dropped his head.

"Tell 'em to come on!"

"May I suggest you lay low. Come with me. Avoid the catastrophe all together. The wave responds in unison. Not division."

"I ain't going nowhere" Kontriss shouted as his eyes stretched wide. "I ain't running no mo'. I've done that. Not again. Not again!"

"I don't like who you've become-"

"-So!"

"Tissamii was right about you-"

"-Who? The Wooden Man?"

"You are iron willed and just as rebellious and balky as..."

"-As what?" Kontriss hollered, jumping to his feet in a rage.

Core paused and glanced to the ground just as Kontriss slammed his hands on the table.

Whom!

"Say it!" He yelled with twitching eyes, glaring up to Core in anger.

"What if I was as stubborn as you? What if I refused to gate to your aid? What if I just let you drop?" Core quizzed.

Kontriss giggled and sniffed uncontrollably. He coughed as he stood upright, putting his hands on his hips. "You think I need you?"

"I suppose not," Core answered as he backed away from the table, looking helplessly to the floor. "Your reluctant character will cost you in the end." He inserted as he turned away.

"Gone fold yo' ass up into yo' self."

279

"Oh!"

"Aww… here we go!" Kontriss bleated just as Core whirled back around.

"Almost forgot. Have you heard of a tyrant by the name of Arola?"

"Nope!" Kontriss grumbled as he plopped back into the couch.

"What about a guy named, Arlo Crane?"

"Core… I'm sure there is nothing that you have to talk about that could possibly interest me."

"7-Dial, or Seven Arola-"

"-Wait. You said 7-Dial?"

"Yes."

"I overheard Vykra talking about a 7-Dial. I'm still not interested, though."

"Arola has implemented a project in secret. This project would be the reckoning of Wavemaker and the Xaris. Possibly the entire Layo Galaxy."

"So?"

"You are a part of Wavemaker. Are you not?"

"Yea… but that shit ain't got nothing to do with me."

"This project could bring about an end to your business." Core announced, placing his hands in his pockets.

"Cool breeze, I've got 700 galaxies under my belt. He couldn't stop this if he tried. Besides, I swore not to return to the Layo Galaxy anyways." Kontriss confirmed as he laid back on the couch.

"But here's the fragmentary…" Core noted. "7-Dial's plan has been tampered with; I surmise. How this became evident bedevils my perceptive science."

"Core!! I. Don't. Give a damn!"

"I know." He remarked. "But this is something I've never encountered."

Kontriss sighed heavily as he sat up, reaching into his boot. He pulled out another vile of cocaine.

"This bonanza of mysteries blundered through the keenest of minds. Some way or another, two of Arola's subjects possess the same documentation. Which means, that the files for this, Crane fellow were duplicated. I mean nearly everything; names, birth dates, ages, hair, eye color-everything. Except, for the actual DNA of the humanoid subject."

"Humanoid." Kontriss whispered as he sprinkled more coke on the table.

"It's too late for blood work. The experiment is done, and the files have been deleted. Permanently. Arola calls it the Carbon Event."

"Ugh huh…"

"The subjects came from the Zulliesa Sanctum. Or the Milky Way galaxy, with planet Earth as its essential fountain of souls. It's like something is missing. What I'm saying is, one of 7-Dial's experiments is a complete twist of galactic fates. A purposely driven wild card." Core lectured just as Kontriss laid his head on the table, inhaling the coke into his antennae.

He sat up with a deep sigh and sniffed, "You know, out of all of my renditions, Vykra's strand is always the best."

"As tiny as this hiccup could be, this may easily spiral out of control. Out of the Xaris control- even 7-Dial's," Core continued.

"In theory, to erase one's memory, the brain must be wiped the first time. In its entirety. If not, then the memories that were severed during the initial abduction could resurface, even after the experiment has completed. Snippets of the subject's past could toggle in and out of their reality, making the hybrid species unstable." Core hypothesized.

"Hybrid?"

"7-Dial is bonding ancient slugs with humans. It's his last-ditch effort to save your subsiding race. I think it's brilliant. But if any of the subjects were to become aware, then we're talking absolute inversion."

"Shit, man... I thought all the subjects died in the abduction. And how come they can't just wipe the brain again?"

"They can." Core answered. "Yet the results would be unyielding. The human cerebrum may become immediately vexed in reconstitution. The mother slug could subdue the host but after a while, free will and inversion would still be the outcome. For the experiment to run successfully, the brain must be wiped in its entirety. The first time."

Kontriss paused, with an intriguing look washing over his demeanor.

"The subject's identity is crucial. Someone knew this, and they purposely altered the wiping procedure. Whoever corrupted 7-Dial's objectives, must be irresistibly stupid. Or incredibly smart."

Kontriss stared up to the mobile void and quizzed with sincerity, "Holy shit… Core?"

"What?" He asked with excitement.

Kontriss sat up from the couch and pointed sternly. "Fuck 7-Dial. Fuck the Xaris. And fuck you!"

"What is this… Fuck?"

Kontriss hesitated. "…Go fuck yourself."

"You will falter at the cost of your hard-headed attitude."

"Yeah. Yeah. Yeah."

"I must be going now," uttered Core as Kontriss shooed him off.

"Bye, hoe!" He boomed as he slouched back in the couch, propping his foot up on the coffee table.

"You have been warned, Kontriss. The Xaris monster lives for your expiration." Core assured as the drug lord flipped him off. While unbuttoning his trench coat, the void whispered with worry, "And just *who is* this… Arlo Crane?"

CHAPTER 30:

Xon vs Azix

"Azix. Xon! Choose a wall." The colonel shouted as I traveled over to the same wall that REB chose. Then I noticed Azix following me. She stared to the floor as she walked with precision.

Turning my back to the wall as I approached, Azix stood directly beside me, still staring at the floor. She placed her hands behind her back in a precise manner.

There was no explanation for this notion. But as far as I could tell, Azix had undoubtedly selected the same wall.

"Interesting," the colonel whispered. "I've never seen this before. I'm currently shuffling this option around... You both have the same wall. That means either of you can simply tap the wall and the drill will- Here!" He shouted. "Let's change the rules..."

"The first to take down your opponent gains the option to tap the wall and set the match. The wall must be touched by hand. Your right hand.

You cannot touch the wall with your back turned. The motion will be denied. You must be facing the wall for your tap to count." He explained.

"Understood!!" He roared.

We said nothing, concomitantly acknowledging his acclimation to the rules.

"Very well," he mumbled as he floated over to the opposite wall.

"On. *Call...*" he whispered with a delay.

The colonel searched behind him with a discarnate face. He paused for a moment, like he heard something, or someone. He glanced away from the wall and then in the opposite direction. He stared over to Rayefill and REB with a stern face of sagacity. He peeped behind him again as his sense of urgency grew.

It seemed like, whatever it was that was coming, must've sped up.

The colonel rolled his eyes to the ceiling, sighing with annoyed gall.

Suddenly, a man folded into reality, and from within himself did he enter the Blackline.

He flopped right behind Guitussami wearing a long brown trench coat, with matching gloves and a big brim hat. His face was as dark and empty as the undefined planes of this room.

His eyes were white, and I could tell he wasn't made of common molecules. Somehow, a vast chunk of outer space found a way to contain itself, within this man...

"WWhhhhaaaatttttttt...." Colonel G grumbled while glaring into the ceiling.

287

The being glanced over to Rayefill and REB, then over to Azix. But then he froze. And there he floated, staring deep into her eyes.

"Speak Core!" Colonel G shouted, rattling him out of his daze.

"I… I."

"Stop stuttering."

"They…" Core chuckled. "Inexplicable. He did it."

"You speak the obvious. *Now?*" Guitussami blurted as he glanced over to Core.

"I have to tell you something."

"The Carbon Event," Colonel G grumbled. "I already know."

Core floated in silence.

"Look Core! They chose the same wall. I'm sure there's an explanation for this. You wanna watch?"

"Do you know how long you've been down here?" Core jeered.

"I was told to take an eternity if needed," snapped Guitussami.

Core lowered his head.

"Would! You! Like to! Watch!!" Guitussami yelled.

"I… I."

"Stop!! Stuttering!!"

"I'd like to watch!"

Guitussami turned to us and with a thundering voice he shouted, "Ljaka!!"

And suddenly... Azix turned on.

Her sockeroo of transmuted blitzkrieg came as inundated solar flares. It felt as if explosions were erupting all over me. When, in actuality, it was her striking me that hard and that fast. The normal being would've disintegrated from her first attack, but my overly condensed body classified every blow, leveling the severity. But Azix had been watching us in secret, learning our moves. While she pretended to be listless and detached, she retained every smidgen of information. Azix had become a silent but deadly, killing machine.

She hit me over a hundred times, as I was too bulky to dodge her liquid form. She moved flawlessly, so elegantly through me. Before I knew it- she had wrapped, pulled and tucked me into a knot.

Standing freely on one leg, she popped up behind me, yanking my foot from the floor.

Poff!

I hit the ground, unraveling myself, as she whirled around to tap the black boundary.

Suddenly, something... an unexplainable urge lifted the ground.

Then, Azix's body snatched away. A vicious, satanic wind crushed her deep into the far wall.

Kavvoooommm!!

Guitussami and Core gawked to each other as I walked over to claim my victory.

Right then, I thought I was touching the wall. But, to my consternation, I was grabbing Azix's face.

Snatching her out the way, my grip slipped through her head.

She responded with a series of combos, striking faster with every blow. Her form was so smooth, she could entice you into death with her damaging style of etiquette. Her unorthodox violence would logically confuse a galaxy. Her attacks were too precise- too controlled, I could only counter a few.

She punched me in the face while wrapping her forearm about my neck.

Immediately, I reached for her blood choking grip.

She hooked her other arm over my shoulder. Then she hopped to the outside of my leg.

She torqued her hips so fast that I flipped clean into the air. My feet flew over my head as I crushed to the ground.

Croom!

The room shook as she landed on top of me, shoving her knees into my chest.

As soon as I tried to lift her off, the bones in her legs converted into a goo.

Her pressure emulated an asteroid when she wrapped her legs over my shoulders. She then released her choke only to apply another one.

This one was twice as bad as she utilized both of her arms. They wrapped around my neck, flopping over each other like damp towels.

Her arms must've made at least three revolutions before the space between my body and hers constricted to zero.

She tucked her head into the loft of my shoulder, and she squeezed away.

"She's killing him!!!" Core screamed.

"SSSssshhhhhhh...." Colonel G whispered. "I asked if you wanted to watch. Not comment."

Azix's grip was deep. Really deep... While peering feebly over to the wall behind me, that incredible urge came again.

A fierce rumble shook the Blackline, and a huge chunk of the wall tore away from the partition.

Azix looked up as the structure torpedoed into her face.

Brak!

Zapping her clean across the room, the boulder decimated into the far wall.

Kafoom!

Finally, freed of her deadly grip, I laid in a daze. But the deadly goddess was already back to her feet.

Rolling over, I stood slowly. My legs shook like flimsy noodles as I walked over to the enclosure. Then, a jetting wind came from behind.

But I was so close to my victory, and I could feel myself touching the barrier.

Suddenly, Azix snatched me away and stood boldly between me and the wall.

There was something, troubling about her...

The sweet, seductive snake of execution could have easily tapped the wall. Even now, all she had to do was turn around and touch the partition, and the match would be set.

But she had no intention...

This fight had just begun.

I rushed her, punching, and kicking to take off her head! But she bobbed and weaved with an exquisite flare so smooth that it seemed as if she wasn't moving.

She ducked and countered my combination, punching me square in the face. But I fought on, unphased.

She countered again with precision, returning several punches to my head and to my mid-section.

That's when I increased my speed, but her skeletal structure turned off when I swung at her.

She bent over backwards, dodging my attack. Her hands caressed the floor and a fumy secretion jetted from her palms, spinning her behind me.

She whacked me in the spine with a front kick, bending me backwards. She stepped over my midsection and with her confining thighs, she locked me in place. She crossed her thighs to secure her position and her overruling legs, clinched me tighter by the second.

Her torso twisted all the way around to face me.

She struck me in the head repeatedly, over and over with no mercy. Every hammer fist, punch and elbow pummeled me closer to the ground.

Contemplating a reduction in her speed would rest in a fool's paradise. For neither of us understood fatigue.

Lifting my feet from under me, we careened to the ground.

Boom!

She landed on top of me, punching me into oblivion.

Pinning my thighs over her shoulders, I shoved her back. But she slipped through my legs with a barbarous punch.

Kloom!

"Oohwww!" Core shouted as her fist shattered the floor, I darted my head away, shifting over to my side.

She reinforced her clinch around my waist; just when I stood to my feet.

She struck me continuously in the head. As I charged for the partition, I aimed to plow through the wall. But she flipped from my waist, grazed her hands against the floor, and her excretions bolted her though my legs. Her ankles latched around my neck as she rammed my head into the wall.

Klackpt!

I placed my hand on the barrier, snatching my head from the devastation.

"Set!!!" Guitussami shouted.

As I peeped over my shoulder, Azix glared into my eyes. While glimpsing back to my right hand caressing the wall, Azix dropped her head. The deadly woman marched across the room. She placed her arms behind her back and stood next to Rayefill in a calm and professional manner. Azix simply desired to make a statement.

Reluctantly, I dropped my hand and journeyed back to my original position, next to REB.

"It's a wonder he's not dead." Core mumbled.

Colonel G snatched over to Core and uttered, "I assure you. This is merely training."

"I don't know, man…"

Guitussami gawked over to Core. Then he floated over to the mobile void, slowly. It took about an hour.

"Is there something else I can do for you, Core?"

The mobile void threw his hands up. "Hey man, I just came to tell you something that you already knew."

"Okay???" Colonel G retorted.

"I guess I'll be leaving."

"That would be nice." The colonel spoke as Core unbuttoned his coat. "We will proceed as planned," the colonel affirmed as he turned to face us.

"Of course," Core replied as he folded up into himself, clearing away from our reality.

Subsequently, we trained and trained over the course of several thousand cycles. Every type of militant, gladiatorial exercise that could have occurred, occurred within this extended class of sharpening. Our training came to an odd end when Colonel G began his last lecture.

"Before you exit the Blackline, and before I give you my seal. I will have you to know…" he paused, dropping his head in dismay. "You are the team of ages. You were designed for the comparable leveling. Every universe will know of you as you will rush to their aid if needed. What one governing body can't do, you will." He said as he began to float away.

"Now," he mumbled while looking to the ground. "There's a chance that I wasn't completely honest with you…" he addressed while looking over the room.

295

And for the first time, I saw Guitussami's eyes twinkle. An inadequate amount of fluid dropped from his face. The substance immediately commuted to a dust. What was happening?

He lifted his head and gawked at us with an unreal face. "There is a war, a secret war- brewing here. This war has been in existence since the dawn of cycles. A group of highly advanced individuals (the gods of technology) seek to rob the universe of all that we hold dear. And Project Rapture will ensure this. But you... the anchor, you stand for something greater." He lectured.

"The Xaris seeks to reduce your race into a powder of genocidal macabre. My men, and women... you are the only thing standing between your species continuation. They will do any and everything to turn you against each other. I've seen it happen. Do not let this occur. You are to stick together. No matter what.

You are married to the anchor. We initially stand to protect and project the pre-existing and yet to form planetary alignments, even down to the smallest organism. This is why the Xaris hate you.

There are spies everywhere and this room is the safest place to deliver the truth." He included. "With that being said, you all must attend graduation. In the Fact Matter Room and directly in front of 7-Dial. Do not look Arola in the eyes. You could die from the mental connection alone. After graduation, you will become known to the public and possibly the Xaris. You have been granted a ship. This vessel is like none other. You are to board this ship. Thereafter, you are to leave this ratchet universe and never return. The Xaris will seek you out. You're better off away from this. Besides, you need to mature in your gifts before taking them on. Hear my words." The colonel addressed.

"You are to destroy evil of any kind, and at any cost. You are the last of a dying race and the only way for you to exist would be to rebel. Whatever you do… Don't let the Xaris have you." Guitussami demanded while backing up to the reflective barrier.

"The moment has come… I'll meet you at the Blackline," he whispered, just before he vanished.

Right then, the large room began to scale down.

We stood straight like soldiers as the barriers squeezed in, converting into a pliable solid. Considering our view at hand, this spasmodic moment could have been a true test of character. But we knew not of doubt, abhorrence, fear or phobias. Without qualm, we submerged into the drowning thick liquid.

The tangibly dark entity of celestial matter took us…

CHAPTER 31:

Demagogue

We zapped up from the Blackline, standing with an attentive gaze of sedulousness. The dark fluid bled down our bodies and into the black strip below.

We were standing in the same exact spot as before, in front of the same wall, in the same massive corridor as if no time had passed at all.

Then, I remembered the beast at the end. That monster, with that worrisome smile...

Peeking down the hall to see if the creature was still there but out of my peripheral, I saw nothing. The setting had become freakishly desolate.

"Anchor. Observe."

We turned to face the opposite direction and there floated Colonel G. His head was lowered when he spoke to us, but strangely, his mouth didn't move.

"Remember your why. Your reasoning for existence. Follow me..." he commanded.

He turned and floated down the massive corridor.

REB, Azix and Rayefill followed behind him.

Just as I lifted my foot from the Blackline, something came...

It was a ghostly feeling. An aggressive immersion of my already complex makeup stopped me still in my stride. Sinking further into perturbation, I peeked over my shoulder, and there he was… The elephantine monster and its bewildering smile.

Carefully, I moved my foot from the Blackline while turning to face the savage hellion.

The barbaric freak of nature sat like a dog, peering deep into my psyche.

From the ground up, I gaped at the creature's arms. They were just as monstrous as the rest of his portrayal.

His hands and fingers were made like paws with very sharp talons withdrawing from the ends. The talons curved with an unrealistic shine, while those veiny arms leapt with extraordinary muscles.

Using the Blackline as a separator, I had backed away from the creature. But somehow, I possessed a desire to fully perceive this leviathan's abnormalities. Then, something snatched my eyes up to the creature's face.

We made eye contact again… then I was immediately hypnotized. The seduction became real, and I couldn't turn away from his inducement. Gently, I crossed over the Blackline, while attracted to this titanic magnet.

The entire while, the monster's grin never ceased. It never weakened. It only intensified as I neared.

Then, I felt another urge, a burning desire to pet this large dog of a monster. Thousands of angels and demons sung together in one emotional choir. The closer I came to the monster, the more my restraint slowed to a creep. The urge was too grand.

An unspeakable rumble shook the hall. A crack split through the Blackline and up the wall behind the monster.

"Don't touch him!!" Colonel G shouted, interrupting my invasive distraction.

My horrific allure ended. Just as I lowered my hand, I glared over to Guitussami. He floated next to the monster.

"This is no pet. Not of yours anyway." He added as I glanced over to the large creature. He lifted his hind leg to scratch his ear. The beast shook his head vibrantly while lowering his leg. His long and pointy hairs thwacked and shuffled lively about before settling.

The creature smiled on without blinking.

"Come Xon. The anchor awaits." The colonel ordered.

Right then, I turned away from the beast to see my teammates patiently awaiting.

"That's going to take forever to fix…" Guitussami grumbled while looking down to the Blackline. He turned away from the terrible rift and followed close behind me.

But something warred within me, on the inside as I wanted to look back. Bad. Really bad…

Be that as it may, I carried on. Away from the Blackline. Away from that haunting smile…

"Zacuther is a very special being. You are only seeing him because he is 7-Dial's protector and aid. Little else is known of Lord Labrys." Colonel G revealed as we approached the rest of the team.

"He seems to be quite fond of you. Xon…" Guitussami nodded as we headed into the great hall. "Or maybe he hates your red compressor shirt," the Colonel continued. "The last being to touch Zacuther cracked! The man went psychotic. Looney. Moonstruck nutty! Ragging on and on about Nazi Germany. I don't know… I'd have to research the matter." Colonel G revealed as we neared the Fact Matter Room.

"You stay away from him." He ordered. "That goes for all of you," he noted. "Zacuther is not a toy. Do not be deceived by that enchanting grin."

We came to a stop just when we approached another bisecting hall.

"Graduation is just down this hall." The colonel announced with a stern face, gesturing his head towards the corridor.

We turned down the hall. But I peeked out of the corner of my eye, back towards the Blackline. And there he was- that monster, sitting attentively- still as a dog. He hadn't moved a bit and his smile hadn't faded. It shined bright as a shimmering sun.

Zacuther watched vigilantly from afar, as we transitioned into the bisecting hall. Even then, I could feel him pulling… mentally. But I dared not entertain the colossal phoenix of a demon and his evil presence.

The course to graduation was extensive. To ease the journey, Colonel G discussed his plan of rebellion with us, several times, telepathically. This plan was easily understood by us all. But what I couldn't understand, was how the screams of one man traveled so far. And the closer we got to the Fact Matter Room the louder the yells became. The screams were occasionally followed by a vocal rant. It sounded like an odd language-quite similar to German.

We stood just in front of the Fact Matter Room's massive doors. Colonel G floated in front of us as the screams continued. He lowered his head and whispered, "That's him…"

Guitussami peeped over his shoulder, and wailed, "The idea is to remain focused. Remember! Don't look Arola in the eyes!" He shouted over the boisterous ranting, "The mistake will cost you dearly!"

Just then, the massive doors of the Fact Matter Room creeped open.

We stepped into the room only to be overwhelmed by the spectacular science. There were at least a million highly skilled scientists with computers, floating monitors, and diagrams everywhere. The technology and the cosmic anomalies combined into a uniformed soup of life bringing masterminds.

The massive doors closed behind us.

Colonel G floated over to a nearby monitor. He spoke into the transparent display and a flash of flickering rays scanned over us.

"Guitussami. Proceed." A voice ordered.

Colonel G nodded his head forward and we progressed to the front of the crowd.

Our unmovable presence took the room by surprise.

The unease of soulful frights steamed from the boffins as their heads turned with dread.

"Stop behind the red," a scientist murmured.

We stopped behind the line and right in front of us was the screaming German, squabbling over the floor. He was shirtless and barefoot, wearing only a pair of brown dingy cargo shorts and a chunky utility belt around his waist. His skin was gray with a tint of dark green and white blotches covering his shoulders. He was extremely muscular, medium built and overly dense. But the ranting German was strongly disfigured. An odd bulge curved down his spine in sections, and with a thread sticking from each segment. While accompanied by two aliens, that struggled to keep him at bay, he wrangled for liberation.

Then, a godlike voice spoke. "Dr. Phlaxlur. Relate your level."

Something watched me as I peeped across the room with my head down. Then, a messy doctor stepped abruptly from the crowd, walking quickly to the front of the room. He stopped in front of the certifiable German.

"*Wer nennt sich Gott?!!*" he hollered in German, while tugging fiercely over the ground.

"Lord Arola. Our findings stipulate major concerns and a problematic juncture in this subject's future." Dr. Phlaxlur urged. The doctor shuffled through his documents while the crazed German continued to rant and rave.

"*Ich bin Gott! Ich bin Gott!*" He whaled. "*Mütterchen Russland fällt! Ich werde auf die sie Scheiße! Nachdem ich verdauen ihre innereien fertig. Sie Plankton. Ich bin Gott! Heben Sie ihre Hand so class ich ihren arm aus Zupfen Kann! Alle Heil den Aufstieg von Nazi- Deutschland!*"

"My lord." Dr. Phlaxlur interrupted. "The subject is not well. At all... He is ill prepared for your purpose of plan."

"Ha!!" laughed the German. "*Dann befreie mich... Ich werde dir zeigen!*" He inserted just before he started screaming all over again.

"Lord Arola!!" Phlaxlur shouted, attempting to speak over the German.

"Aluevis." Arola spoke subtly.

305

The German failed to respond. He only raged on, screaming, and shouting obscenities to the top of his lungs.

"Release him," ordered 7-Dial.

Just then, the heavy-handed aliens freed the German. Surprisingly, the lunatic settled to a calm.

"Speak freely, Craiser." Arola instructed as I looked up to the kneeling German.

The deranged man faced 7-Dial, then he glanced over himself. It seemed as if he had just encountered a psychological introduction. He laughed hysterically while staring into his hands.

"*Ich spure alles. Was hast du mit mir gemacht?*" Asked the German.

"My Lord. I motion to have this subject re-wiped. This evaluated study has been nothing short of a complete and total fiasco. A snafu waste of intellect." Dr. Phlaxlur interjected, aggressively tucking his clipboard under his arm.

"I can speak whatever language I choose. Because I understand. Who is *your* God?" The German asked in Layian.

Phlaxlur bolted over to him, and the crowd responded with murmurs.

Just then, the German stood to his feet in obvious anger.

Phlaxlur bellowed quickly, "Lord Arola. The subject has been contaminated. The entire labor crew brands this theme as defective."

"Defective?!" Craiser boomed. The demented German lifted his hand to Phlaxlur.

A thick pole shot from his palm, striking through Phlaxlur's forehead.

Clunck!

The crunch shook my body.

The gore wiped away as the silver staff retracted from Phlaxlur's forehead and back into the German's palm.

The hole in Phlaxlur's head was so tidy, you could peer clean through it as he dropped to the floor.

A fearful distemper swept the room as Arola's men jumped to apprehend the German.

"Stand down!" Arola shouted.

The men held still, as Arola's orders were not to be mistaken.

The German stood motionless with his hands in front of him. While I, in other minds, fought hard to avoid this, this inward debate. My crave to look in Arola eyes became stupendous, and I just couldn't turn away. Something begged and pleaded for my eye's acquaintance.

Just then Guitussami whispered, "This means you, Azix…"

His voice plucked me from my indictment as I glimpsed over to see the deadly woman advancing forward. She stopped at once, falling sadly back into the lineup.

"I have seen it. I've seen it all. Every fragment. Every equation and formula. The skies have opened to me and my mental capacity." Craiser yelled from afar as he paced the floor, contributing his sinister spiel.

"I am the result of your so-called... miscalculation. The perfect mistake in error. The matchless, Aryan- superlative soldier. I am the head of all races and full of your advanced science. [Lithuanian] *Siekiate sutaupyti mirstancios rases.* [Swedish] *Ar det racen ariska?* [Afrikaans] *Nee?* [Estonian] *Muidugi mitte ...*
[Czech] *Zaslouží si být zničen.* [Maori] *Te horoi i tenei whenua...*
[Vietnamese] *tạp chất ...* [Swahili] *Ni jukumu-* that I will deploy myself." Rambled the psychotic German.

The mad man walked freely about the Fact Matter Room. His mental expansion leapt to an unfound level as he spoke over seven different languages. Craiser accommodated this knowledge so fast that within a matter of moments, he fully comprehended Layian Telepathy. And I could tell...

The noteworthy German tossed around his idea of Nazi superiority, taunting the scientist and doctors as he continued his monologue.

"I…" he stuttered while wandering by a monitor.

He turned to face the image, perceiving the truth in his appearance. Craiser walked over to the doctor's desk and violently snatched the monitor from the wall.

Skassshh!!!

"I…" he grumbled again, touching his face in a distasteful manner.

Craiser walked back to the front of the room, looking down into this monitor. He held the reflective screen so tight that his hands shook. The mad German rocked back and forth, swaying into a woozy daze.

"Let him see." Arola commanded.

The deranged German fell to his knees, dropping the monitor in between his legs. Tears plopped into his reflection as he glared into the screen, rocking back and forth, screaming to the top of his lungs. "*Ich bin ruinieit,*"

Craiser jumped to his feet, chunking the monitor.

The medic dodged out of the way as the monitor crashed into his station.

Blazsh!

"*Meine haut!* … Who is responsible for this harebrained mold of departing knack?" wailed Craiser. "Huh?! Speak!" he shouted. "You fucking coward!!"

"I am responsible." Arola politely announced.

309

Craiser looked over the room briefly. And just as he looked on to 7-Dial, so did I... We both gathered our perception.

The Tyrant's feet were human and extremely masculine. His legs covered my essence with untampered power. His skin was brown and without blemish. Suddenly, before my eyes could climb any higher, something apprehended my rationale. Over to the side of the godly tyrant. There he was again... that monstrous smile.

The beast of unmatched riddles sat like an obedient dog and only a few feet away from the side of Arola. It was him; this overpowering gawp of a beast had been beckoning for my attention the whole time.

"I'll run your ass smooth over Arola! SSssmmmmmoooth!" Craiser shouted as I fell into Zacuther's mesmerizing gaze.

"You should fire yourself. Your efforts are subordinately inspired. I hate you, **Arola**! You are no God. You're not even a tyrant. You don't deserve half of the respect that you think is owed. Look at me, 7-Dial! I'd invite death to your bedside, but I'd be too busy taking its place- Kiss! My! Ass!" Craiser yelled out of the blue. He unbuckled his belt and unzipped his pants.

The crazed German mooned Arola.

The room gasped with a holler. But the whole time, I was locked into the attractive glare from the monstrous hound. And at that eldritch instant, I saw a specter...

It was a kid.

"Xon!" A voice shouted as small child peeked from the rear of Arola. The child darted up the side of Arola's throne. My eyes followed helplessly as they were ruled and governed by another…

The child settled amongst the thick mass of mane that seemed to extend forever on top of Arola's head. The dismal kid frolicked about the vast span of hairy space, just before tumbling down to Arola's forehead. Then, the kid vanished. And that's when it happened, I glared right into the tyrant's eyes and I was pulled into a portal, a void…

Interdimensional strands of DNA, formulas, particles, and molecules reducing to their simplest forms, while converging all at once. An indescribable surge of knowledge, way worse than that of the anchor, came rushing into my mind, into my understanding. But then, a thousand firecrackers went off.

"Xon!" The colonel shouted.

Turning my head away from the cerebral attachment, I logged back into reality. Craiser had stared into Arola's eyes for so long that an informational overload exploded in his face.

This data transfer was so vast that it shoved his brain into several chain reactions. His head cracked back and forth. Then, Craiser's face erupted. The mishap repeated over a hundred times, deforming the ranting German even more. Craiser fell lifelessly to the floor, with his pants hanging on by a thread.

A colorful smoke lifted from the German's face as I ogled with a voided mindset. It was baffling how I ventured away from the anchor's lineup, only to stand beside this occurrence.

"So sets this section of rectitude. Craiser. You and that blasted *staff* of yours just killed one of the greatest minds to ever walk the lower quadrant.

You have however, eased the opprobrium of graduation. You see, Phlaxlur had been plotting against my goals for over a thousand cycles. His death comes as no surprise. For that, I will spare you.

But then… you undermined my conquest, the men and women of the Fact Matter Room, Zacuther, Guitussami and my precious anchor. For that, you will live in a constant state of excruciating pain. The deformities in your face will forever torture you. Your brain will expand and contract so fast that light speeds will never measure your attempts to comprehend the immense amount of knowledge, that you- *just recently*, downloaded into your subconscious.

I am very disappointed in you, Aluevis. I give you gifts. The ability to exist in Layain immortality, modus operandi, and you…" The imperative tyrant sighed. "And you scared Zacuther," Arola grumbled. "Look at his face."

I glanced up to that demonic smile of his, and it burned just the same. The monster's face hadn't changed at all.

"Craiser, I can't allow you to exploit even a fraction more of this space. You have denounced your own creator. Why, Craiser?" Arola asked with a trembling voice. But Craiser hadn't spoke, since he was leveled to the floor.

The smokey fumes dwindled to a colorful steam as I glanced down to the German. His facial cheeks had been pushed back beyond the width of his head. And the ends of his facial deformity resembled that of jagged fish scales with sharp prongs protruding from the ends...

"Don't bother responding. Zacuther can no longer stomach your obstreperous spirit. Damn demagogue!" Arola ordered. "Take this... Myrmidon to Atomics."

The same heavy-handed aliens approached the mad German and lifted him up by the arms.

"Let him drop," Arola added.

The aliens nodded in agreement. Then, they hauled Aluevis off with his feet dragging the floor and with his pants collecting at the ankles.

"Lord Arola? What of Phlaxlur's body?" Asked a nearby doctor.

"Leave it," Arola answered with his dangerous eyes staring at me. "Guitussami, bring the anchor forward." He demanded.

Then, I felt Zacuther, that hell in a dog, staring as well.

"Seems like one of you are already up here," Arola stated.

313

The massive doors of the Fact Matter Room opened as the aliens hauled Aluevis out. "And fix his pants!" Arola hollered.

With my head lowered, I glanced over to see REB approaching my side. Then to my other side came Rayefill and next to him stood Azix.

The large doors slammed shut, when Guitussami appeared in front of us.

"Lord Arola. I'd lik-"

"-Hey!!!" 7-Dial interrupted. "You!!"

Lifting my head, I saw Guitussami standing in front of me.

"Keep your **head** down." He hissed.

My posture improved as I stood sturdy, with my chest forward and my head down.

"Lord Arola. Allow me to introduce your anchor," Colonel G redirected.

"Guitussami," Arola countered.

"Yes, my lord?"

"Why was this man up here so fast? Is he, *defective?*"

Colonel G froze as well as the rest of the Fact Matter Room. Another cold discomforting silence dashed in as Guitussami struggled with the questionnaire.

"Hey!" Shouted Arola, sitting up in his throne. "You defective?"

"No, my liege. Xon is a warrior like none other. He was only preparing to rid you of the German's insolence." Guitussami responded.

"Oh…" Arola mumbled while sitting back to a calm.

Guitussami was still staring at me. But then he finally turned to face Arola.

I caught a glimpse of Zacuther making eye contact with 7-Dial. The demonic dog freak rolled his eyes away from Arola and back on to me. That damnable smile came ironically in tone as I snatched my eyes to the floor.

Then, the tyrant coughed. This was indeed strange. The god of creation does not fall to the need of medication nor is he ever numbered among the sick.

"To my left is the head of the anchor. REB. A.K.A. Big Bang. The successful experiment has over several thousand rare molecules (including the god particle) infused into his palms. He can manufacture prodigious, unprecedented chemical reactions with but a simple swipe of friction. I believe he may have access to another spiritual realm. An occultist… dark art of necromancy. During our preparation stages, REB, impressively claimed ownership over the Blackline." Guitussami announced as he floated in front of me.

"Nice," Arola whispered.

315

"I believe you already met your regulator, Xon. Your strong arm. This subject seems to be several steps ahead of his counterparts. His grasp of Layian Telepathy has excelled beyond the norm. I have yet to witness the effects of the implanted Xano Chip. Though, I am sure that the device is working fine." Colonel G explained. "Xon will have to encounter a true exertion of strength before the Xano activates." Guitussami included.

Colonel G floated by with his introduction as I gazed at the floor. "Infiltrate and Retrieve. The Tierun duet. First, we have Rayefill. He has an undefined speed index, making him the most efficient speed machine in all existence. The subjects' momentum increases over an extended period of time. The Tierun fuse multiplies his tempo in eight accelerations per movement. With proper muscle memory, he could easily exist simultaneously- in two different spaces. Then, we have Azix…" Guitussami paused with a grin. "It's safe to say that you've outdone yourself with this one my Liege…"

"Really?"

"At first, I assumed she may have been inoperative. But I think she works, *too* well." He chuckled.

"Uh huh," mumbled Arola.

"The Flavius respond perfectly with her chemical and molecular makeup. I consider her to be extremely dangerous." Colonel G added with pride.

"Really?" Arola probed. "Show me…"

"Of course, my Lord. What will you have of her?"

"Ciomaka!" Yelled Arola.

"Yes, sir!" Shouted a nearby doctor who stood quickly to his feet.

"Come forward please…"

The doctor immediately dropped what he was doing and sprinted to the front of the Fact Matter Room. He stood in front of 7-Dial, bowing his head in allegiance.

"Stand up straight!" Wailed Arola.

The doctor stood to attention as 7-Dial spoke on. "Ciomaka?"

"Yes, my lord."

"Would you mind letting Azix kill you?"

"Huh?!" The doctor retorted with a puzzled face.

"Do your thing." Guitussami gestured over to Azix, who had already stepped out of the lineup.

Just as the doctor turned to us, Azix kicked over his shoulder, wrapping her leg around his neck. Then she stepped up on to the doctor's hip.

The doctor fell to his knees, gasping for air, just as Azix folded over to his back.

Azix grabbed the doctor's arm, broke it, and then punched the doctor's arm into his own back.

PIFff!!!!

"Aaaaagggggghhhh!!!!!!" He screamed.

The entire room shouted with disturbing yelps as Azix thrust her head into that same gap.

The doctor's chest tugged and bulged as Azix unsnarled her leg from his neck.

Suddenly, her head popped out of the doctor's chest. Her shoulders and arms followed, inching, twisting and turning out from the gash, feeding her entire body through the small aperture.

She stepped out (one foot at a time) while untangling herself from the small congested orifice within the doctor's chest.

She stood, ferally drenched in blood. She gripped the doctor's shoulder while redirecting his arm through the orifice. Then she grabbed the doctor's hand and yanked his arm through the small hole. His body jarred with every tug she made. Finally, the jerking ceased. And the tantalizing woman of death stood with the doctor's heart beating in her hand.

The medic's blood spread out to an evident puddle, dying the floor with gore. The queen glared motionlessly down to the doctor's twisted corpse. Then, she placed his beating heart back into his own hand, which reached out from his chest cavity.

Azix faced Arola with her eyes fixed to the ground. And with mastery, she placed her hands behind her back, while the carnage ran slothfully down her sleek structure.

This moment took a vicious turn for the worse. Everyone gawked with a petrifying gaze as the odor of death lingered in the air.

"Clean her!" Ordered 7-Dial.

Just then, several barefooted angelic maids came from the rears of Arola's hair.

The women were of several different races. Their skin was flawless. Their hairs were tied up into a bun. And they were all dressed in silky smooth gowns that covered their bodies in a flowy, mysterious aura. They carried gold buckets of water and virtuous cloths of white perfection.

Azix held out her hands as the angelic women hustled over to her. They wiped her down to a spotless gleam. But she, without blinking an eye, glared on to the floor as if she saw nothing. Nothing but the vision of blatant macabre.

The angelic servants wiped over the floors. Then, they rushed back to the rear of Arola's throne, vanishing into the planet of hairs stemming from the tyrants' scalp.

Guitussami floated over to Azix and nodded his head. "Thank you," he mumbled.

And without question, the chaperon of death walked elegantly over to her initial spot. Next to Rayefill.

And there we stood, with a solid face, staring to the ground with humbled eyes of terror. The flustered look of excellence, enigmatically online with the cosmos.

"Splendid! My anchor. I'm sure they are more than capable of mission finesse. I'on know what was up with that other guy," mumbled Arola.

"Thank you, my liege. Permission to board Anarqkis?"

"Permission granted." Arola answered with a smirk that I couldn't see- but feel. "Zacuther will show you out."

The massive smiling hound popped his neck.

"Clear a path!" Arola shouted. "The anchor doth my bidding."

Zacuther glanced up to 7-Dial just before stomping down from the mighty platform. And with a heavy thump, the dog from hell trotted on, into the crowd of scientists.

"Anchor. Face," ordered Guitussami.

We turned to exit the Fact Matter Room.

Colonel G floated in front of us while that speechless hound stomped on, just a few feet ahead of the colonel.

We walked, side by side, and in a studious manner as the massive doors of the Fact Matter Room creeped open.

Scientists and doctors watched in disarray, fright, agitation, and some in total grief.

The ferocious beast stepped to the side as we approached the doors. He sat with that uninviting smile on his huge, wide, face. And I could feel something… something that I couldn't describe. "Guitussami!" Arola shouted.

"Anchor. Yield," he whispered. We stopped in our tracks as the ancient being floated around to face 7-Dial. "Yes, my lord," he quizzed with lowered eyes.

"No one liked Ciomaka. He was always using the microwave."

"Yes!" hollered a random doctor.

"And his food would stink up the break room. I got over a thousand complaints." Arola inserted. "Did you know he was a spy?"

"No, my lei-"

"-Yea!" Arola heckled. "He was working with Pias and Dr. Phlaxlur, with hopes of aiding Project Rapture. That was until that deranged butcher chopped everyone into souse meat. Damn co-joined twins. Chop-Man! That's what I call him. Chop-Man. I'm sure Azix knew… she sensed it. So did Xon. Well… the war is here now. No escaping that, old friend. There are spies everywhere, Guitussami… *Everywhere.*"

The colonel floated with his head down.

A major discomfort swept through the room, but that hell of a bastard hound just kept smiling. His eyes tore my psychological plane into cat sushi.

"Carry on old friend," chimed Arola from afar.

"Anchor. Proceed," Guitussami whispered.

CHAPTER 32:

Anchor. Abord.

Moments later we trekked through another massive hall with walls that journeyed far up into the black heaven. This, yet to be understood, passage came as a host of turns and mazes. But our formation held the same. Zacuther led the way while Guitussami floated beside him, and we followed close behind.

We soon came to a concave wall.

Zacuther walked over to the side wall, and he sat there with that horrible idea of a smile stretching over his grotesque face.

We waited and waited for a moment and that dog of a beast didn't move a bit. Nor did his smile ever weaken. He must've turned off. Or maybe he went into some state of sleep.

He glared straight ahead into the depressing wall. Then, Colonel G floated over to the monster, and he stared him in the eyes. Strangely, the dog snatched away from Guitussami.

Another moment of silence prevailed as the dog of disaster glared off. Suddenly, the concave wall vibrated, and the outline of a perfect circle formed within the ground before us. A massive cylinder-shaped structure lifted from the ground, revealing several massive hallways.

Colonel G faced the growing channels while the hell hound stepped to the center of the growing halls.

Now, there were three different tunnels before us.

Zacuther sat for another moment as if he was lost. Or maybe not. Either way, my antennae extended out of the top of my skull.

Zacuther lifted his leg to scratch his head. Then, he peeked keenly over his shoulder, glaring directly into my eyes, psychologically crashing through my crux. He pulled away with a snarl, walking leisurely into the right corridor.

We followed close behind him...

This savage abnormality trampled in front of us with his strong ubieties. Those shoulders and hips lifted and dropped while his hairs danced over his back. His muscular fascia became paralyzing, a mind staggering retrospect to body mechanics. The longer I traveled behind him, the more of an unease flattered my anatomy.

We came to a bisecting hall.

The massive monster stopped at the edge of the intersection with his back against the wall. He sat with that same disturbing smile on his face.

And there, we waited again... silently observing the build of inquietude.

Moments later, Colonel G floated over to the beast. It appeared as if the dog had turned off again. But before the Colonel could approach the hellish hound, Zacuther turned down into the bisecting hall. There again, we followed close behind the hell binding beast of voiceless potter.

We must've traveled for an entire cycle before we neared a set of double doors. A very subtle blue light peeked in with a sneaky calm of moisturized air.

As we neared, the hellafied guardian from Satan sat against the wall, a few feet away from the massive doors.

Guitussami slowed to a stop, with his eyes fixed on the hound. "Are we where I think we are?" The colonel asked as the doors swung open.

The beast smiled on as a beautiful setting developed before my eyes.

A fountain of blue shades covered the lands by the billions. A towering flow of air came with a noticeable dew complimenting this impressive vibe.

Up into the sky was a crystal blue sun- a boiling sphere of exuberant light. The rays shouted with joy as its essence ignited the ahs.

"In all of Layian lands… a Water Sun." whispered Guitussami. "This sun fuels a great deal of existences. It's believed to be the foundation of Tierun. How in the lands of sand did we get here?" Quizzed Guitussami.

The colonel gazed over to Zacuther. The devilish miscreant only stared straight ahead into the gorgeous setting with that same villainous smile.

"I've always wanted to see this before I died. And now... I have embraced such a setting. Thank you, Lord Labrys," Colonel G whispered.

The dog glanced away, blushing with that same smile.

Then, from the fogs of the Blue Lands mocked the presence of a glowing rectangle. The enormous plane lowered from the midst with a transparent glow.

"Anarqkis," mumbled Guitussami.

The now apparent vessel slowed to a smooth hover, grazing gently over the ground.

Guitussami sighed, "Anchor. Proceed."

We walked out into the Blue Lands and straight towards the mother of all spacecrafts.

The lineup was the same as before. Reb walked to my side while Rayefill and Azix traveled on the other.

Zacuther sat still as ever, staring up to the sky, breathing in the air, with slow and deep breaths. His head lowered as I passed by. His demonic eyes fixed to my body like a targeting system. The creature trounced my inner phrenic when my walk grew incredibly slow.

Just then, the spacecraft's bay door opened.

A glorious light spread out of the fogs ahead and a shadowy figure stood within the ships' loading dock.

"Anchor. Aboard," Guitussami ordered as a malevolent, dominant presence overtook me.

What's happening? Was I walking next to REB? Or was I… strobing in place? Whatever it was, it obstructed the anchor's lineup easily.

Suddenly, a huge hand clutched my body, and yanked me back.

CHAPTER 33:

Enuvion

The hand flung me back into the massive hall. The doors slammed shut behind me as I tumbled through a white light, and into a round silver room.

The window of light zapped away as I sat up to a mammoth ogre of a smile, charging right for me.

In my attempt to stand, the demonic hound was already attacking.

His arm extended beyond the average reach and his hand grew as he snatched me into the air.

Then, I captured this globed room. It was embedded with small to large circular vents, shifting over the floor as I lifted into the sky.

Suddenly, I stuck still, in midair. Glaring down to my midsection, to discover a spike rammed clean through my stomach. My blood trickled down the thorn while thousands of spikes protruded from the room's elliptical vents.

Within a flash, I slipped away from the spike as they retracted into the vents. But that smile glared up to my aerial plop.

The deadly minister of horror galloped up the side of the curved barrier while the circular vents shifted.

Before I hit the ground, the beast leaped off the wall, stretching his arm out for me.

His gigantic hand grabbed me by my leg, slamming me into the same wall he dismounted.

Woommmmm!

The vents stopped moving as the monster landed.

He launched his other hand over, snatching me by the feet. He slung me over to the opposite side of the room.

Platt!

I smacked to the curved surface just as hundreds of spikes erected from the vents.

Shicnk!

One pierced through my shoulder. Another shoved into my thigh, and another missed my head by a thread.

He gripped my feet together and yanked me down, raking my body over the spikey cluster.

The spike in my shoulder ripped through my flesh like a moist towelette. At that same moment, the spike in my thigh tore open to a wide gash.

He continued to hold me firmly by the feet as he snatched me down. Just then, the spikes retracted.

Placing my hands against the room's surface, my suction came with an infringing cling.

Zacuther pulled and pulled but my adherence was too strong.

The monster released me as I glanced down the curves of the room and over to my side. And there he was, orbiting over the globe's surface with a hazardous gallop.

331

He stretched his arm over and grabbed me by the head, predominantly my entire upper body.

Right then, the circled vents began shifting over the room.

The hellhound tugged to displace my adhesion. The tension grew as I held firm. But the vents came to a still, with one stopping in the center of my hand.

The spikes jetted out fast, piercing clean through the center of my palm, freeing my grip to a waste.

Zacuther slung me across the room.

My back slammed into another group of spikes. Several skewers nailed though my bicep, left pectoralis and my already injured thigh.

He snatched me off the spikes and hurdled me to the base of the room. But the spikes approached so fast; I couldn't steer clear.

My face slammed into the cluster.

Güshhh!

One spike plunged into my chest and another into my other thigh. Another spear shot through my eye and out the back of my head.

Gripping the spike by its base, I backed myself up from the long thorn. The keen point plucked from my eye just as the spikes retracted into the vents.

Right then, the circled orifices started relocating while his oversized hand came abruptly, whacking me into his ferocious grip.

WhaKm!!

He tossed me high into the air as I flailed uncontrollably.

Just then, the circular vents locked in place as I anticipated the spikes. But somehow, I bolted off into a mysterious vortex. And that dazzling smile of his faded away.

From a dark mist I spat out, landing on my back and just in front Guitussami, who only glared with disgust.

This vicious attack happened so fast, and no one was prepared.

"Core! They're onto us!" Guitussami shouted.

"You think?" another being wailed.

Floating behind me was the same entity from the Blackline. He had on a large brown coat and a big brown brimmed hat. His face was a darkened void of starry space, that mentally wandered astray. He just finished buttoning his coat when he looked down to me, shaking his head.

"What happened to him?" The Colonel quizzed.

"Lord Labrys," Core answered. "Luckily, I hacked his TPD just in time. You wouldn't believe where he took him."

"Where?"

"Enuvion."

"The Round Death?"

"Yes. Zacuther meant to kill him. And he might've if I had been a second late."

"Not quite. This was more of a tortuous sentiment and highly uncalled f-"

"-Da fuck!" a woman disrupted as she entered.

She was of slug descent, very shapely and a bit different from the rest of the anchor. For one thing, she could speak…

"Come! Take him to the light table. And start this ship immediately!" Colonel G howled as he floated back to the open bay doors.

The young woman rushed over to me as Guitussami continued. "Core. Warn the others. The rebellion is here."

"Done," Core replied as he unbuttoned his coat. He folded up into himself, disappearing in that same instance.

The woman sat me up just as my antennae twitched.

"C'mon, Chobe,"

Right then, behind Guitussami, I saw a silhouette through the fogs of the Blue Lands. It looked like a mammoth herd of shoulders approaching.

"Mechanism. You're responsible for the knowledge transfer. Each member of the anchor should know how to fly the ship with ease." Guitussami advised.

"But G, I-"

"-No excuses! You get him to that table!"

"Yes, sir," she answered as she started to drag me off.

Yet, that black shadow of a figure was approaching way faster than I figured. It was then when I finally understood the thing in the distance. It was not a herd. It was one. One single individual galloping so fast, that it kicked up the dust of a thousand stampedes. But the first thing that I really gathered, was that smile. That hell of a burden found us.

He trampled towards Anarqkis with a furious fire, igniting the flames of damnation.

The Mechanism sped up in her efforts to haul me away. But Colonel G kept speaking as if he had yet to notice the approaching disaster.

"We'll rendezvous in the safe zone," he noted just as gusting noise of Black Matter sounded.

An enormous projectile shot from Zacuther. The object traveled quicker than Rayefill.

"You get this s-"

"SSSssshhhhhhhiitttttt!!!" The Mechanism interrupted with a bellowing scream. Dropping me like a brick, she sprinted over to the control panel.

A brute of a double-edged battle axe entered the ship.

As I redirect my sight over to Guitussami, the flying adz chopped clean through the colonel's brain and heart.

335

Shaasssz!

In two separate slivers, did the colonel toppled out of the loading zone. The barbaric blade followed behind him ricocheting off the walls, and into the Blue Lands.

Zacuther screeched to a halt as the bay door slammed shut.

Mechanism rushed over to me. Lifting me up by the arms, she screamed at the top of her lungs…

"Rrrrraaaaayy!!!"

CHAPTER 34:

Earth's Return

Bright were the lights above as I sat up, rubbing my shoulder, the back of my head, and my eye. Every injury had been completely restored.

Squinting cautiously over the ultra-clean white room, I noticed that I was floating on a thin light table. A holographic display on the side of the table, flashed a message (in Layian).

Translation:

Status_
                Complete.

The device shot back into the panel as the table of light sat up quickly, standing me to my feet.

Then, the table slid into the floor.

My vigor flooded the ultra-clean room as my Layian ESP jump started.

Suddenly, a door swiped opened in front of me, revealing a massive hall.

In the distance, facing another door, stood a young child.

Traveling slowly down the hall, I finally approached this unnatural presence. This specter wore an all-white dingy nightgown full of aged bloodstains. The phantom suggestion kept its head down with those flagrantly thin and filthy hairs concealing its face of taciturn thrill. Something was off with this youngling.

Fathoming how the kid subsisted, here, obscured my grip of Layian telepathy.

Right then, the door swiped open.

Glancing to the door and back, I found that this kid had vanished… For a moment, I stared into the empty space before entering the room ahead.

The door swiped close behind me.

Moving planes of light, shaped the flooring beneath me. They shifted constantly, up, and down, and left and right as I traveled through the room. Suddenly, a small light twinkled in the far corner of the room. The observation brought me to a slow. A being stood in this corner with his back turned to me.

He wore a long, all white quilled cloak with razor shreds infused into it. The large robe covered a great deal of his physical mass.

Over a dozen monitors circled the individual who typed into each screen as they orbited. Atop of these revolving screens floated a solid black and pink polka dotted ball. The sphere hung without aid as it rotated on its own axis.

As I came to a stop, so did the shifting panels beneath me. With a strict eye, I examined the individual, surmising that he piloted Anarqkis. To consider the vigilant, or the wakeful, the being stopped and lowered his hand.

Then, I recognized the contrariety of colors in each of the being's palms. It was REB.

As he peeped over his shoulder, another panel popped up next to him. He typed into it as the other panels whirled about him. He placed his fingers at the base of the panel and swiped up.

A door opened in concert and right in front of me.

Erratically, this doorway of a portal, was nowhere to be found at first. To be unequivocally correct, I was yards away from REB, and any opposing wall. As he stood with his fingers pressing into the panel, waiting with reverie, a voice echoed from the doorway.

"And now I've gotta break this to Core."

Glancing over to REB, whos' scientific declaration persisted, he turned to me in a disturbing manner, and I finally entered the portal.

The doorway shut behind me as I entered the bridge of Anarqkis.

The same panels of light flowed evenly. They made up every instrument, apparatus, engine, tool and contraption associated with the ship's controls.

Way in front of me sat a huge transparent window, supplying a view of the endless galaxies streaking by. Underneath this window sat a large light panel, a control deck with thousands of tiny squares floating over it.

To the right of this table stood Infiltrate and Retrieve. And to the left was Mechanism. She sat slumped over in a light chair, crying and sobbing.

"But I can't... I can't tell Core, that Z-Man killed Guitussami. He's gone. The pain is so unreal, God, erase the image. Agh!! God! Why!" She whined as she sat up from her slouching, throwing her head back.

She peered into the ceiling and cried. "Oh God, I don't even know how to say something else... He was like my floating daddy. But I couldn't pay him. I couldn't play with him either, because he didn't have any arms or legs... God no! I don't wanna!!" She bellowed as the tears ran down her face.

Mechanism had been pouting and wiping her eyes for a while before she decided to settle down.

"I'm in no position to lead this team. I'm no Guitussami," she sniffled.

"I can't coach... Chobe's gone. Colonel G. Zacuther. In the hangar. With the battle axe. That smile..." she voiced with a frightening tremble.

Her face went blank as the thoughts took her away.

Then, that same smile jogged through my memory, but it had no effect on my mental mulish.

"Oh. Hey, Xon!" She blurted with a wave.

It was odd how quick her crying ceased.

Stepping over to the light table, I stood before the desk, glaring down to the controls.

"You healed up nicely," she added.

She then burst out crying all over again.

She yelled and yelled to the top of her lungs. While slumping to a new low, she grabbed her stomach and bent over in agonizing grief.

Infiltrate and Retrieve glared at each other with the meanest faces just before they stared back to the floor.

The Mechanism fell slothfully from the light chair and onto the floor, graveling in miserable contrition.

"Gguuuuiittussamiii!!!" She hollered. "Somebody kill me!"

Just then, Azix started over to Mechanism. The Speedster grabbed her quickly by the arm. Azix stopped in her tracks, but her face was still fixed on Mechanism. Death boiled over in her eyes as she stepped back into place.

"Chobe… you look so good over there!" Mechanism cried, still sobbing in cheerless sorrow.

Rayefill released Azix and she placed her hands behind her. Standing still as an effigy, she eyed Mechanism with a cruel stare.

"Agh! Take me, Chobe! I can't!" She grumbled as she stood to her feet, propping her hands up on her knees.

"Geez. You guys don't talk much, do you?" She asked. "REB has the coordinates for the Safe Zone," she said as her crying turned off like a faucet.

Suddenly, all the squares on the control desk flipped over with a domino effect.

In her inspection, Mechanism stood up straight. "We just merged into a timed galaxy. We're here." She said as she retrieved her TPD. "Everything is clocked now." She included. "My job is done. I'm not up for any of this."

Right then, a bright window opened a few feet behind Infiltrate and Retrieve.

REB stepped from the door of light with that black and pink polka dotted sphere floating about him. The orb spun in front of him as he tapped into the sphere. Then it changed in coloration with every rotation it took.

"Thank you, Mechanism. We appreciate all that you do for us. With yo' fine ass!" Mechanism blurted. "Aw shucks! No problem, guys. I wish I could do more. I just can't take this, *Silence of the lambs!*" She chuckled. "Get it? Silence? ... Aghh, never mind." She asserted while typing into her TPD.

Just then, the polka dot ball rolled to the center of the light table. The sphere morphed into a translucent map, unveiling this galactic arrangement.

Mechanism started crying again.

We looked at each other and then back to her. Neither of us understood her tears.

"That's so beautiful," she cried while typing into her TPD.

REB swiped his index finger through his palm and the map responded. The hologram recentered while zooming into the planetary systems.

"Oh, hold me, Chobe! That's so sexy," she grumbled while walking over to me with her arms out.

The whiffler's interest and emotions were all over her. She hugged me around the waist, burying her head in the center of my chest.

Glancing down to her, I peeped over to the rest of the anchor.

REB kept swiping through his palm. Rayefill was already looking at me, while Azix kept her eyes fixed on the light table.

The planetary search stopped when a planet centered the light table.

REB dropped his hands.

"That's it. That's the safe zone," said Mechanism as she pointed.

She walked over to the table and stopped next to the floating hologram.

"Where you land is up to you. But you guys are moving at over a zillion teraflop. If you land at this speed, you'll split the planet in two." She paused as Anarqkis began to slow. "The thing about Anarqkis and timed galaxies is... once you slow the ship down, it tends to advance time. It's actually a defect. We've been trying to fix it for eons." She spoke. "You can either land in the future, prior to your initial arrival or you can land in the present using the chronometer. Your choice." She whimpered, wiping her mouth.

And there, through the window, was the sustainable planet. Earth. This planet was small. We could cover the entire space within minutes. Plus, Earth only had one sun to orbit.

To us, this meant that the planet was spinning out of control. We could see every revolution the young planet took. One day made one complete rotation. This would take some getting used to. Seeing that, in contrast, the Layo Galaxy doesn't revolve. It is the center of all gravity for millions of multiverses.

"Azix. Rayefill. Xon... REB. It was grand. And sad," she huffed while tearing up. "You guys are creepy..."

She turned her back to us while typing into her TPD.

Suddenly, a widow of light opened in front of her. She turned around and asked, "Aren't you guys gonna say bye?"

We stared at her with bland expressions.

Rayefill folded his arms.

"I can't do this anymore. It hurts too much." Mechanism grumbled, dropping her head.

She gazed out to the planet in view, with a tear rolling down her face. She turned and slowly entered the window of light.

The door diminished symmetrically.

REB walked to the center of the light table, stopping beside me. He swiped through his palm again and the transparent map recentered. A large island came into focus.

The land was thick with vegetation.

REB glanced over to Infiltrate and Retrieve and then on to me. He brushed his hands together in a cleaning fashion.

The topographic map reformed, shaping back into the polka dotted sphere.

The sphere lifted into the air and floated over to REB.

Infiltrate and Retrieve headed over to the large control desk. They began typing into the small squares of light while the polka dotted ball stopped just in front of REB.

REB stood motionlessly in his alchemistic white robe.

He double tapped the sphere and it boomed to the table like a compacted heap.

Fwoomm!

The sphere simulated the gravitational weight of the planet. Then, the entire ship flashed light blue and then back to white.

My body felt lighter.

The sphere adapted the Earth's gravitational pull and synchronized it with Anarqkis.

A pulsing came in my wrist as I glanced down to a small black knot, bulging, and throbbing for my attention. Peeping over the room, I noticed everyone pressing this button. Just as I repeated the action, the button turned red and sunk back into my dense skin. Then, my heaviness, the weight of my anatomy returned with an overall distinction.

REB gripped the sphere and turned it twice in one direction. The orb detached from the table and lifted into the air. It floated over to him like a chemically receptive accomplice.

Infiltrate and Retrieve turned to face REB.

He reached over to the far end of the light table and gently placed his hand against its surface.

An odd chronometer displayed within the table.

REB slid his hand slowly along the sleek design and a bright light flashed before us.

Just that fast, the chronometer altered our arrival. We landed just in time, and in the center of a tropical island.

We stood in the bridge, staring out of the window and into a thick foggy setting. The environment was full of moisture, flowing through our reality but awfully dissimilar to that of the Layo Galaxy.

Infiltrate and Retrieve ventured out into the environment to obtain various items for research purposes.

During that time, REB showed me around Anarqkis, teaching me how to pilot the ship.

He showed me how to access the Light Void. Which is an instantaneous operating system used to generate a doorway to any area within Anarqkis. There were hundreds of codes and frequencies I had to learn, which didn't take long at all. He also showed me how to fly my own Haylo Jet, housed just underneath my boarding room.

With the use of REB's floating sphere, we gathered loads of information on cultures, languages, and advanced technologies.

The sphere could also communicate with Anarqkis on several different levels, which allowed us to synchronously monitor every planetary event.

REB and I gathered in the bridge, monitoring the global events through the hologram emitting from the light table.

Just then, Infiltrate and Retrieve returned with various objects to examine. We picked up on the prehistoric data quickly, as our technology debunked the planet's advancements by a trillion life spans.

Explorative studies revealed that nearly every act of violence was planned and calculated. Humanity, the animals and even some inanimate objects were already being affected by the

Xaris. Even now, their reach prevailed on a subconscious level. But the true question is, and for better inquisition, are the Xaris physically here, among humanity? Or is this just a simple instance of their influential infection? Their 'mental sway' could easily corrupt the fledgling- up and coming, embryonic minds of man.

CHAPTER 35:

Hell's Steed

The next morning, a particular case stuck out among the rest. This was no bomb. This was no hurricane or a mass shooting- all of which we deemed unworthy of our aid.

But this one thing had been ravaging the Earth, even before our arrival. This monstrosity had been killing for two whole days. And now, its rate of destruction had become infectious.

We gathered around the light table while REB researched Equus Ferus Caballus. The facts that we uncovered trounced the norms by leaps and bounds.

The average Clydesdale stands just over sixteen hands.

This thing stood over twenty.

The average horse can weigh up to two tons.

This thing weighed over eight.

The average Clydesdale can produce up to ten gallons of saliva in twenty-four hours. But this Clydesdale produced ten gallons of saliva within two hours, and without dehydrating, tiring, or sleeping. This horse's blood circulation rushed through his veins like a pressure washer. This sped up the horse's aging so that a year came equivalent to a month. In addition, the average horse can run up to thirty miles per hour. But this Clydesdale could move almost as fast as Rayefill...

Almost.

REB and I sat in our light chairs, observing the Clydesdale through the hologram.

Infiltrate and Retrieve stood, surveying from the opposite side of the table.

We waited and waited.

Within the next few hours, the Armed Forces intervened.

We did nothing, nothing but observe.

REB's Ormica (or Medicine Ball) accessed hundreds of satellite feeds.

We watched a sniper shoot this horse dead in the center of its head, but the bullet bounced away. Then, a tank entered the scene while two F-14s scrambled in the sky.

They blasted the horse with a gang of missiles, blockbusting him into a building.

The structure demolished on impact.

The dust cleared swiftly as the horse stumbled back to its feet, unphased.

REB commandeered the visual feed from one of the soldier's headsets. He zoomed into the midst of this wild battle to observe the horse's hooves.

They weren't hooves at all. They were more like fingers.

We noticed the horses' injuries healing before our eyes.

Suddenly, the horse took off like a lightning bolt.

Immediately, the tank turned and opened fire as the horse trampled over an army of men, their bodies burst with gore.

The Clydesdale rammed into the tank, flipping the weapon on its side.

Another army of men opened fire just when the horse zapped to the front of the tank.

The bullets bounced around as the horse bit into the tip of the tank's cannon. It dragged the tank out into the street, backing into a spin.

We watched vigilantly as the steed defied the laws of certitude. This monstrous idea of a Clydesdale hurtled the fifty-ton weapon into the sky.

REB stood to his feet. The light chair vanished as he paced the floor.

By this moment, the Clydesdale had killed another twenty people. At first, we figured the horse to just be mad, but this was more than anger. This was more than Xarchanzian influence. This was something else...

REB hooked his index fingers together, disconnecting the feed to the soldier's cam. Then, he swiped lightly through his hand with his fingers.

Our view switched to an aerial perspective as the Clydesdale zapped across three states within a matter of minutes.

Rayefill crossed his arms. He and his counterpart peered over to REB who had come to a mysterious rest.

REB lowered his hands and looked over to Infiltrate and Retrieve. The intergalactic alchemist dropped his head as the duo walked out of the bridge.

REB stirred his fingers through his palm as I glanced out of the bridges' window. Two Haylo Jets (one emerald blue and the other smoke gray) streaked off into the tropical thickets.

A fluff of smoke cooked up from REB's palm as I studied on, ogling into the light table hologram.

The juggernaut of a horse galloped with a spring of energy down the middle of Park Avenue. Just then, the horse stopped. It turned and trotted over to the sidewalk and stood.

Some fled in terror, seeing that the horse was out of the norm. Others sat mesmerized by the Clydesdale, and unaware of the trotting disaster.

Suddenly, the horse took off with a bolt of red lightning, clobbering through tables and chairs, paving dozens into a bloody mush.

Turmoil screamed over the lands as the Clydesdale's havoc wreaked anew.

REB hadn't viewed into the hologram. He was busy fabricating something within his hands. He sped up in his endeavor as the Ormica floated over to him. It stopped in front of his midsection.

He poked his finger into the sphere a few times. Then he swiped his hands together, splitting the orb in half.

He grabbed the top half and sat it bottom side up on the light table. He scratched the edge of the half, resting on the table, and it floated up into a slow spin. He sat the other half on the table as well. Then, the Alchemist lowered his hands.

We gazed on into the hologram as his Ormica spun away.

The monstrous atrocity killed another thirty people.

The National Guard shot the horse with everything they had. But the Clydesdale stood even stronger, with a translucent and unmerciful presence of rage.

The horse climbed up the side of a tank. It stomped into the roof and bit into the hatch, peeling the lid off like the top from a sardine can. He flung the hatch away as the army fired.

Bullets ricocheted over the streets just as the Clydesdale stuffed his head into the tank.

The demonic horse bit into the soldier's head, snatching him out of his seat.

"Aaaaaaaagggkkkk!!!" The gunner wiggled and screamed for his life.

Pugshhazzz!!!!

The steed plucked the soldiers' head off. His body slid down the side of the tank. Blood gushed from the headless stiff like a thermal spring as the Clydesdale chewed the soldiers head up to a guck.

The army continued to fire as the horse zapped from the tank and up the side of a building.

After reaching the roof of the building, the horse leapt into the air, crashing into two F-14's as they passed.

The horse scrambled over the jet, stomping into the front and rear of the aircraft.

The pilot pulled the emergency latch as the jet dismantled.

The hatch flew off, but the horse whirled around, plunging his head into the cockpit.

The Clydesdale ripped pieces of the pilot's body away.

Then it stomped repeatedly into the cockpit, warping the pilot into a clump of porridge.

Spiraling out of control, the jet crashed into a skyscraper.

Kabloooom!!

The explosion killed dozens. But the Clydesdale tore out of the smoky wreckage, tumbling recklessly down the side of the skyscraper.

The steed came to a controlled still, defying the laws of gravity. He stood along the side of the building with muzzling chunks of debris and sparks of red zipping around him. Then suddenly, the steed bolted down the side of the structure at a freakish rate.

Crashing into the streets, Archipus stood fast in the smokes of woe with scraps of destruction filling the setting.

A fiery red glow emitted from his indomitable eyes as a militia with several tanks encircled.

The army opened fire.

Sight of the Clydesdale ran thin as a soldier called a cease. But sadly, the horse had already kicked through the soldier, who disintegrated on impact.

BaLaasshhhh!!!

The smash flipped a tank to a roll, crushing dozens over into a sliding gore.

The remaining men ran for their lives as the horse trotted in mindless circles. "Somebody nuke that thing!" A man shouted.

The Clydesdale stopped to face the fleeing army, then he took off like a bullet, tripping over his own legs.

The unhinged steed clambered back to his feet, glancing about the streets to locate the aggressor. It turned again to see the remaining soldiers hiding within the gory detritus.

A host of choppers circled above as the beast kicked and bucked with no control.

Archipus glared up to the choppers, then it took off again, only to be sideswiped into a building.

Kclooom!

The disastrous horse crushed deep into the structure, tumbling head over heels.

Landing belly down, the horse stood quickly, shaking its head, and bucking furiously.

He stopped and glared over the empty room. He shook his head again, gazing directly into the eyes of Rayefill...

The speed demon stood just outside of the dilapidated entrance. Debris fell lightly as he stepped slowly into the abandoned building.

Suddenly, the horse flew over.

Before the Clydesdale could make a full gallop, Azix slid underneath his belly.

She gripped his front legs and yanked back.

The mighty steed flipped over, squirming chaotically through the air.

Rayefill spin kicked the steed through the ceiling and into the second floor.

Klac-Cclloommm!!!

The horse dropped fast, with ceiling fragments scurrying about him.

Azix slid in on her back, catching the beast with her feet.

Viscid secretions blasted from her palms as she planted her hands to the ground. The propulsion streaked her and the steed over the floor. She lifted her hands and flipped to her feet, launching the Clydesdale clean through the rear wall.

Flooom!

She stood inert, with her hands behind her.

Rayefill walked up to Azix. His antenna twitched as she exited through the front of the building.

I peeped away from the table hologram as REB opened his hand. Then, the cosmic alchemist just stood there. I peered back into the table's holographic feed.

The gargantuan horse stumbled to his feet as Rayefill stepped through the wrecked barrier and into the back alley.

The beast spun around to face the speedster while Azix snuck up from the rear. The horse shook its head then he took off.

In swooped the duo, crossing the horse's legs up.

The demonic bronco crashed head-first to the ground.

Bllushk!

Then, the horse stood tall, bucking violently.

Azix wrapped her body around the steed's front leg while the speedster lost his grip and jumbled into the air.

Suddenly, a window opened behind me.

Out stepped the speedster…

But I glanced back into the table's hologram to see the Clydesdale kick the Speedster into the distance.

Bamf!

I glanced back over to the speedster and a soft steam simmered up from his chest. While clenching a chunk of hair in his hands, the window of light wiped away. The speedster brushed the follicles into REB's awaiting palm.

The two carried on while I was still batting my eyes.

REB walked over to the halved spinning orb, dusting the hairs into it as it floated.

A strange array of clouds fumed up from the concoction.

At this instance, the orb heated up to about 12,000k.

The ancient theurgist tapped the bottom of the halved sphere and it reversed in rotation. A thick, yellowish pus bubbled up from it as REB walked over to the light table with the halved orb spinning beside him.

He slid his hand vertically against the light table. Then, the hologram toggled over to the far end of the table. REB clapped his hands and the halved orb stopped spinning. He caught it as it dropped from the air. Then, he walked over to the other half of

361

the sphere. He poured a liberal amount of the yellow pus into it and another hologram projected up from the light table.

We studied the imagery of a self-replicating DNA, an advanced strand of molecules that could modify and code switch at will.

REB sat the orb next to its other half. Then, he took his middle finger and slid it through his palm.

The hologram zoomed into a subatomic level and there it was. A cancerous poison. A mutated, pulpy corporeity that I couldn't catalog exactly, but REB knew exactly what it was.

Rayefill and I watched as a very small black marble floated up from the halved sphere that sat on the table.

REB stroked the marble with his finger, and it spun over quickly.

Suddenly, another hologram popped up within the light table. There, displayed the cancerous singleton with ancient dialects, descriptions and formulas surrounding it.

REB immediately interpreted the scriptures.

Zachamor4uia: the highly unstable and treacherous substance, better known as Ultra Zach, ran coarsely through the horse's circulatory system. This four staged- alien beefing steroid can remain in a victim's system for nearly four earth months before the host would encounter any side effects. The complete absence of any weakness, super speed and strength would all come to a halt, over the time allotted.

But the amount of Ultra Zach injected into the horse mega factored the equation, which turned this timetable into a debacle. In retrospect to Earth, everything here is time-based, not cycled. By this gospel alone, we were severely behind.

REB turned both halves of the orb clockwise once and counterclockwise twice.

The small marble plopped back into the halved orb.

At the same time, all the images in the light table vanished and the holographic view of the hell driven Clydesdale recentered.

Reassessing the quarrel, I discovered that Azix had been holding her own the entire time.

Despite her immolating dexterity, not even she could vanquish the steed alone.

REB stared into the hologram while lifting one half of the orb from the table. He flipped the half over and placed it on top of the other half, turning the top until the orb locked in place.

It was then when we all accepted the facts… Zachamor4uia is not from Earth. Mainly because the elements needed to generate such a substance had yet to exist in this galaxy.

We were now beyond killing the Clydesdale. It had to be cured.

The Ormica morphed into a Rubik's Sphere that systematically unraveled itself.

Still engulfed in the holographic battle stemming from the light table, I finally lifted my head.

Rayefill and REB stared at me. Then, they turned to each other. Rayefill looked to the floor while tapping the medallion on his chest. A window of light opened behind him. He backed into the portal and the doorway closed fast.

REB stared into the altering orb. He walked over to the light table and propped himself up. And for a moment, we both monitored the massive horse.

REB stood upright as his heavy cloak concealed him in such, questionable thriller. He turned his head to me in a very cold and ghoulish manner.

And that's when it hit me!

It was my turn...

Standing from my light chair, it flipped away into the floor.

REB lifted his hand and a transparent panel populated out of thin air. He typed into the panel and a doorway opened next to me.

Entering the portal, I trekked directly into a lower hanger. The portal shut as I walked over to my Haylo Jet. Placing my foot on the hood, the windshield morphed into a liquid.

A set of light stairs popped up as I walked through the aqueous windshield. They vanished as I stepped down, leveling with the ship's controls.

From the flooring configured a sophisticated pilot chair. While sitting in this seat, I turned to face the control desk, and the entire Jet lit up.

Two spheres (about thirty inches in diameter) lowered from the ceiling. Then, a faint alarm sounded. A red light flashed in the windshield as I stared up to the Layian message.

Translation:

> *'Obstruction in rear transformer grid.*
> *Yueqatti conversion revoked.*
> *Remove Interference. Remove Interference.'*

The message cleared as another message populated. *Translation:*

> *'For deployment-*
> *Accept or Decline notice.'*

Reaching up to the windshield, I pressed decline.
The message wiped clean, and the Haylo Jet powered up.

Right then, the hangar floor flashed away, and the aircraft dropped into the rainforest.

The jet soaked up the Earth's gravity fast as it lowered to a smooth.

From the pilot seat, I reached up to the spheres above. They bolted to my hands like magnets. Gently, I pushed them in, and the Haylo Jet zapped off.

Merging through and between the trees, I boomed across the seas. The Jet, bent, spiraled, and distorted itself through the streets.

Before I knew it, I was sitting in a trashy alley.

CHAPTER 36:

Archipus
Part 6

The Bronx, New York

Sudden vibrations, screams and explosions, roared from the street ahead. With scrutiny, I viewed out of the jet's windshield, and into this intersection.

A red spark of lightning streaked across the sky...

Then, something... stood me up from the pilot seat, which recycled into the Jet's floor. The orbs detached from my hands and traveled back into the ceiling.

To the rear of the ship, I walked and waited there for a moment. Turning to face the transparent window, I took another step back, pinning myself to the rear wall. And there, I waited again... Another streak of red lightning zipped through the sky.

Suddenly, I sprinted for the windshield.

Bolting out of the jet, I collided with the passing Clydesdale.

Croom!

We shattered glass everywhere as I tackled the horse into a bar, destroying its foyer.

Beneath the horse I found myself dodging from shoulder to shoulder as he sought to stomp me to paste.

Weaving my arms around his front legs, I stuffed my feet into his belly.

Monkey tossing the horse over, I landed with my knees in his chest. As I punched the horse in the face, he kicked me in the back, bolting me through several buildings.

Klissshh!

Blooshhh!!

Ckooom!!

Clutching onto various objects to keep myself from flying off the Earth, I slid to a screeching halt. Briefly I stood in the center of a demolished restaurant with dozens of Earthlings hiding within the rubble. Glaring into the wall ahead, I saw a clear path of destruction. The Clydesdale kicked me clean across town.

Sprinting from the dismantled wall and up the side of a building, my secretions jetted from my hands and feet, propelling me up to the roof. The slimy secretions gushed from my pores again, jetting me from rooftop to rooftop.

Swiveling around the side of another building and up to the top of a skyscraper, I stood amongst the clouds. Sprinting to the opposite side of the roof, I leapt off.

The misty winds flowed gracefully as I yielded myself over to Earth's gravity, tucking my knees into my chest.

My target neared. This destructive plummet couldn't have been better timed. Seconds before the clash, I fully extended my body, brutally bashing into the horse's back.

Booosshh!!!

The horse crushed into a deep crater.

We squabbled within the cavity, while I put the steed in a rear naked choke. As he clambered out of the basin, Azix slid in, wrapping her arms around his front legs. Oozy emissions dashed from her feet, snatching the horse out of the hole.

Rayefill sprinted up, wrapping his arms around the horse's hind legs, he yanked back while Azix tugged. The steed's body held static in the air.

Releasing my choke, I swiveled over to the horse's neck, gripping the Clydesdale by the snout. I punched him in the head, shattering his skull with every blow. The injuries healed before my eyes.

Infiltrate and Retrieve continued to tug as a peeling tore through the airwaves.

His 'impenetrable' skin gradually ripped as I glanced to the horse's midsection.

I mushed his head up just as an acidic sphere materialized from my palm. The ball soared underneath the horse.

While the monster struggled for freedom, I catapulted to its underbelly.

The acid bubble revved up into the horse's laceration as I hopped to the ground. Repositioning my stance, under the sloshing acid, I shoved both of my hands into the gap, tearing his skin a sunder.

Ssskaaaaaasssshhhhhh!!!!!!

The front half of the horse toppled over Azix while the rear half tumbled to Rayefill's side.

Drenched in blood, I bolted over to grab the rear half, and I flung the severed legs into space.

Blood rained moronically in tone as I turned to the scuffling horse's front half. It galloped klutzy down the street with a trail of innards trashing from its offensive opening.

Infiltrate and Retrieve followed close behind the bloodcurdling sight.

Just then, a strange gushing of muscular fascia developed quickly from the horse's severed half.

We rushed the Clydesdale, but before we could get in reach, the horse had completely regenerated.

The monstrosity kicked Rayefill rapidly, snapping him back into a building.

Bbooooooommmmmm!

Then, the nightmare of a bronco looked demonically as he turned to stare...

He doubled in size, blowing violently through his nostrils with those slaughtering eyes of decimation.

We charged the steed of hate.

The beast ran me over. I collected his head and neck in my arms and lifted the steed to an upside-down position. I fell back with a vertical suplex, cracking the ground open.

Whom!

The steed scrambled back to his feet as I held on to his neck.

Azix slid in as the horse kicked with his rear legs. She sidestepped and dodged. Then, the Speed Demon plowed into the horse's side, spinning the steed and I over to building.

Klooooom!

We crashed through the wall.

The suction in my feet brought us to a stop, flaking the floor to dust. I cupped my arms over the horse's head, gripped his triceps, lowered my hips, and suplexed him over my head again.

Bloooooo!!!!!

We crashed through a wall and several floors.

Bishhh!!

Ka-Foomm!!!

Wrapping myself around the horse's neck-

-Ba-Cufff!!!

We crashed into a basement.

FfWuuuuuummmm!!!

As Infiltrate and Retrieve landed, I clenched the horses' mane and slid up to his head. But he clambered to his feet. Folding my legs around his masseter, I dug my fist into his eye; plucked his pupils out and tossed them afar.

His eyes restored instantly.

Rayefill and Azix grabbed his front legs and pulled in opposite directions.

Replacing my grip, I stuffed my feet into his jawbone. Gripping his snout and teeth, I pulled with a stretching tug. But then, the Clydesdale surged with power, snatching Azix to the ground. With her grip still intact, the Speedster ran over to Azix. He lifted her up and ran in reverse, smacking the horse to the floor.

Plap!

Rayefill zapped back over to the other leg. Then, the duo tugged again, aiming the horse's limbs to the rear.

The bronco dragged to a skew, just as REB entered the basement. He came, creepy in his approach, with that orb floating behind him. The Ormica had smaller globes circling and bulging like clumps of thew.

But I was still forcing the steed's mouth open, and with no success. It was surely my strength versus the Ultra Zach, and the monster grew stronger by the second.

The Clydesdale stood upright as Infiltrate and Retrieve struggled to keep him at bay.

Suddenly…

A red light filled the setting, and a menacing sound shook the land.

BBBbbbbbbbeeeeeeepp!!!!!!

An indescribable surge of barbaric strength overtook me.

Lowering my head into my established grip, I elongated my body, and snatched the horse's mouth open.

SKassssssssshhh!!

The steed's muscle fibers ripped to shreds, snapping through the air as I disintegrated his jawbone.

REB glanced over to his Ormica, and the ball tunneled briskly into the horse's mouth.

The orb spun until it macerated away.

The Clydesdale gagged and coughed, regurgitating blood from his esophagus. His omnipotent, powerhouse of strapping legs fell limp and a host of colorful bubbles fizzed up from the steed's neck. The horse's head and I, teetered away from his body like hot wax melting down the side of a candle.

Infiltrate and Retrieve released their grip, but my clench was still fixed to the horse's mouth. Even then, I was seeing red, until the Speedster stood over me. That's when the red glare began to dim.

Rayefill stared into my eyes just before he dashed up the wall behind me and into the streets above.

With the Clydesdale's head in my lap, my ferocious grip came to a rest. Then, I sat up to my knees.

REB stood in front of me, dropping his head, shuffling his fingers around in his palm. He trailed off into the spooky shadows, the same ominous hall in whence he came.

Soaked in the blood of this weird triumph, I glared onto myself while the leviathan of a horse shrunk in size. Azix entered my view, standing with her arms behind her. With such a piercing look, she ever so slightly nodded her head. Then she jogged over to the wall behind me. She scaled through the floors and into the streets above.

In seclusion I sat, numbing to a still, ensuring the end of this… demonic- crazy horse.

CHAPTER 37:

My brother

Meanwhile, septillions of galaxies away-

The crazy horse aberration was found successful in the eyes of Xarchanzian minds. However, Archipus was only a diversion, which related to a deeper Symbassy plot.

The American Government (or any government for that matter) had yet to locate their universal launch codes. And every weapon of mass destruction had mysteriously vanished from the face of the Earth. This could've been the main reason Archipus was never nuked in the first place.

This discovery united the Earth, while revealing Horace Vaydin to the world.

But in the end, every Xaris noted the occurrences. And the wiles of Project Rapture, induced the multiverse.

At the same moment, along the outskirts of Layain lands, rests the defined boundary of Atomics.

The barricade is noted for being one of the most dangerous spans in the Layo galaxy, seeing that the region is full of atom-based mines. Hence the name, Atomics.

Bitter and rude was the accompanying sandstorm that battered against the body of Attica James.

The wanderer drifted oddly, but confidently through the tortuous climate. He had been studying Atomics for over a thousand cycles. He, almost, knew exactly where every mine was.

Attica's quest came with a profound detection of an unsettled mass, an undefined weight within the mines. And besides his apparent knowledge, the findings of such a thing kept him in debate.

Near the edge of the Xarchanzian proximities was the hump of undefined mass. His knowledge base became stupefied, for Attica had yet to evaluate this area. From here on, every step that he made through the boundary could be his last. But his curiosity, his unyielding desire for the misplaced thing- verified his compulsion.

About six feet away from the abandoned lump, Attica accessed his time twisting watch.

He tapped into the device and turned the dial counterclockwise.

The sands froze still as *his* clock ticked away.

Attica dashed straight for the mass.

He took out his TPD and typed into it briefly.

Just behind him opened a window of light.

He tucked the TPD back into his coat pocket and lifted the sand covered mass.

Attica gawked in startling realization as the grainy dust fell from a Gray Garden slug. It may have been defective and even near death, but the wanderer had no time to debate.

Right then, his time twisting watch clicked to an end.

In apprehension of the fading slug, Attica triggered several mines, spawning a chain reaction of explosions.

Ka-Fllooommm!!!!

Boooooommmmmm!!! Boooom!!!

Bllllooooommmmm!

The immense booms lifted the grainy turf, plunging Attica and the slug into the portal.

The void closed instantly.

Moments later...

"Former Olympic gold medalist. Pole vaulting. Discus and Javelin throwing. Extremely Bad-tempered. Hateful-Nazism... Abducted into a hybrid mollusk. Alarming amounts of knowledge and abilities. Phlaxlur cast as defective." Attica noted as he closed the manila folder. He passed it to a fellow Xaris while lowering the black scarf from his face. He grumbled, "Aluevis, Craiser?"

The German slug opened his eyes to a dimly lit ceiling. He laid on a pure gold bed with his eyes fixed on a familiar flag that hung above the room's entry door. Below this flag and directly in front of him, stood a host of men who appeared to be members of a particular soviet regiment.

The men all bore the same symbol on the flag- but branded into their faces.

The slug smiled painfully. As he sat up to his newfound confederates, he mumbled softly-

"*Meine Bruders...*"

Sup!

Dis Kontriss.

Knowhatumtalmbout?

I know you aint supposed to talk to the bad guys.

Well, I like kids. And I turned one of my space lots into a homeless shelter. I'm working on changing, while some of yawl probably hoping I die. And some of yawl thinking me and the Mechanism bout' to get booty and have a lotta chulrin.

That shit aint eva' happening.

I'on know. It might, in the next book. I guess it depends on dat' stupid ass author. And the reviews.

I heard…

Now dis' just what I heard. But every time you share an honest review, you save a tree from cocaine.

So, feel free to leave a review on Amazon, Goodreads, or anywhere you find Evolving Crane. And if you have friends, unlike some of us, be sure to share your enthumiasm.

How you say that word?

Shit. Yawl knowhatumtalmbout.

Well, um bout to re-up. Holla' atchawl' catz later. Be cool.

And don't do drugs.

Unless your folks were killed by a herd of deadly Poki-

-Acknowledgments

I'd like to think the almighty first. Without life, and the imagination, there would be no science fiction. I'd like to thank my absent mom and dad, and my immediate family.

I'd like to acknowledge my fans: Tamara Hohn, Devon Ford, Sam Bristol, Bernardo Gomez, Chris Frischkorn, John Haze, Randall Burton, Michael Evan, Derek Gillespie, Malina Avery, Marisa Enlow, Bubby Mitchell, Dee Clark, Morgan Hazelwood, Adrian, Tom Biondonillo, James Reid, Jason de Gray, Sam Stokes, Jason Cummings, Lakeeta Williams, the entire street team, my newsletter subscribers, Dorie, Ayodele Shaihi, Michelle Kidd, Tina Holmes, Nadine Russo, Antonio Perez, Joe Baxter Sr, Derrick Clark, Tugako Yosida, Cedric Hill, Tiger Catz, Bryan Johnson, Yoel Yehuda, Richard Spillers, Tom Waite, Kristopher Lobzun, John Shadeck, Simon Kennedy, Richard Breeze, Mike Portsmouth, Yasuo Fukuda, and all the fans of M.O.S.

I'd like to thank, Lamar Harvey, Anastasia Boone Talton, Mary Cain, Milton Davis, Marquita Ward, Dion Douglas, Ty Smith, Quinten La Mar Culpepper, Lance Darden, E.G. Stone, Johny Lewis, James Maddox, all the women named Denise, Levi Welch, and Bridgette Simpson.

Thank you, guys, for your constant motivation.

For Correspondence:

Dave Welch

P.O. Box 6402

Macon Ga. 31208

www.itsdavewelch.com

Email me: adaptorstudio@gmail.com

Review your purchase on

Amazon

excerpt_B

Evolving | **Crane**
Book 3 | Triple Beam

"The devil deals." Muttered Kalor.

His counterpart took her bulky nunchucks from their holster and the blades sprung from the ends like volant flits.

Goodrum screamed with rage, "Fire at will!"

But before a single bullet nicked the limo, Ix careened to the front of the shelling.

She flailed her bladed nunchucks with tuned exactness, reflecting bullets back into the swarm of officers. Her merciless twirling rebounded death just as fast as the bullets arrived.

From inside the limo, Horace typed on into the TPD as this blood thirsty quarrel commenced.

The helicopter crew filmed from a high when an altered portal opened above its propellers. The portal vacuumed the rotor wings off, twiddling the aircraft beyond control.

From behind the crowd of officers came Kalor and Efr, launching shurikens into the crowd of officials. She killed by the handful as a shotgun cocked-

-*Blam!*

An officer blasted her in the back of the head.

She fell into a forward roll.

Suddenly, the officer's head popped off as Kalor unsheathed his devilish sword.

Efr stood next to the demonic merc, poised, unphased and presently surrounded by a multitude of agents.

Foooomm!!

The helicopter croomed to the ground, pouring violent spates of explosions over the cemetery. Then it came. A dicey, foul, and revolting game of hand-to-hand combat.

Kalor swiped as an agent approached. The official's chest opened quick as he fell back into Efr's side kick.

Spak!

Snapping the man's neck like a twig.

Another man shot Kalor in the chest.

The bullet darted off as the merc snatched the man up.

He slammed the agent into a large tombstone that cracked on impact. He stabbed his sword into the top of the man's head, through his body and into the ground.

The merc yanked his sword out as Efr triple kicked another agent. Round housing him into an aerial spin, Efr hurled numerous shuriken into the official before he hit the ground.

Shots fired continuously and blood spritzed like hell as Kalor stabbed another official in the midsection. A bright portal opened above the official's head, sucking a portion of his body away.

The window dispersed as the merc snatched his sword from the gore gushing corpse.

Efr headed to Canieya's grave, blasting a shuriken in an agent's face as she passed.

The man's head sprayed off as the female assassin bolted in.

389

She ducked and dodged through the gunfire, swinging her bladed nunchucks, decapitating everyone in her path. While somersaulting up to her counterpart, he flipped over an agent's head, stabbing his sword in and out. The merc landed firmly as his counterpart sliced through an officer's upper body, which see-sawed horrifically to the grass.

Shell casings dinged as several agents charged the demonic assassin, knocking him and his sword to the ground.

Ix flipped over to the pileup. Whirling her bladed nunchucks, she whisked the men into bloody grates.

Gory shavings chucked over Kalor as he rolled backwards to his feet. He bent rearwards to collect an agent by the ankles. Lifting his legs over his head, he kicked the agent to the ground. His feet caved into the agent's chest as he stood. But the merc held onto the man's ankles, only to rip his legs off.

He slung the severed limbs away. Then, the demonic assassin reached for that diabolical sword, and it snapped over to his accursed grip.

Ix grabbed an agent by the arm, flipping him over her shoulder and into Kalor's slash.

Swish!

The officer's head swept aside.

Milton Keynes UK
Ingram Content Group UK Ltd.
UKHW010127080324
438930UK00019B/39